SHE L

SEE DOWN THERE

SHE
DOWN
THERE

Lynton Francois Burger

Penguin Books

Published in 2020 by Penguin Random House South Africa (Pty) Ltd
Company Reg No 1953/000441/07
The Estuaries No. 4, Oxbow Crescent, Century Avenue,
Century City, 7441, South Africa
PO Box 1144, Cape Town, 8000, South Africa
www.penguinrandomhouse.co.za

First edition, first printing 2020
1 3 5 7 9 8 6 4 2

ISBN 978-1-4859-0435-9 (Print)

ISBN 978-1-4859-0445-8 (ePub)

Cover design by Jacques Kaiser
Author photograph by Lukas Mueller
Text design by Chérie Collins
Set in 12 on 16 pt Adobe Caslon Pro

Printed and bound by Novus Print, a Novus Holdings company

It is quite conceivable that underwater man will be spiritually transformed by his activity, that from his intercourse with the sea he will receive an unexpected gift: a certain wisdom, a different way of thinking, judging and making decisions.
– Jean-Albert Foëx, *The Underwater Man*, 1964

'Yeah, underwater woman too.'
– Claire Lutrísque, 2000

Commander Islands, Bering Sea – North Pacific Ocean
August 1768

She is there this day. To witness what is about to happen. She, who lives in the minds of men, glides through the clear cold water, drawn to the calls – plaintive whistles, little grunts, no more. She approaches, barely touching the stalks of the kelp forest. When she surfaces she looks out over that forlorn bay, to where the two sea cows, rotund spindles floating in the fronds of kelp, are drawing closer to each other with gentle swishes of their broad tails. She Down There feels the water trembling as their age-old courtship begins.

The male sea cow matches his mate's every move. When she dives, he follows. Surfacing, she feigns escape, but he stays by her side. She stops. Rotates her bulk to come to rest in a clump of kelp. Light breaks through the leaden sky to catch the drops falling from her stubby flippers held aloft. Coming around from behind, he slides up her with a sudden surge, his tail fluke thrashing. His weight pushes her half underwater. He nudges and bites her. They clasp each other, and he begins his slow thrusting. As one, they lift and sink in the swell, sending ripples out, and their snorts and hurried exhalations carry across the quiet water.

When he is spent, the male sea cow slides backward like a newly built ship. He disappears underwater for a moment while his mate rolls onto her stomach. Surfacing next to her, he exhales a full breath. It hangs in the air for a while as a mist. They drift close together, bump and begin to wallow and stuff kelp into their bristled mouths with their flippers. A white gull, head down, flutters above the male, lands to pick off a sea louse embedded in a fold of his bark-like hide, but then flaps away. A dark shape is approaching over the sea.

When she feels the rhythmic splashing carrying through the water,

She Down There knows, and she shudders. All winter, ever since the sailing ship ran aground, the little rowing boat has come out from the shore to find the sea cows.

Two of the men are seated side by side with their backs to her. Between strokes they glance over their shoulders past the third man, who is standing up in the prow which lifts and cuts the sea with each stroke. He alone has a crude hat made from sea-otter fur. They all have full beards, and their padded coats are faded and patched. Their faces are lined, burned by the sun and the wind, and their long salt-set hair lifts in the breeze.

She sees the two metal hooks the hatted one holds. They are round and rusted, but for the points, which are sharpened to silver. The thick ropes tied through the eyes of the hooks snake between his legs into the boat. A cold dread grips her heart.

She Down There ducks down. Weaves as fast as she can through the kelp stalks towards the boat. The hull of the boat bumps her aside as she intercepts. But the men do not see her. They are only interested in the sea cows. Without slowing, she spirals onto her back and fins furiously under the hull. She hears the oars being shipped overhead. Her outstretched hands touch the sea cow's side, and she looks up into the narrowing grey sky between the boat and the creature. Straight into the eyes of the man with the otter cap. A vacant hunger is all she sees in those pale-blue Siberian eyes.

The hatted man starts, blinks. Was that the face of a seal he just saw? A sea lion perhaps? Or was it the saddest human face he's ever seen …? The hook hovers in his raised hand. He closes his eyes and brings it down.

She Down There jackknifes and dives as the boat passes over her, feeling as she does the shudder as the male sea cow is impaled. Followed by a dull thump as the boat's prow hits his side.

Above her, there is the thudding of boots on wooden hull. Oars dip down and swirl the boat around. In a froth of bubbles, she speeds to the female, who remains by her mate's side. She Down There grabs her from below, strains to turn the female sea cow around so she can urge her to flee. But all she can see in that deep-set eye is a complete lack of fear – a being who has never known a foe.

The sea cow is confused. Her mate is calling out to her as if she isn't near. A strange floating thing has come between them. Below her, through the clear water, the comforting sounds of the reef come rushing up to her. Her eyes close involuntarily as a blinding pain arcs across her back.

When She Down There feels the female's convulsion, she cries out as if she too has been impaled. The plangent sound carries through the water and up into the air. The rowers look at each other. They shrug and reach for their oars. And the hatted one rearranges the ropes in his hands, keeping his eyes on the pebbled beach where more men have appeared.

Feeling infinite grief, She Down There holds the last great siren of the north, last of the species they will name Steller's sea cow, with all of her love.

The rowboat crunches onto the beach and other men come down to take the trailing lines. They form two teams and, hand over hand, they pull the sea cows, who don't resist, into the shallows.

She Down There stays alongside the sea cows as far as the kelp's shallow edge, where their undersides touch the shore. The men lean back as they haul. With one final heave, the creatures are beached. A final tug of war won.

She swims aimlessly around the desolate bay, unable to leave. When the men strip the flesh from the sea cows, whose hearts have finally stopped beating, she too is stripped. Her heart aches with each outgoing tide. Not only for that which is lost, but also for the weakening of humans' place in the natural world.

But as each tide comes in, there is a softening. A reminder of the force present in all that remains, and with it the promise of new life. When She Down There brushes the kelp as it grows, she feels the pulse of life in the cells. When she swims among the flashing herring as they school, she hears the urgency in their pull. She sees the fury, the blur of bubbles as air is forced from a sea lion's fur when it gives chase to a lingcod. The shock waves thud through her chest when the storm swells reverberate back off the cliffs. Then, when it is calm, she rests on the reef that never sleeps and listens to the gentle splattering of rain on the silver ceiling above. And the sound of a million pebbles shifted by the receding surge, the gentle *conkle-conkle* on the shore, infuses her everlasting sigh. The same sigh that speaks to the hearts of all humans on all shores, without them knowing why.

She lingers in the bay through the last days of winter. She hears the merriment around the fires at night as the men barbecue the meat with delight. When spring warms the air, and little purple and yellow flowers appear above the high tide to track the sun, they launch their boat one last time. They row out to their ship, repaired now, with chunks of smoked sea cow at their feet. Their minds are filled with the tales they will tell – of endless abundance, of fantastic sea creatures. One man, adjusting his fur hat, holds the face of the sea-wraith he saw. When he gets home, and he is filled with drink, he will speak in awe of pretty mermaids. But not of the face, set in grief, which haunts him when he closes his eyes to sleep.

The echo of the last Steller's sea cow lifts from the bleaching bones and joins with the melancholic call of She Down There as she leaves this place. To be with all the sea creatures in all the seas. And to retreat into the shadows of human consciousness, itself retreating with each generation from its place in nature – which is everything, and all that there is.

Further south, on an island where the gnarled cedar trees spike the mist, a Haida shaman sits in deep contemplation, her wide, weathered face lit by the glow of a small fire. Her lips repeat the name of SG̱uuluu Jaad, Foam Woman, the sacred being who was there when humans first appeared out of the sea. And with these invocations, she enters the dream place, which cannot be seen but which exists in the depths of the oceans. Here there is no veil between the spirits of humans and the spirits of the other creatures. This is the realm of the supernatural creatures, the ChaaGan XaadaGay. She frowns as she senses a great imbalance in this place. Fractured words of warning swirl in a mist. And then, without warning, she hears the mournful cry of She Down There coming through the shroud. The one her cousins, the Aleut and the Inuit to the north, call Sedna. Ruler of the Sea Creatures. As the voice of Sedna grows, the shaman's eyes twitch, and she winces as an icy fear grips her heart. For the voice she hears speaks of the ultimate death of a sea creature, of a kind. And of the dawning of a dark age of greed. With her arms outstretched and her head bowed she begs forgiveness. She knows there will need to be a reawakening within the hearts of women and of men. She wonders how many lifetimes this will take, for she knows it will not be in hers. And she searches her mind for the stories that must be told and passed on. So that when the time comes, the message they carry will be heard.

So too, at this time, across the world in southern Africa, a wizened artist crouches in a small cave on the edge of the Great Karoo. The cave is set into the side of a flat-topped ridge overlooking a dry riverbed and beyond this a sweeping plain. He has gone within himself to become one with the stars and the wind and the living, dry land of his ancestors. For he wants to capture the essence of the strange-looking people he had seen hunting fish in the deepest rock pools on his recent forage to Tsitsikamma, the sacred meeting place whose name means 'place of much water'. There, from his hiding place, he had seen them go underwater for longer than any person could. When they dived, he'd glimpsed not feet but what looked like tails, like those of a sea creature. And as they floated, he'd heard them speak amongst each other in a peculiar, clicking dialect – a mixture of Dolphin and his own |Xam language.

When he is ready, he dips a supple twig into the ochre paste in the ostrich shell he holds, and lifts it reverently to apply the pigment to the rock. Stroke by stroke, the mystical abhumans emerge. A reminder to be left for his grandchildren, and theirs, that life is not always as it seems. And he wonders if perhaps one day one of his people will find a way to go where he could not. Down there, into that dark-blue, mysterious sea.

– HALF-AWAY WOMAN –

Southern Haida Gwaii Archipelago, British Columbia, Canada
18 July 1991

Claire Lutrísque shields her eyes with one hand against the white sky, so she can see where his smashed bones were placed. There, at the top of the pole, in the wooden box set into the apex. 'This is how it was done back then,' they'd told her.

She was nine when she first came here, with many questions, such as, *Were there any bones left up there?* But she'd never asked. Even then, she could feel the reverence that this place demanded.

The Haida mortuary pole stands in a clearing a little way inland, surrounded by rich green evergreen trees, Sitka spruce and western hemlock, which extend into the interior of the island as receding shadows in the mist. This dripping rainforest, which harbours voices from the past, grows right to the edge of the intertidal, where the sea licks the dark rocks and the pebbled beaches. Sometimes a deer will come out of the shadows without a sound and reach down to the drying rocks for salt.

Claire's dark, silken hair hangs to frame her upturned face, set in settled concentration as she studies the cracked plaque of the burial box. She blinks, then closes her eyes, feels into the growing disquiet that she's carried for weeks now – this gnawing knowledge that all is not well in her realm. But no answers come. It is like being in murky water in the presence of a sea creature who doesn't want to be seen.

She remembers desperately wanting to climb the pole to see for herself. She'd meant no disrespect; the inquisitive baby sea otter in her almost got the better of her, that's all. She'd imagined clinging on and peering through the gap in the plaque, the same one she's looking at now, into the burial box, and seeing how the blood and soft tissue would've soaked through to become one with the cedar wood, leaving only mouldering bones, remnants of hair and skin. She didn't tell her father and her grandmother, her beloved Náan, of these imaginings when she quietly joined them as they sat picnicking on the shore that day.

Náan had told her that the pole belonged to a legendary Haida whaler. One of the fearless hunters who once rowed out in dugouts, out beyond the horizon and into the vast expanse where myth merged with the sapphire sea. There where leviathans rose up from the depths to be battled with blessings and wooden spears tipped with bone. This is why he, like revered chiefs and shamans, has his own mortuary pole.

Claire opens her eyes and squints at the pole's crests, the carved motifs of the supernatural beings who honour his life's story. She calls forth his presence which lives on in this place, and in her veins. For this is her great-great-grandfather's pole.

Remembering why she is here, she brings the plain wooden box she holds to her chest. She takes a deep breath and opens the lid to reveal the grey dust. *No different to the cold remains of an evening's fire*, she thinks.

'Put some of me on the land, here by my grandpa's old pole, then spread the rest of me in the sea,' Náan had instructed them that day. 'I want *you* to do it,' she'd said, staring at Claire. She can hear Náan's cackle still, sounding out like a herring gull.

Claire's bare feet slip off the rotting branch she's standing on, and she has to tuck the box close and steady herself by holding on to the pole. She finds herself staring into the face of Frog, who squats as the base crest. His round mouth is opened in an eternal sigh. With the smell of crushed moss and rotting leaves rising to fill her nostrils, Claire dips her hand into her grandmother's remains. She feels the grit between her fingers as she spreads a fistful around the base of the pole. In the sniffing stillness, she is quite alone; with each breath, each powdered gesture, she reaches out beyond the forest, beyond the quiet sea. When she spills the third handful, tears finally well. Claire closes the box, places it on the moss by her feet so she can rub her eyes with the back of her arm. She steps back to take in the pole's crests, one by one.

Above Frog is Bear, the Elder Kinsman, looking menacing with his non-retractable claws framing his face. Honoured by the Haida as one of their own people, he exudes courage and strength, traits her great-great-grandfather would have had. SGaana, supernatural Orca, is halfway up the pole. He is the keeper of Ocean's living treasure. The one the Haida whalers would have conferred with in their meditations before a hunt, would have asked permission from. Astride SGaana, radiating ascendancy, is a squatting man. This would be him: her forebear. His round eyes stare anxiously out over an everlasting sea. And at the top, just below the burial box, and silhouetted against the misted glare, is Raven. His proud beak juts out into the clearing, and his carved wings unfurl right to the edges of the plaque. Náan had explained to Claire that without Raven there would be no stories at all, for in the beginning, as a Masset Haida creation myth goes, the sacred trickster pecked open a clamshell to release the physical form of man into the world.

A man's voice carries through the forest. Claire keeps her squinted eyes on Raven, but listens. She can't hear what he is saying. But that tone, the lecturer's drone, becomes a bumblebee in her chest. She asks Raven under her breath, 'Is it him? Is this what the trouble is? Is it?' But when Todd stops talking, there is only the forest dripping quietly.

Claire retrieves the box at her feet and turns from the pole. She has only taken a few steps when she hears the sound of powerful wings stalling. She swivels her head and flicks her hair over her shoulder in time to see a large black raven alight at the top of the pole. She has to raise her hand once more, and as her eyes adjust, she looks straight into those smoke-filled holes glaring at her. The raven opens his beak a crack – a salacious smile – and a tinge of rose appears on Claire's high cheeks. He shifts his glossy weight and his talons bite into the cedar wood. His throat hackles balloon. The echoing cry carries around the clearing, into the misty forest and out over the still sea, 'Aak, aark, aak! … Aaaark!'

The raven lifts his tail and a pale white blotch appears on the wood between his claws. It slides down the front of the plaque, alongside the other fading faeces. Claire clucks at him, breaks eye contact and turns away, continues toward the shore, picking her way over the roots and the branches covered in verdant moss. The raven watches her receding back, then falls into the air and beats overhead.

Claire steps over the line of driftwood on the edge of the clearing and onto the pebbles. The two men by the stubby aluminium dive boat look up as she joins them.

'Hey.' Claire makes eye contact with Todd, then tracks the raven as it circles behind him.

'How was it?' he asks, straightening to his full height. He scratches his greying beard, unkempt from being in the field.

Howie, their young skipper, lounges at the stern with his hand on the outboard motor. He squints into the glare, says nothing.

'Yeah, special. Thanks. Beginning to rot in places.'

'To be expected, I suppose. Did you, um … do the deed?' Todd's ice-blue eyes show momentary interest.

'Yes.'

'Well, we better get going. We need to get in the water while the light's still good.'

Claire steps into the sea, finds her footing to help Todd push the boat out. When she feels the pebbles let go of the hull, she turns to him, 'Thank you for agreeing to do our last dive around here. It means a lot to me.'

'A pleasure, my Haida girl.' He smiles briefly. Pats her twice on the shoulder.

They climb aboard, Howie starts the outboard and shifts the tiller to turn them seaward. The boat lifts and cuts a frothing white wake over the still water. Todd settles next to Howie up at the console. Claire sits at the stern, hugs her box with one hand and squints at the raven, who is following with slow, deliberate flaps.

They clear the cove and ride the wide, easy swells of the exposed seaward shore to the north. Claire's nostrils flush with the crisp ocean air, which carries the unmistakeable fresh-cut watermelon perfume of *Melibe*, the hooded sea slug. The delicate, transparent creatures will be clinging to eelgrass in the shallows, exposed by the tide.

'Stop the boat!' Claire is pointing at the dense spread of kelp they're passing to starboard.

Howie looks over his shoulder, pulls back the throttle. Claire has to snatch the gunwale to prevent spilling the box as the boat slows suddenly.

'What is it?' Todd asks.

'Thought I saw a sea otter. Over there.'

'Impossible.'

'Seriously … in that thickest clump.'

Howie brings the boat to the edge of the kelp, and the glistening brown fronds lift and drop with the surface of the water as the wake makes its way through it. The stillness hangs in the air.

'You must have imagined it.'

'It's just. I could have sworn …'

'There have only been five sightings of sea otters since the early seventies … in the whole of Haida Gwaii.' Todd shakes his wrist, looks at his dive watch, and back at her when she speaks.

'I'd like to spread the remaining ashes here, if that's all right?' Her face flushes.

'Sure. Go ahead.'

The two men watch as Claire kneels by the warm outboard and spills the rest of her grandmother into the water, bangs the back of the box, then submerges it. She lets it go and swirls her hands through the grey cloud spreading on the surface and dissolving down into the kelp.

Claire looks up through her tears and sees her grandmother's last breath, the finest dust, hanging like the exhale of a sea creature. She searches beyond this for the otter. But there is nothing.

'Goodbye, my Náan. Goodbye.'

Claire remains kneeling, staring blankly into the clear water. She runs her eyes down the kelp stalks, all the way to the seafloor where they are rooted to the rocks, and where small fish swirl between the wafting weed of the forest understorey. And she remembers the first time she looked underwater.

She'd been with her father and Náan, somewhere off Skidegate, or HlGaagilda as it's called in Haida. On her father's boat. She must have been seven or eight. He'd finished diving and was shifting the crates of urchins around when Claire had grabbed his mask and leaned over the side to peer into the water. The two adults had cracked up when she whipped her dripping head out and announced loudly, 'It's so beautiful! I saw a big orange starfish, like the sun. It had lots of legs. I want to go down there. Can I? Please … can I?'

Claire wipes her face, fills her cheeks and blows out. She turns around to face the men. Without making eye contact she tells them, 'I'd like to dive right here.' This time there is no flush.

Todd's eyes narrow, 'Are you sure you're okay to dive?'

'Yes.' Claire wipes her face. Lifts her chin.

'Fine. We're not far from where I planned to do this one anyway.'

Howie eases the boat to the edge of a thick kelp bed, where the water shimmers shades of emerald. He kills the engine. Steps forward to drop a steel anchor from the bow. The splash is followed by the clattering of the anchor chain and the quiet zing of the line running through the bow roller. He leans down, grabs the line as it slows, lets out another few metres before tying it off around a cleat.

The raven flaps toward the nearby shore and swoops into the tree line to land heavily on the bough of an old spruce growing out over the intertidal. He caws loudly, and Claire looks across at him. The raven cocks his head, studies her face a second time - sees the full force of life in those dark, almond-shaped eyes. They narrow.

Claire mutters as she turns away, 'Why are you so interested in me?'

Howie looks to Todd, who shrugs.

She and Todd move about the deck in a familiar routine – adjusting the dry suits they've stepped into, readying gear. In the stillness, the sound of metal on metal rings out as Claire shifts a scuba tank against the aluminium hull. Standing up straight, she twists her hair into a tight bun and pulls the hood of her dry suit over her head, shoving the stray hair into the sides with a few deft movements.

'Do you think they'll listen to us?'

'Why wouldn't they?'

She forces a smile. 'I don't know, I just don't trust them. We've been here two weeks now and it's pretty obvious to me they should extend the national park into the sea, and—'

He cuts her short, 'It might seem obvious. But let's wait and see what the data tells us.'

'Yeah, I guess.'

'Good. Now let's get down there and gather some information, shall we?'

Will I forever be his student? The thought announces itself, blinking. Like a seal lifting its head out of the water. Claire sniffs, reaches for her fins at her feet.

She and Todd sit on the gunwales on opposite sides of the boat while Howie helps them shoulder their tanks. They inhale from the regulator mouthpieces, clenched between their teeth like bits, to test their air. The short, sudden release of compressed air startles the raven. He settles, fluffs his feathers, doesn't take his eyes off Claire.

Todd holds a tape measure and a clipboard with waterproof paper and a pencil on a string. Claire balances an underwater video camera on her knees. They spit in their masks so they won't fog up, lean down to swirl some seawater in them, then pull them over their heads. Claire jams her neoprene gloves into her armpits to work her fingers further in. Her eyes meet Todd's behind the glass of his mask. They exchange nods, inhale, and in unison fall backward off the boat.

The raven launches into the air and his scratching caw recedes until there is misty silence once more throughout the forests and over the sea. With slow wingbeats, he heads back to the clearing. The sun breaks through the swirling white, and he looks down to see an otter bobbing on her back like a cork, her body wrapped in glistening kelp. She holds a spiny urchin on her furry stomach, and in her front paws a rock, a little bigger than the urchin. With a few swift blows, which submerge her body enough to send ripples out onto the calm water, she smashes the urchin, drops the rock, and feeds with relish on the orange flesh.

Claire gasps as the water hits her cheeks. Ocean's cold fingers creep over her scalp, wetting the bundled hair. She is in her embrace again. Floating on the calm surface, she looks down to follow the kelp stalks stretching to the reef below. Rays from the sun, which has broken through again, angle into the emerald depths like thin columns of translucent alabaster. Claire comes back to the boat and holds on to the side, looks under it to where Todd's finned legs swirl as he hangs off the other side. Simultaneously, with the instinct and ease that come from being both lovers and dive partners, they release air from their buoyancy jackets and drop down through the water.

She pinches her nose with gloved fingers, blows gently to equalise the pressure on her eardrums. Down they go. To the reef. To her beloved sea creatures. Into the soup of life, which now includes her suffusing Náan.

Claire drifts into her diving reverie. Unable to talk for the next hour, she goes inward to commune with all that is Ocean. Feeling as comfortable underwater as she is on land – especially after the many days of continuous diving they've done on this trip. When she reaches the seafloor, sunlight still streams through the kelp, swaying in the surge around her. Brown and red seaweed form a dense understorey, a thicket where fish dart and settle. Her breathing steadies as she adjusts straps and releases a little air into her buoyancy jacket to lift her off the sea-floor.

As they begin their transect, finning slowly through the forest of stalks, she tunes in to the sounds of the crackling reef, punctuated by the quiet rasping inhalation and louder upward explosions of their breathing.

Claire feels particularly at home in these waters. She considers the Haida her people, even if her father is Quebecois. 'You might be a half-breed, but you're twice the Haida I am,' Claire's mother often used to joke, not realising how the word stung each time. A Haida boy in her class told her one day before school that she was neither White nor Haida First Nation. 'Not this, nor that, but in the middle. Like a tide that doesn't know if it's coming in or going out.' He thought that was a really smart thing to say. Until he felt the pain when her flung fist landed on his nose.

Náan had called her a 'Half-Away Woman'. But the way she said it made it sound magical, something to be proud of.

'You know who you are,' Náan had told her. 'We are sea people. Through me you are a descendant of the first people who came from the breasts of SGuuluu Jaad, Foam Woman, from between the tides at Xd'gi, the sacred reef near SGaang Gwaay. Ninstinsts, as they call it now. You are Haida, because I say so.'

Náan's body may have departed from this earth, but she comes to Claire in her undersea dreaming, and today she is full of stories. Her weathered face, a sea of creases, forms in Claire's mind. Náan's eyes, although misted with age, speak of mischief. Claire could never fathom how she remembered so many stories without reading a single book. She knew the lineages, who was connected to whom, how humans fit in to the natural and also the spirit world, which she referred to as 'the realm'. And her stories were always filled with detail and delight.

'Let me tell you the story of Sedna, Claire.' She can feel the presence of Náan acutely now. It's as if she is sitting by her bedside. Her eyes glint as her mouth forms that wide, turtle-like smile. Claire has heard the story many times but never tires of it. 'The story of Sedna comes from our northern cousins. But I'll tell you a secret ... I believe Sedna dwells here in our waters too. Many old people say they have seen her. Or have heard her. I thought I did myself, the one time. Not far from that cove where your great-great-grandfather's mortuary pole stands. On the seaward side, there where the bald eagles like to sit with their heads under their wings in the dead cedars. I was there with your grandfather. We were out on his skiff, fishing for salmon one misty morning. I swear I heard a woman calling through the white. It was the saddest voice I have ever heard. It made my hairs stand up. I called out to her. Your grandfather thought I was crazy, talking to the mist ... to the sea. And when we saw ripples coming across the calm water, he said it must have been a sea lion. Or the sea otter that everyone talks about but never sees. But in my heart, I believe it was her. Half-Away Woman. She Down There. That's why I call you by that name. That's why it's a special name. You, my Claire, remind me of Sedna. You want to live down there and serve all those sea creatures, don't you just?'

I do, Claire sends the answer through the water.

A rock crab the size of her hand scuttles away on its eight pin legs, disturbed by their looming shapes. Claire slows and hovers in mid-water as Todd ties the line at the leading end of the measuring tape to a kelp stalk with a slip knot. When he tugs hard enough on it at the end of the dive, it will come loose. She comes down to rest with her knees on the reef and watches him as he writes on his clipboard with the pencil. *I do love this man*, she thinks for the second time today. They share the desire to understand how it all works down here. To explain the ecology of the place, and use this knowledge to protect what is left. Yet lately ... *Is it the commitment?* She dismisses the thought. *No, I've made my mind up.* He still seems keen. It's time. She is feeling the stirring. And she's seen how good he is around kids.

Does it have to do with the move then? Away from this place of her youth, her people? To the city where Todd has been offered a tenured post at the University of British Columbia, UBC. Her alma mater. No, it isn't this either. *I've known for a long time that I would leave. And I can visit.* What is it then? This feeling, this sea creature in the mists of her mind, remains elusive. It retreats when she focuses her attention on it. So, she lets it go. It will show itself when it needs to.

Todd glances her way. She gives him a quick A-okay signal. He turns and flicks his fins to swim through the kelp forest, trailing the tape behind him. His job is to swim out the fifty-metre tape and to record the fish he sees on either side of him. She will swim after him filming the reef. They will classify it later based on substrate and habitat type. They have swum hundreds of these transects this summer.

She switches her video camera on, glancing to make sure the little red recording light is flashing before she follows Todd. A movement catches her attention – a school of herring pass overhead like a silver veil. Claire keeps the camera steady on them. They change direction and their bodies turn to dull grey, then back to shiny silver. This magic murmuration draws back the curtains of her mind to once more reveal the face of Náan, whose eyes have that faraway look. The same look that used to come over her face before a favoured tale. Her familiar, frail voice calls out in Claire's mind.

'Sedna was the most beautiful young woman in the village. She kept her black hair in two long braids. Her face was open to the world and her eyes had the lustre of deep water. Despite her beauty, she had done the unspeakable. She had refused to marry any man. She had always been different. From a young age, she had been seen whispering to the unseen in the forests and on the shores in a voice only a few elders in the clan could understand. She fell in love with a stranger who turned out to be Raven. He had seen her beautiful heart and disguised himself as a handsome whaler visiting from another village. When this mysterious man spoke to her, he looked deep into her eyes in a way that no other man had ever done, nor could. She stole away with him to one of the furthermost islands. There where the salmon gather before they journey up the rivers to spawn. Once they were on the island, he revealed himself as Raven. Bewitched, she stayed with him, and they were happy.

'When they learned that she had been taken, the elders instructed her father to fetch her. He set out in his canoe with their words of rebuke ringing in his ears. In truth, he had struggled for many years to accept and love Sedna as his daughter. He paddled on, furious and filled with shame. When he reached the island, he found her alone, as Raven was out hunting for food. With silent force, he bound her, thrust her into his canoe and started paddling back to the village.

'The canoe appeared across the bay, cutting a wake across the still sea. The father knelt, intent. His paddle dipped first one side and then the other. All was still but for the rhythmic sounds of his paddle entering the water and his heavy breathing. Sedna glared up at him from where she lay, trussed up at his feet, her thick braids lying like two ropes by her sides. He couldn't meet her eyes.

'Before he could reach the village, a raven came flapping low across the water. And, as he drew near, he transformed and filled the sky above them. The great spirit bird flapped around the canoe, screeching and beating the surface of the water in a fury, so that the sea rose up, becoming one with the mist. Her father was terrified.

'Sedna looked up at Raven. She pleaded for him to stop. But Raven knew he had lost her, that his true form had been exposed. He could hear the veiled chanting of the village shaman, intent on harming him, and his eyes smouldered with rage. If he couldn't have her, he thought, then neither could they, so he beat at the water with all his magic.

'Sedna's raised voice, this shrieking apparition who wasn't his daughter, brought a chill to her father's heart. His eyes grew wide, and he struggled to breathe. No longer thinking, he untied her and threw her overboard, as a sacrifice to Raven, to make him stop. When she hit the cold water, her scream carried through it and over the surface of it. A pod of orcas heard the call and they slowed in the water, their breaths hanging like wisps of mist in the white glare. The crackling of the reef below stopped momentarily. A deer, licking salt from the rocks in the intertidal not far off, looked up. Sedna called out across the water again. She grabbed the side of the canoe, her knuckles growing white.

"'Don't leave me!" she shrieked. "Don't do it!"

'The orcas listened. A whale wallowed, waiting. Two sea otters ceased their kelp rolling and looked on. Her father tried to paddle away so hard that the veins and tendons on his arms welted up like reef worms. But Sedna clung on resolutely. Avoiding her eyes, he dropped his paddle and took his skinning knife from its sheath, leaned forward and hacked at her knuckles. The sound of the heavy blade hitting the wood of the canoe rang out like dancing sticks talking – *Clack-clack-clack-clack!* The blooded knife fell from his fingers and clattered to the deck. He reached down to where her still-warm fingers lay and hastily threw them overboard. Slumping back into his seat, his whole body shuddered as he cried out to the sky as if impaled. When he paddled away, it was with difficulty, even though the sea had become strangely calm, for the blood of his daughter lay between the oar and his hands. A thick mist drifted in from the forest and settled over the water.

'Sedna and her severed fingers drifted down into the cold depths. One by one the fingers turned into sea creatures. A sea lion, a seal, an otter. One thumb became a rockfish, the other a grey whale. One finger turned into a whole school of herring, while another became an orca. They all circled around Sedna, whose braids were unravelling, the dark hair swirling in the current. They were joined by the other animals of the ocean who heard the orcas and the whales calling out her name. All the creatures swam with her in a mighty vortex, and from then onward she was Sedna. Ruler of the Sea Creatures.'

Náan's voice fades. Claire slips through the water, her fins hardly moving, as the swell lifts and eases her down. She glances to the side as a wolf eel peers out of its hole. She catches the reef with her gloved left hand and steadies her body in the water so she can frame him in her camera viewfinder. His peg teeth are set in gummy jaws, which open and close as he breathes in water, and his marbled grey eyes glare at her from his bloated face, just like a little old man's.

She resumes swimming along the line, and her Náan whispers to her one last time. Words she has heard so many times, they are etched in her memory.

'She is Half-Away Woman. Her name is her destiny: half woman, half sea creature. Down with the octopus she dives. She swims out beyond the waves with the sea lions and the orcas. She rolls with the sea otters in the kelp. She rests in the intertidal – that place which is half sea, half land. When the winter storms set in, she shelters on the reefs, deep below the thrashing waves, with the rockfish and the wolf eel. She sees all in the sea. She feels all. And she is forever destined to be the voice of the sea creatures, the one the shamans have to dive down to each spring to appease, to ask to release the animals for the summer hunt.' Her voice fades as she ends: 'You, little Claire, remind me of her.'

Claire shakes her head, blinks, as if awakening. She drifts through the kelp. Takes a deep breath. The silver bubbles of her exhalation rise in the water column. With a few flicks of her fins she clears the forest, then films the transition to the deeper rocky reef, which is coated with filter-feeding invertebrates. Sponges the size of bread loaves, wafting soft corals and pouting anemones, arranged in a splay of red, orange and white. Ahead of her, Todd has reached the end of the transect. She switches off her camera and swims to join him as he jerks the tape free. She hangs next to him, staring over the reef into the gloom while he winds it in. Her mind is a beautiful blank.

Claire cocks her head as the eerie shrieks interspersed with pitched whistles carry clearly through the water. The sound is unmistakeable. And near. Todd stops winding. She turns to him and then to where he is pointing. Catches sight of the huge shape. The magical being. *Holy crap!*

They look at each other, eyes wide. Claire clutches Todd's arm. Draws closer. Bubbles of shallow breath fly from her regulator. *SGaana* – the word forms in her mind as the smooth black form with white markings comes into view over the reef. The magnificent animal catches the shafts of light coming down through the water; they play along his sleek side. His tall black dorsal fin seems to quiver as he alters course to face them. The orca's jaws open imperceptibly to reveal the rows of pure white teeth. He glides in. Hangs in the water before her. She feels exposed, examined, as the rapid chatter-clicks and squeals echo in her head. The orca turns sideways. And when that round black eye locks on hers, it is as if her heart has stopped. She is standing naked in a misted forest with loud unseen birds calling out around her. She feels no fear, just a vague sensation that her brain is being tickled. She says his name out loud and the sound resonates in her nose, comes out as voiceless bubbles.

The orca thrusts his broad tail fluke, turns from them. Claire follows him until all she can see is the white underside of his tail. Then nothing. She searches the water column for further movement, wondering if he was ever there. The voice of Chief of the World Beneath the Sea, the mournful squeak-whistles, lingers. Until this too recedes. And it is just the sound of their rattling breaths, and the quiet crackling of the reef.

She hangs in the water, as her heart and breath settle. Feeling his absence acutely. Words, shaded distribution maps, photographs of markings on dorsal fins – these can't possibly capture the profundity of this encounter. Searching to make sense of the experience, her mind goes instead to the depiction of Orca in traditional Haida woodcarvings. She sees the cedar mouths split by stylised teeth, polished abalone-shell eyes flashing ferociously, and the carved curves painted in earth-tone reds and black. Depictions that can summon a distant chant can begin to connect the essence of Orca with the essence of Human. Yes, these carvings more accurately capture the impact of meeting SGaana in his kingdom.

They take the cue from the encounter to ascend. She catches Todd's eyes behind his mask. She blinks a smile at him, to show that she is glowing too. As she rises, she feels the release of pressure on her body – Ocean letting go – and at the same time a reluctance to leave. She wants to stay with the sea creatures. To hear her grandmother's voice.

A pale jellyfish comes into view, passes, pulse-pulsing in the water with a sexual urgency, trailing its deadly tentacles like a lover with the burden of past loves. Claire closes her eyes. Prepares to re-enter the world of air which awaits up there. She arches her head back, removes her hood and her mask so her hair spills and spreads into the water, and when she blows a ring of bubbles toward the surface she is filled with an ineffable happiness. She reaches up to the silvery, grey-blue mirror that is the under-skin of the sea. And for a moment, as the light catches her gloved hand in the water, it appears fingerless.

Claire leaves the paved road north of Lost Lagoon to step onto the mulched crunch of one of the forested paths of Stanley Park. She slows the pace of her running to inhale the mossy freshness and lean into her stretching legs as the trees rise to greet her. She's enjoying the break from diving. The novelty of fresh clothes on skin that's actually dry. The bliss of a bed with crisp sheets after three weeks of hips compressing the thin foam of a camping mattress. Resting muscles worked hard by shifting tanks, hauling the dive boat, swimming kilometres underwater.

The state she enters underwater is an integral part of Claire's inner journey. But feeling the air in this remnant old-growth forest, so reminiscent of the Graham Island of her childhood, is helping make sense of her recent underwater trances. She frames the orca in her mind again. She's had many magical moments in her five years as a field biologist, but this one certainly stands out. It keeps throwing up questions, the synchronicity of it: Ocean revealing herself so profoundly, just at a time when Claire's internal state is so unsettled. The answers will surely come if she keeps going within.

Claire isolates the forest birds' calls as they carry through the stillness between the trees, then her footfalls, and finally her breathing. But random thoughts persist. It would make sense to live around here. Near Todd's parents' home, where they're staying at the moment while he attends meetings at UBC between their two summer field trips. Todd could cycle to work. His face had been aglow when he came back from being shown his new office two days ago.

Then she could run here often. Claire glances joyfully at the mossy hide of a tall hemlock. *We take them so for granted.* She turns her head back to the path. Hears the gentle sound of the surf at Third Beach filtering through the forest.

Perhaps Náan was right. *I do think too much.*

She recalls the smell of the homemade perfume, mint and eulachon grease, which Náan had been wearing that evening, not too long ago, when she handed Claire the little whalebone carving of Sea Otter. 'Get out of your beautiful head, my Claire,' she'd told her. 'Find your own voice. Remember your crest, your totem. Flow like Otter flows. All you have to do is to express your inner truth. I hope this reminds you.'

What is your totem? she'd asked her grandmother.

I've always identified with Turtle, she'd laughed. *Even though they're not common around here. Turtle is the messenger. That's why I have that print of Spirit Turtle above my bed – to remind me to tell stories.*

Memories flood as she picks her way along the path coated with wet leaves. The summers at Náan's wooden cottage, set back from the beach … pricking her fingers gathering wild raspberries out back. Gathering eggs – and facing the angry cock who came out to protect his hens. She chuckles as she recalls how Náan once disciplined her two brothers for some misdemeanour by making them compete to see who could chop the most firewood in an hour. She can clearly remember that face, bursting to giggle while pretending to be stern. And Náan's loud gratitude that day a local Haida fisherman dropped off a fresh Chinook. The respect written on his face when Náan bless-ed him in Haida. After he left, Náan explained to Claire that he'd been to residential school, where the language had been all but beaten out of him. Not many could speak it now.

Náan's cottage couldn't accommodate the whole family when they descended for the summer, so her brothers and parents would pitch tents in the meadow. But Claire got to stay with Náan. Each night there would be stories: recipe stories, silly stories. And Haida stories of old. Náan said that the sea was inhabited by many supernatural creatures, the underwater people or ChaaGan XaadaGay. Creatures from a time when the veil between humans and other animals was thin. Most stories revolved around how the Haida sacred ceremonies allowed them to 'put on the skins' of their animal brothers and sisters and venture into their world, including underwater.

Náan became animated when she told the story of Claire's whaler forebear. Her hands flew and her eyes grew wide as she told how the great whale had smashed the long canoe, carved from a single tree, as if it were a matchstick. Claire would swear she could hear the men screaming when her grandmother paused for effect. They had been, far out to sea, the old lady related, almost as far as Bowie Seamount. 'SGaan Kinghlas, as we Haida call it. Supernatural Being Looking Outward.' The only reason Claire and Náan were both around was because other boats were there that day to pluck Grandpa out of the water, she cackled.

Náan also told of descendants decimated by smallpox brought by the early European traders, leaving only a few hundred Haida to take them into the twentieth century. And at least once each summer, she would happily relent and tell their favourite – her version of the story of Sedna, of She Down There.

The image of Náan's hands comes to her. Soft and wrinkled, and for-ever busy. Making, baking, scolding. Náan's bedtime storytelling would sometimes end with her saying a personal prayer for Claire. In these moments, when Náan rested her cool palm on Claire's brow and the old lady's face settled and spread to honour her blessings, she would feel safe, even as an adult. Connected to a boundless and all-powerful strength. She remembers the feeling of those hands that final night as the old lady placed them with such reverence on Claire's chest. Those clouded eyes that twinkled in the candlelight. Claire had known it was the last time they would be together.

Náan's cremation ceremony had taken place at the beginning of the summer. All her family and a few Haida elders and villagers who knew her well gathered at her home. It had been a short but fitting blessing to a long life. When Claire walked away with the boxed remains in one hand, she'd also taken emotional leave of the place. It wasn't the same without Náan, and her parents had announced shortly afterwards that they'd be selling it.

Another woman runner appears up ahead and Claire whips away the tear. They greet with a quick smile and a 'hey' as they brush past each other. A few paces further, a squirrel scampers across her path, almost tripping her. Claire lifts her hand to make sure the otter pendant is still there, tucked into her sports bra. She feels the chain jumping on her chest as she runs, and silently repeats the Haida word for sea otter, like a dove's call … Kuu.

'Remember, Otter is one with Ocean,' says Náan's voice. 'She flows with the current, rests in the kelp. And she likes to play. You are too serious, my sweetheart. Just because your science man lives in his head doesn't mean you have to as well.'

That makes her smile. Her science man is probably still dozing in the delicious bed she crept out of half an hour ago. The Japanese maple she stretched against this morning reaches Todd's childhood bedroom window on the second storey; if a squirrel running along a branch a minute before six had looked in, it would have seen her straddling him. The tree is the same age as Todd: a gift to his father from a close friend, a Japanese whaler captain, on the occasion of his birth in 1953. In the fall its leaves gush a rich red.

Arne Storstrand had been a captain of one of the 'chasers' belonging to the Western Whaling Company. But the retired whaler no longer brags about his personal tally of 821. 'We didn't know any better back then,' he'd told Claire, close to tears, that same night he fell in love with the idea of his son marrying her.

They were called fish back then. Claire had learned this when she examined the book of records up in Nanaimo, at the Department of Fisheries and Oceans. Pages and pages of 'fish' – lists of dead whales – neatly inscribed by a man called Gordon Pike. *I guess that's what biologists did in those days.* When the world war between men ended and the war on nature resumed in full force. When humans used the new technology, which had brought them back from the brink, to drive other sentient beings close to theirs. Better boats equipped with better sonar. Better explosives to more accurately blow out brains. When she flipped through the Kodak photographs in the old box, she'd identified the species being hauled up on the slipway of the slaughterhouse in Coal Harbour: blue, fin, sei, sperm and humpbacks in various stages of dismemberment. Todd told her he'd been there many times as a boy. That it was the reason he wanted to create marine sanctuaries.

She hears the gulls calling on Third Beach. Makes out the bleaching logs tumbled like pick-up-sticks on the shore. *Follow my normal seawall route, or keep to the trees?* She decides to keep this morning forested and turns onto the path that heads north, up to the Siwash Rock viewpoint.

Claire runs with a quiet mind for a few minutes, concentrating on her breathing. She contemplates their upcoming trip to S<u>G</u>aan <u>K</u>inghlas. They're going to dive to the depth limits of scuba on that remote pinnacle, and she will stay down longer than she ever has before. She wipes the sweat from her face and pushes her body up the slope to the viewpoint. She glances at her watch. Making good time.

Claire slows to a walk, steps off the path. Out over the sea to the west, several container ships are lining up in the roadstead. Below her, she sees the basalt sea stack that was once a man, Squamish legend has it. His name rolls off her tongue as her breathing slows. 'Skalsh.' Ocean is calm this morning and washes a subdued white around his feet.

Náan told the myth of Skalsh each time she heard Claire was going to Vancouver. She explained how he was a great father, firm and resolute but considerate, even-tempered. Spoken about by all the clans, up and down the coast. So exemplary a father was he that Q'uas, the supernatural being also known as The Transformer, who had the power of turning humans into animals or inanimate objects, had turned him into a rock, to henceforth be: Skalsh the Unselfish. Claire snorts. *Bit shitty to be turned into a rock in the sea as a reward for being awesome.*

She steps back on the track, which winds up to Prospect Point, and focuses on her breathing. Feels the easy contraction and relaxation of familiar muscles. She is present, but releasing all thoughts now, going within to that intertidal place of the mind where the sea of myth meets her deep rhythmic breathing, to invoke pure gratitude. And although she knows he isn't a god, she calls on Q'uas, The Transformer, to do his magic. Acknowledges that he may have started already. And she begins to smile inside as the forest around her hums and crackles to meet the rising heat of the day, and her drumming feet and her breathing combine as a mantra. By the time she reaches the Vancouver Aquar-ium, the sweat is pouring and her mind is quiet.

A magnificent bronze orca, rendered in Haida traditional style, looms large outside the aquarium. The artist, Bill Reid, also had a European father and a Haida mother, she recalls. She walks round to the plaque and reads, as if for the first time, the words etched there: 'Skana – The Killer Whale known by the Haida to be chief of the world beneath the sea who from his great house raised the storms of winter and brought calm to the seas of summer. He governed the mystical cycle of the salmon and was keeper of all the oceans living treasure.'

Tomorrow evening she'll be back here for the marine-parks planning meeting that Todd's chairing – the first she's been invited to since completing her master's degree. But right now, Claire's looking forward to Todd's mother's berry pancakes when she gets back. She steps back on the path and heads through the last bit of native forest. The sun is well up by the time she hits the streets of West Side. She pushes past the parked suvs, the prim dog-walkers, the clipped sidewalks and the painted postboxes, fully engaging her muscles. She'll feel it tomorrow but she doesn't mind: soon she'll be at sea for ten days with no chance to exercise.

The mere thought of going out there lifts her spirits. The offshore trip to Bowie Seamount will bring her and Todd together. She knows he loves her, had felt it this morning. He'd been lazy and tender, had waited for her. Like most times. She can feel his commitment; he knows how much it will mean to her if Náan's ancestral land is protected. *Todd will be a great father too. Like Skalsh.*

But the unease is still there. And from this unsettled sea, the fresh question breaks the surface, dripping, to confront her. *Who is it that Q'uas would have me be?*

Claire gives it all she's got, all the way down the street to the weatherboard home with the Japanese maple. Gasping for air, she collapses on her back under its boughs. As she looks up into its spreading branches, silhouetted like arteries, she notices the first leaves – red as blood.

Vancouver Aquarium
1 August 1991

'Did you know that the orca named SGaana who lived here was, in fact, a she?' Claire points to the plaque, hoping to stop Todd's pacing. She tugs down her dress, which keeps riding up her thighs. Earlier, as they walked through the forest in the dying light, he'd told her she looked lovely. She imagines this is what it will feel like to be 'going away'. After the ceremony. They still haven't agreed on anything.

'No. I didn't.' Todd's crisp white shirt flashes from under the navy blue of his jacket sleeve as he thrusts out an arm to check his dive watch. 'The others are late,' he grunts.

Claire studies his neatly trimmed beard, face tanned from all the time in the field. *Handsome.* She has to concentrate not to lick off her lip gloss. 'Yeah, she died here in 1980. Left quite a mark.'

'How so?'

When he turns to her, his eyes flash pale blue in the building's exterior light, and she is taken back to when they started dating. 'He's got such beautiful eyes. It's like looking into the sea. I see his passion for Ocean there,' she'd told a girlfriend.

'You remember Dr Paul Spong, right?' She shifts her weight on the heeled shoes to ease the pinching.

'He was that neuroscientist who worked here. On the orcas.'

'Yeah, I attended a talk of his a few years ago.' Claire pauses, but Todd doesn't respond. 'Anyway, he shared how he'd come here to study SGaana in the early seventies. But found himself studied instead.' Claire had been so taken by what the gentle New Zealander had to say that she'd gone up to him afterwards to find out more.

'Sounds like a flake,' Todd says, glancing at his watch again.

Claire frowns, tries to look him in the face, but he's scanning the paths. 'He said that he developed a special bond with her, convincing him that cetaceans are as intelligent and emotionally sophisticated as humans. That hunting them is an act of murder. He said he wanted to influence the activists who were protesting nuclear testing in the Aleutian Islands; shift their attention to whaling. So, he introduced SGaana to a journalist named Bob Hunter …'

'The guy who started Greenpeace? Vancouver hippie?'

'Yeah. Apparently Bob and SGaana hit it off instantly. Were soon rubbing heads poolside. But one day SGaana rose up and held Bob's head in her jaws – "like a crystal goblet in a vice," Dr Spong said. Later, Bob told Dr Spong that a lot went through his mind in those long seconds before SGaana let go. That it changed his life.'

'Sounds like a bit of an exaggerated story, if you ask me. Where are these damned people?'

'I think it's incredible that Greenpeace's first anti-whaling efforts stemmed from this personal encounter between a captive orca and a man. And that it set off a series of events and relationships that have reverberated around the planet. And that because of this, thousands of whales have been saved.'

Todd turns to her, smiles for the first time. 'You really have an active imagination.'

Claire returns the smile but doesn't say any more. She looks up at the carved face of SGaana and wonders what it would feel like to have an orca's peg-like teeth clamped on your scalp. She turns away as the aquarium director saunters toward them.

Claire stops when she enters the boardroom. 'Wow, impressive!' she says to no one in particular. The thick glass takes up most of the long wall – a clear view into the orca enclosure. *Hope it inspires everyone to think and say what's best for Ocean.* Claire chooses a seat facing the glass. The other participants take their positions. Todd, at the head of the table, opens the meeting by asking everyone to introduce themselves.

Her face flushes as she rushes to say her name, adding 'Todd's field-research assistant'. She counts the ten faces. Government officials, academics. And the host, the affable aquarium director. She is the only woman.

Five minutes into the meeting they appear, and Claire is transfixed. The large male Hyak 2 and his mate Bjossa glide toward the glass and stop midwater. Their black-and-white bulks are set in shimmering turquoise. Everyone looks around in awe and Todd has to bring them to order.

The two orcas come and go throughout the meeting. Claire drifts in and out of the conversations. She has a vague sense that the session is going well. Everyone seems to agree that marine protected areas are a good idea.

'But do we need *all* of these "no take" zones you're proposing?' a fisheries manager across from her asks. 'Don't fishermen have the right to do what they've always done? And will these restrictions apply to First Nations?'

They all turn to Todd. As he outlines the plan to consult with 'all stakeholders', to seek 'workable compromises', Claire wonders if the others can hear the staccato clicks whenever there's a pause in the talking. Like the orcas are trying to have their say.

The meeting drags on, and Claire becomes more and more agitated. Has to reach for her glass of water to wet her mouth. She imagines what a cacophony it must be for them, their pulsed clicks bouncing back at them. Echoes with no location. When she closes her eyes, she sees the vitality of the majestic orca she met on their last dive, and a distant chanting begins to grow in the recesses of her mind. She opens her eyes, tracking theirs as they shift their bulk across the glass. *Ocean's greatest predator confined to life in a swimming pool.*

As Todd begins to wrap up, gets agreement on the date and time of the next meeting, an unfamiliar warmth emerges within her. It seems to rise up her spine and out through the top of her head.

When he pauses, she lifts her chin and looks across the table to the aquarium director. Speaks for the first time in the meeting. She doesn't recognise the voice that carries when she opens her mouth.

'I was wondering, Director, have these two orcas stopped whistling? Do they only communicate with the quieter clicks of their complex vocabulary? For surely the louder and more penetrating continuous-tone emissions they use out there in the open ocean would drive them insane, bouncing around the walls of this box.'

The room is hushed. Pumps hum in the background, pushing sea-water through pipes. She holds the director's eyes. All of the men are looking at her.

'I, uh, I don't know,' he stammers.

'And tell us, why has Hyak's dorsal fin collapsed since his imprisonment?' Before he can answer, she adds, 'And why did their calf die in 1988?'

'This sometimes happens,' he answers quietly. She can see he is bewildered. This isn't the sweet, inquisitive student he got to know when she was a volunteer here that summer during her undergrad. When he was delighted to have someone of colour out there among the public.

'Let's call it an evening,' Todd almost spits, gathering his pieces of paper with deliberate intent. 'I want to thank you all for attending. For giving up your evening.'

As the men stand and parting conversations start up, Claire goes to the orcas. She presses her forehead against the cold glass, to hear their clicks more clearly. Spreads her arms wide as if to hold the two forms as they nudge the other side of the pane. She closes her eyes.

'I am sorry,' she finds herself repeating. Honouring their female calf who starved to death two weeks after birth because Bjossa couldn't produce enough milk in captivity.

She doesn't see Todd's controlled rage as he turns and strides out of the room.

Her trance is broken when she hears a polite cough behind her. Claire turns and stares at the director as if she's seeing him for the first time.

'I … I need to lock up, Claire.'

She takes one last look at the orcas, and makes for the door. At the threshold she stops in her tracks, turns to him, and says, 'It's not right, Dr Fletcher, it's just not right. And I know you know it.' She doesn't wait for his response.

She walks as if in a dream to the yacht club where they have a table reservation. Todd isn't there, so she turns and wanders barefoot, her fancy shoes in one hand, through Stanley Park to his parents' home. Listening for night birds and insects in the shadows of the forest; feeling into this new voice that has appeared within her.

She's never seen the veins on his neck stand out like this. She sits on the side of the single bed, hands clenched in her lap, as he paces the room he grew up in. It feels small, like the walls have come in closer to support his fury.

'Are you stupid, or what? Do you know how important that meeting was? What were you thinking, Claire? What got into you?' She doesn't wipe the drop of spittle that lands on her forehead. He doesn't allow her to answer: 'And what was with the bloody chanting? Acting like some hippie!'

She can't meet his eyes, which are boring down into her. She has the thought but doesn't say it: *Didn't you hear them calling?* For the first time, she is scared of a man.

'I am sorry, Todd. I couldn't help myself. After meeting that orca underwater in the wild …'

'We didn't *meet* the bloody thing! It came to check us out. It was just a curious predator in its natural habitat, for fuck's sake. We're lucky it didn't take us out.'

'I'm sorry,' she whispers, studying the patterns in the faded bedside rug. And as the tension lingers, she whispers under her breath, 'He would never have attacked us. I felt it.'

Todd only calms when he sees she's crying, trying not to make a sound. With a final 'fuck it' he sits down on the bed next to her, puts his hand on her bare shoulder. For the first time, she wants to pull away. But she dare not.

'I'm sorry too, Claire. But you have to understand. We are so close to getting buy-in from these guys. It's all politics to them. We have to play their game. We are scientists. We have to act the part. I would have thought you—'

'Yes, I understand. I … I am sorry. I …'

'Let's forget about it for now. I'll call them all in the morning to fix it. Let's go to bed now, okay. It's been a long day.'

'Yes, it has.'

He strips off his clothes, stands in his underpants before her. 'Please don't ever show me up like that again, okay?'

'Okay.'

When he is spent, when his tense muscled weight has lifted off her, she pulls the sheet to her bare chest. Feeling her heart beating faithfully beneath her clenched fingers, she stares at the ceiling where the silhouettes of maple leaves dance with the dim street-light.

'Our work is so critical, Claire,' she hears him saying, as if from across a vast sea.

'Yes, but what is *my* work?' she whispers when she hears his first snore. Closing her eyes, she surrenders to the waves of doubt. As she calms, an image remains: wracked seaweed, washed up on the rocks.

Claire is wandering around campus while Todd attends his meetings when she sees the notice. An evening talk by a visiting academic on the conservation status of the Sirenians, 'with a particular focus on the endangered dugongs along the coast of Mozambique, after recent fieldwork'. What an apt name: the Sirens. Manatees and dugongs, the mermaid family. Ocean's only vegan mammals. *Mo–zam–bique. Wasn't that the title of a Bob Dylan song?*

She's disappointed to see the talk was two weeks ago, but gathers from the blurb that the speaker is based here at UBC for a six-month summer sabbatical. She makes her way to the Marine Studies building and enquires after Dr Adam Eishmal.

It's been four days since their 'blow-up', as Todd called it, and they've agreed not to talk about *that* evening again. Over breakfast this morning, he reminded her that a marine park would help protect her grandmother's heritage. She had not responded. She wishes he'd leave Náan out of it. This is not what drives him. Not really. It's actually all about *him*.

When she reads the typed name card slid into the brass holder, her knuckle hovering after the knock, she has a fleeting premonition that this seemingly random meander may hold some significance. Before she can grasp what it may be, the door opens.

'Hi, Doctor Eishmal?'

He's older than she'd expected, with a jet-black, immaculately trimmed beard. 'Indeed, how may I help you, my dear?'

She registers the English accent. Anglo-Indian?

'I was in the field when you gave your talk. I have a few questions. Would you have a minute?'

'Of course. Of course. Please do come in.'

She steps onto the faded Persian rug. As he closes the door behind her, she takes in the cosy academic office lined with books, with its smell of printed paper and yesterday's coffee.

'You are Claire Lutrísque, aren't you? You're with Dr Storstrand.'

'Yes. I'm his field-research assistant and fiancée.'

'Ah, delighted. I recognise you from your photograph in the *Marine Parks Journal*. From that recent article. Fascinating. Please do sit down,' he gestures as he sinks back into the chair behind his desk. 'I met your lovely man in the tearoom this morning. Thrilled to hear he'll be joining the faculty here in the winter. I have read several of his papers. I mean, *your* papers. Forgive me. Congratulations to you both for the work you are doing here in BC. I would have loved to see more of your beautiful province. Sadly, I'm heading back home soon, to Edinburgh ... Yes, the talk ...' He lifts his head, laughs. 'Well, at least twelve people attended. Mostly undergrads. Which is encouraging, I suppose. Would you like a copy of my notes? I have a few copies left. Somewhere here ...' He rummages around on his desk.

'Thanks, I would appreciate that.'

When she feels his hand through the stapled sheets of paper, there it is again, for a second – a whisper of significance. But it's gone when she notices the framed poster behind him.

'Were they really *that* large?'

Five spindle-shaped animals fill the poster: the four extant Sirenia, three species of manatee and the dugong. And the fifth, dwarfing them all: the extinct Steller's sea cow.

'The sea cow? Yes, I believe it's an accurate depiction,' he says, turning back. 'I've studied Georg Steller's original notes and sketches, you know. And touched the skeleton at the Smithsonian. Thirty feet long. You are familiar with their fate, I imagine?'

'Vaguely. I know the last ones that lived were somewhere up north. Near Alaska, right?'

'Yes, a fascinating story. They found them quite by accident, as you may recall. Russian sea-otter fur trappers ran aground off what is now Bering Island, one of the Commander Islands near Siberia. They were stranded there for the winter. On board was the German naturalist Georg Steller. We owe all we know about these creatures to him.' Claire studies his neat face as he gets into his stride. 'It was 1741 and they were returning from Alaska to Kamchatka, loaded up with furs. When they came ashore, they discovered these docile creatures surviving on kelp in the sheltered bays. The sea cows put up no fight when they were hauled onto land. None at all. The meat sustained the men until the spring. When they returned home in their restored ship, the story spread and many fur traders from Siberia followed, because they could now extend their time in Alaska by overwintering on these islands if they needed to.' Dr Eishmal looks down at his desk. 'The last Steller's sea cow was killed in 1768. Gone within twenty-seven years of being discovered.' He pauses, looks up blankly at her. 'But I'm rambling on. Fire away with your questions, my dear.'

'I hadn't heard the full story before. It's tragic. What I do remember reading is that they were a lot like their living cousins, the dugongs.'

'In some ways, I suppose. Steller described their mating, for example. Said they formed close couple bonds and mated face to face. Dugongs do that, you know.' He winks at her. 'I have seen this myself in Mozambique, where I spent two months last year on a research grant.'

'I'd like to know more about that. Our work here in British Columbia has been purely ecological. Habitat mapping, zonation, that sort of thing. Fisheries management, really. But I'm becoming more and more interested in the people aspect. How to get buy-in from local communities. How to involve them with marine parks management, the role of education ... I'm intrigued to learn how this works in other places. In Africa.'

'I can't say I'm an expert – I'm a population modeller. But during my time on the island of Bazaruto, I could see that this aspect was vital.'

'Bazaruto. Sounds exotic.'

'Oh, it is. Stunning little island in southern Mozambique, just north of the Tropic of Capricorn. I was assisting a local colleague, Dr Benito Mutara, with a marine-mammal census. The situation is dire. We found that dugong numbers had halved since the previous census, back when the park was established in 1971.'

'Is that him?' Alongside the Sirens is a framed photograph, a simple snap of two men posing in the shallows next to a faded blue boat with the name *Dugongo* painted in red on its prow. Dr Eishmal looks ten years younger, thinner, grinning under a broad grass sunhat. The African man next to him is laughing out loud. Something, she suspects from the ease of the expression, he does a lot.

'Wonderful fellow. Has virtually no funding, works on the smell of an oil rag, you know. Cheerful as hell. Religious. Christian … lovely chap. The locals are dirt poor. I saw for myself how little they live on. So, can you blame them for eating turtles and dugongs when they get caught up in their nets? A major focus of Dr Mutara's outreach work is addressing this difficult issue. When I was there, he was starting to work with schoolchildren …'

Claire has the thought, as he continues to share his anecdotes, that it must be terribly lonely sitting here all day writing scientific papers. She keeps glancing at the photograph of the two colleagues. It's the face of the other man that holds her attention – this Dr Mutara. It's as if he is staring straight at her.

Dr Eishmal is telling her how the country has opened up after years of civil war, creating opportunities but also problems. How the Chinese are moving in, buying up land, creating demand for marine animal parts: turtle shell, shark fins, dugong penises.

Really? Dugong penises? She's about to ask more about these when there's a knock on the door. Dr Eishmal stops mid-sentence.

'Two visitors in one day. What a treat!' He lifts out of his chair and opens the door. 'Well, well. Hello, Dr Storstrand. We meet again. What a lovely surprise. I am having a wonderful chat with your fiancée. About dugongs.'

Todd smiles across at Claire. 'Mildred told me you were here. Sorry to disturb, but we have that lunch date with Professor Mellon.'

Claire rises, taking one last good look at the picture, at Benito Mutara.

Down and down the fifty-pound lead weight plummets, leaving a trail of froth like a diving seabird. A red cord, as thick as Claire's pinkie finger, trails with it, until at thirty-five metres it crashes onto the top of Bowie Seamount. Onto the black volcanic head of SGaan Kinghlas, Supernatural Being Looking Outward. If it had landed a few hundred metres away in any direction, it would now be dangling in the midnight-blue void, off to the side of the revered Earth Beast, whose broad base rests on the sea-floor at a depth of three kilometres. For hundreds of kilometres around this seamount, there isn't anything but open ocean. It's a long way to Haida Gwaii, over 180 kilometres, and further still to Prince Rupert on the mainland.

A yellow buoy with a fluttering flag – red with diagonal white stripe, indicating 'diver down' – leans and straightens as the line settles in the current. The skipper of the *Storm Dodger*, the twelve-metre longliner Todd chartered to bring them out here, is up in the wheelhouse. His creased, bearded face is set out to sea. With hands wrapped around the wheel, he leans into the turn, his arms scarred and sunburned. A mild-mannered man from the Canadian prairies, he needs space, so he is at ease out here.

When the boat comes around to point toward the marker buoy, he throttles back and drifts closer to it. He leaves the wheel to look out of the portside window. Scanning the blue, he picks up the wide wings of a black-footed albatross as it tips the cresting swells. The bird arcs around the stern.

Her keen eyes, set in her exquisite geisha-like face, search endlessly for fish. A pair of storm petrels flutter and pick for zooplankton in a trough off the bow. Apart from the seabirds and the animals

47

swimming unseen below, they are utterly alone out here: a small bobbing object in a vast blue wilderness.

The *Viking Princess*, the longliner they'd passed on the way out, had told him they'd 'filled up' with rockfish. The skipper is envious. He'd rather be fishing than serving these marine biologists. He steps back into the wheelhouse and peers through the window down to the aft deck to see how they're doing.

A red inflatable dive tender with a diver sitting in it sways below the davit. One of his crew, a thin, rolled cigarette in his mouth, is at the controls. Another is steadying the tender. The skipper mutters into his beard, 'Not bloody comfortable with putting people in the water all the way out here. *Dodger's* a fishing vessel, not a bloody dive boat.'

His crew has dubbed this week-long trip the 'holiday cruise'. If they'd been fishing, the aft deck would be painted with blood and guts by now. Heavy metal would be blaring to get them through continuous eight-hour shifts of hauling lines and packing fish on ice, rain or shine.

The skipper's eyes go to the stern where a dive platform, resembling a high-rise window-cleaning lift, has been suspended. Todd and Claire lean against the railings of the platform to keep their balance. They're fully kitted in their dry suits, tanks strapped to their backs, fins on. The sound of their metal dive lights, attached by straps to their wrists, clanging against the metal rungs of the railings carries up to the bridge. The boat wallows.

Claire can feel the steel platform vibrate beneath her finned feet as the ship's engines idle. She is sweating profusely inside her dry suit. The gloved hand with the dive light clutches the railing. In her free hand, she holds the underwater writing slate. They've exchanged roles for this dive: Todd wants to make a short documentary of their trip, so he now has the video camera. Their task is similar to the other survey work they've been doing this summer. Except here, on this remote reef where fewer people have dived than have walked on the moon, they will focus on identifying as many species as possible – to show its significance as a biodiversity hotspot. Which will, hopefully, support the creation of a marine protected area.

'You look a bit nervous.' Todd shuffles his fins to adjust his balance.

'I'm fine. Just can't wait to get in the water. Ah, there we go.' Claire gestures with the slate at the dive tender being hoisted off the deck.

Brian, their standby diver, waves at them from the tender. He is one of Todd's older colleagues from UBC and was largely responsible for securing Todd's tenure at the university. His relaxed manner makes Claire feel safe to be in such experienced hands. He will wait topside to pick them up after their dive, and retrieve them if they come up off the line for whatever reason. She knows he'd rather be diving this morning, or sleeping in like Howard, the fourth diver on the expedition. He'll get his chance on the second dive. Because of the depths involved, the four divers will each only dive once a day, so they can maximise surface intervals between dives.

Brian's grey hair disappears as the tender is lowered over the side. A few seconds later, Claire hears the outboard engine starting, and the lines that lowered it come swinging back on board. The captain leans out of the wheelhouse and shouts down at them, 'I'll holler when the buoy comes along the starboard side, all right? If you hop in then, you'll be upwind of it when you hit the water.'

Todd gives him the thumbs-up and turns to Claire, 'All good? Five minutes max bottom time at fifty metres, right?'

'Yep. Can't wait. I'm boiling in here.'

'Let's keep it safe, eh? We've still got a whole week out here.'

'I will. You too.' But he's turned to look up at the wheelhouse.

The skipper's head appears through the wheelhouse door. 'Let her rip! And for God's sake be careful!'

They slip their masks on, adjusting the neoprene of the hoodies around them to make sure they're sealed. Claire finds Todd's pale eyes behind the glass of his mask. She can see how amped he is. He gives their trademark 'let's go' chin-up nod. Smiles. They shuffle forward, and Todd steps off the platform and into the sea.

For some reason she hesitates for a few seconds, her fins over the edge of the vibrating metal platform. For a moment, Náan's creased, expressionless face appears before her – a brief but vivid flash. Then she takes a deep breath, her regulator rattling loudly in her mouth, and joins Todd with a white splash. The fishing boat floats ahead, and they're two lone divers bobbing in an open ocean. The marker buoy appears off the starboard quarter. Brian is clipping the bow line of the tender to it, then sits and waves to them. The gentle breeze catches his wispy hair as they swim over.

At the buoy, Claire grabs hold of the rope. She clears her mask quickly, looks down to take in the vast blue below her. She clasps her nose and equalises even though they haven't started descending yet. Realising she's holding her breath, she breathes out. *Relax. A bit of nerves, that's all.*

Todd takes his regulator out of his mouth and looks up at Brian, 'See you later.' He turns to Claire, winks, and without another word releases the air in his buoyancy jacket.

Claire is out of sync with him and has to shift her hands to find her air-release button. She hastily lets out all her air and jackknifes down to Todd, who is already several metres below. She hardly notices the soup of see-through animals she's dropping through. The salps, the sea squirts, the small jellyfish and the comb jellies. In among them are the near-transparent larvae of many species of fish and invertebrates, surviving till it's time to drift back to shore and settle on the mainland reefs.

At three metres, she passes the first two stand-by scuba tanks. A few metres lower, the second pair. These are here in case they go into 'deco', or decompression, and need spare air, as they plan to dive to a depth of fifty metres. If they came straight up after spending the amount of time they're planning to down there, they'd get decompression sickness. The nitrogen would fizz out of their tissues and blood in large bubbles. 'The bends' is an excruciating way to die.

Claire catches up with Todd as they sink below fifteen metres, turning to watch their exhalations rise. Round, reflective plates of air, wobbling eagerly upwards before splitting into ever smaller bubbles, eventually reaching the surface as froth. As she drops through the water, Claire relaxes into her normal yogic dive state, anticipating what is about to be revealed.

Gradually, she starts to hear the gnashing of myriad crabs, shrimp and fish. A sleek, oceanic blue shark appears from behind and undulates slowly past her; its black pupil, set in pure white, swivels to take her in. The shark veers suddenly to avoid Todd. Two, three more come in from different angles. Soon they are surrounded by blue sharks. Their petite lower jaws, set well back from their noses, hang almost comically. A few come in closer to check them out – inquisitive, recognising their presence, but without any aggressive intent – before angling away to circle endlessly. Like all sharks, they have to keep moving or they'd sink into the depths.

Claire looks down. A blur of brown emerges from the ultramarine depths – faint movement, a swaying field. SGaan Kinghlas revealing himself. The marker-buoy weight has landed in a sloping arena of feathery red algae, wafting in the ebb and flow of the swell. They drop down and land in it like skydivers. Claire rests on her knees, and the solidness of the sacred seamount rises up through her body. Gives her comfort. She can hardly believe she is here. She looks up to where the sharks, silhouetted now, are still circling.

Todd has switched on the powerful light mounted on his camera, transforming the layers of juvenile rockfish, which cloud over the algae, into tinsel. Larger adult yellow-eye rockfish and grey widow rockfish come and go from view.

They adjust their buoyancy to hover comfortably just above the kelpbefore swimming over the drop-off, where the volcanic bedrock slopes into the depths. Here the seaweed is replaced by colourful encrusting reef invertebrates. Claire scribbles names down furiously on her slate, looking up to identify more. Clusters of giant barnacles coat the lips of overhangs, where gangly brittle stars hang in clumps.

Attached creatures coat every square inch. When the beam from her dive light finds the orange lips of an open rock scallop, they snap shut. A moss crab, its legs and carapace decorated with live sponge, trundles along between the fingers of soft corals that sift the water for food. She touches an extending white plumose anemone with her gloved hand, and its tentacles retract like closing fingers. A banded tiger rockfish fins out of a hole toward her beam, looks at her, turns and returns to the safety of the reef. She's in awe in the intimate presence of all this teeming life which makes up Supernatural Being Looking Outward. She imagines for a moment that she's swimming through his close-cropped hair. Tickling his temple when she touches the bedrock with her gloved fingers.

Claire is already starting to feel the intoxicating effects of nitrogen narcosis, the 'narks', that strange drunkenness that results from breathing compressed air at these depths. The air tastes metallic. Her mind is becoming dreamy, and she looks toward Todd to give the A-okay sign, which he returns. *He'll be feeling it too.* Her light plays over a splaying sea fan, stops as it illuminates a translucent yellow-brown egg-case attached by tightly coiled strands at each end. She angles her light from behind. The silhouetted skate larva wriggles in its yolk. It's the first time she's seen a live mermaid's purse. *Cool!* She looks up to show Todd, but he is some way off, further down the sloping reef. She leaves the purse and fins to catch up with him. *We need to stay together.*

Her heart swells as a large yellow-eye rockfish, close to a metre in length, swerves out of her way. The fish is gravid, her belly visibly swollen with live young. Claire has read about this species being viviparous, but hasn't seen it for herself. *Precious, pregnant life. So many firsts here.* Her whole being sings with the joy of being immersed in this fecund soup swirling around the seamount. *So little time down here.* With each few metres of depth, the endless water grows a darker shade of blue. When she plays her light over the reef the colours are that much brighter.

They come upon a discarded fishing line, probably from the *Viking Princess*. A few hundred metres of longline with baited hooks floating up off the reef, never to be retrieved. The first few stainless-steel hooks glint naked in their beams. They clear a rise and see the rockfish, hanging hooked but still alive. They draw near, and the rockfish flails to get away, is pulled back abruptly by the line in its mouth. It gives up, exhausted, rapidly opening and closing its mouth. Todd hands her his gear and fins over to it. He grabs the line and draws the exhausted fish closer until he can tuck it under his arm. With a few twists he frees the hook with his other hand. The rockfish bursts away and disappears from view, leaving behind a shower of scales which glint in her light. Further along, there are more. Too many to free on this short dive. Some are dead.

An albatross, the barb of the hook protruding out of the naricorn on its beak, grows larger as they swim toward it. Its splayed wings are frozen in a last desperate struggle to swim back to the surface. When Claire holds a wing and swivels the bird on the line, a few bubbles escape, and the bird's dead eyes stare at her – she has to look away and take a deep breath. As the sound of her escaping breath fades, she hears, coming through the water, a faint call. She cocks her head to the side, a bit like a dog. Searches the blue gloom, but there isn't anything. *Probably a far-off whale, that's all.* She returns her attention to the swaying line of ghosts, and kicks to catch up with Todd.

Finning along, she asks herself, *Would people still eat fish if they could see this carnage?* And, *I wonder if they'll listen to us? To protect this place?*

Out of the corner of her eye, Claire catches movement – a huge Steller sea lion barrelling straight toward her. She barely has time to lift her arms and scrunch her eyes closed as she braces for the impact. The sea lion veers at the last second, but Claire is still knocked back in the water by the force. She sucks air, opens her eyes. Her heart is thudding in her chest. The sea lion is hanging in the water in front of her. A large male. His bulging, chocolate-brown eyes glint in the beam of her dive light as they face off. Quite still, he studies her. And then without warning, he barks. White teeth flash to produce a burst of bubbles, which trail as he pirouettes and twirls away. Claire starts. A second, smaller sea lion appears by his side, as if out of nowhere. *His mate?* She begins to relax as they perform before her. They glide in, turn on themselves to twirl and arch and spread their fins to fly away once more. Forever moving. Forming shape-shifting silhouettes in the blue halo of surface light. *Master freedivers*, she thinks. *And at fifty metres!* She turns to see if Todd has seen them. He cocks his head once. She can see him smiling.

A movement on the reef catches her attention. Tentacles as long as her arms are extending, attaching, oozing the giant Pacific octopus forward. Claire guesses from the large size that it's a female. The octopus keeps her raised cat-like eyes on Todd, who's dropped down to film her. Her skin shift-shapes as she slinks. Then freezes. Turns pale white. Blends once more. Four other eyes are following her covert creeping: there's nothing a sea lion likes to eat more than an octopus.

The octopus disappears into the shadows, forcing her body into all available cracks and holes. All suckers latch. Her siphon flares and billows while the rest of her is still. A shrimp dances out of the way. Todd is low on the reef, but pointing his camera up at the sea lions as they rush past Claire, mouths agape, teeth bared. The larger sea lion hits the octopus at speed. Rips her from the reef and shakes her violently. He lets go as black ink appears like magic. The octopus jets out of her dark cloud, a phantom of herself, and down to the reef. But before she can reach it the other sea lion intercepts, attacks her tentacles and flies away with two of them trailing from the side of its mouth. The larger sea lion, close behind, snaps hard into the octopus's head. Her three hearts shatter and her blue blood bursts to suffuse the sea along with her ink. The sea lions keep coming in, ripping her apart until all that remains of her is a tightly curled, writhing thing. Drifting ever downwards.

Todd is well below Claire, engrossed in filming the sea lions. She dare not follow. Her dive computer has started flashing and beeping.

Fifty-eight metres. Right at the limit for safe diving with compressed air. *We have to go up,* the thought comes clearly. Claire holds up her air gauge, confirms again that the needle is edging into the red – she barely has enough air for the ascent. Her eyes bore through the water, wanting to catch his attention, but he's facing away. Todd and the seals, and what remains of the octopus, are moving ever deeper. Fading from view. Vague thoughts form … drift away into the thickness. *He won't be thinking straight. Should I go after him?* The myriad pale anemones and little feather stars that dot the dark reef appear to her as actual stars … planets, constellations. In a far-off galaxy. She squeezes her eyes shut. *Focus on breathing. Stay calm.* She forces herself to look up, into the lighter-coloured water where her outbreaths are rising. *Must go there.* Her eyes come down and search the darker depths. Nothing seems real, as the rapture of the deep beckons.

Faint patches of lighter colour in the midnight-blue gloom could be his rising exhalations. *Or not.* She glances at her dive computer, which is flashing the word 'ascend'. She decides to count out ten seconds. *One, two, three …* Every second feels like an eternity in this twilight zone. *Four.* She desperately searches, wills him to appear. *Where is he? What is he doing?* She looks up again. At the light. Takes another precious breath. *Five, six.* Her regulator rattles as she draws out the dense air. *Must conserve air.* Her mouth is gummy, dry. *Seven.*

At *eight,* a woman's voice comes to her. 'Go up, Claire. *Right now!*'

Claire squeezes her eyes closed as madness beckons. Pure instinct drives her legs as she begins to fin back up the slope. *Must find the line.* Disorientated, she slews sideways, crashes into the reef. The audible clang of her scuba tank on rock brings her out of darkness. *Don't panic.* She looks at her dive computer. The numbers make no sense to her. *Just swim up!* After what seems like ages, the thin dark stripe that is the ascent line appears miraculously before her; she flails the last few metres to reach it, grabs hold of it, close to tears, and begins her ascent. As the narcosis lifts, the screaming in her head becomes confused voices, then fades to lucid numbness. She knows she can't ascend too fast. She has to make sure she isn't overtaking the small-est bubbles of her own breath, which faithfully rise and rise to the light. Wide-eyed, she slows, scans around her. There is no sign of the blue sharks. With one hand on the line, she pivots as she comes up, searches, begs, for his air to join hers. But there isn't anything. The stand-by scuba tanks come into view, and above them the silhouette of the dive tender.

Náan doesn't come to her. No sea creatures visit her. She has to hang there, clipped to the decompression line, breathing. Breathing inter-minably. Suspended in a blue void. The tender, with Brian on board, is a mere few metres above her on the under-skin of the sea. When she looks up past her rising exhalations she can see it clearly. But she can't go there. Not yet. She has to degas for thirty-five long minutes, according to her dive computer. With desperate hope, she searches the sea that holds her. But there are no telltale bubbles. The minutes tick by and her brain, numb with distress, finally says the words … *He is not coming up.*

She has to control her crying. When the emotion grows too in-tense and her mouth contorts in grief, her mouthpiece leaks at the sides and she splutters, at risk of breathing in water. Claire calls out from her heart for the one who has the answers but remains hidden, but there is only an impenetrable darkness behind her closed lids. She Down There remains in the shadows.

Claire's air runs out, and she switches to one of the stand-by tanks, tastes the fresh bottled air.

Suspended, reluctantly breathing, her essential life force, her effer-vescent Otter spirit, wanes. This part of her wants to die, and she lets it go. Wills it to die. But it won't. And then, for a moment, she bargains, desperately. With whom she is not sure, doesn't care. *If you release him, I will give it all up. The questions. Please!*

But the endless blue remains silent.

Below her, massive SGaan Kinghlas squats, and she submits to his omnipresence. To Ocean's embrace. And the line she clings to with gloved hands becomes an umbilical cord.

She closes her eyes and breathes out the minutes. Knowing that when she rises up the cord it will be to a new world. To a life without Todd.

- THE BUSH MERMAN -

Boesmansvlakte Farm, Karoo, South Africa
December 1980

The old iron windmill, like most in the Karoo, has the name *Climax* inscribed on the vane in faded red. It stands at the base of the flat-topped koppie behind the farmstead where Gwen and her parents live. In this exact place, the polished Y-shaped stick pulled down heavily in the diviner's hands to point to where the water lies. The windmill draws from the vast, brackish sea trapped deep below this dry, weathered land. Once a swamp inhabited by dinosaurs, but hardly vegetated now.

Nineteen-year-old Klaas Afrikaner, still discovering his well-muscled frame, has climbed the windmill as high as he can and hangs off into the air. Closing his mouth, he takes measured breaths through his broad nose to calm himself, hardly noticing the overwhelming fragrance of dry honeybush that fills the air. His hazel eyes, unusually light for a man of mixed race, are fixed on the winding line of the dirt road stretching to the horizon. He's seeking the telltale dust wake of her father's car, bringing her home from boarding school. A long summer holiday stretches before them, before she starts university in the new year. It has been many months, but she has written. And there were those hearts and kisses. The creaky blades barely turn behind his head as the wind decides. Her name and all it means fills his head to bursting ... Gwen!

From up here, he can see where they were born: she in the big farmhouse, he in one of the stone huts with the flat corrugated-iron roofs clustered behind the tractor shed. This is where his father and the other Coloured farm labourers are housed. It's also the house where his mother died giving birth to him, her only child. He came into the world before Gwen, by almost a year, but he's always felt two steps behind her. When he was growing up, the other farm workers nicknamed him 'Hottie' – short for Hottentot – on account of how his face resembles his mother's Khoisan forebears, who lived in this area for centuries. And because he could be a bit hot-headed, like the famous Baster rebel leader Klaas Afrikaner, a direct ancestor on his father's side, after whom he is named. When Gwen learned at school that the word Hottentot is derogatory, almost as bad as the 'k' word, she forbade anyone on the farm to use it. They still do though, behind her back. But when they say it, it's with a tone of endearment, respect even.

The sun is low in the dry December day. Its orange light lingers on the far hills, above the deepening shades of khaki and grey on the flats. A shifting wind dribbles a rolling tolbos this way and that between the stunted bushes and tufts of bleached bushman grass. It snags on the rusted barbed wire of a sheep fence, strung between hardwood posts. In the brief stillness, when the wind is elsewhere, there is, if you're attuned to it, the whisper of forgotten stories, of mythical creatures long gone, and of water.

The wind turns the blades that crank the piston to probe the earth, lifting water up its sheath to spill into a wide circular dam. The dam has a whitewashed concrete wall, yellowing where it's been patched. Such pumps and their dams are the lifeblood of the Karoo. Without the water they bring, there would be no stories. Klaas has no idea on this day that his story will be shaped by a far more watery world than this farm dam.

He sees the car! Slowing to pass over the bumpity iron trusses of the cattle-grid entrance to the farmstead. How had he missed it? So close already. His heart thumps and thumps. His chest heaves as he sucks in big air. His palms are sweating. He switches hands to adjust his stance, leans out even further as the car pulls up, and his eyes caress the long blonde hair as Gwen gets out. He's so engrossed, he doesn't feel the wind pick up, shift direction and swing the vane around. The windmill comes to life, and one of the blades clips him hard. Its rusty metal edge slices into his neck, behind his right ear.

He has no sense of calling out her name as he falls – only of the strange world he sees when he opens his eyes.

He's in a cool, all-encompassing wetness. It's strangely familiar, comforting. He opens his eyes and blinks. Thick curtains of stringy green stuff, which he knows as 'paddaslyk', hang in the gloom. Behind this are darker spaces. Tadpoles wriggle in all directions, like sperm, across his vision. A black creature comes into view. It floats up, then claws the water furiously with paddle legs to get back down. Only to float up again, and fight to be down once more. Does this endlessly. It holds a glistening silver dome on its rear end. A water beetle with an air bubble, he later learns. A long-legged frog stretches across his vision. *So, this is what it's like underwater.*

It all begins to fade. But in the moments when the fantastical underwater scene before him is darkening, as unconsciousness beckons, another scene plays in the recesses of his mind. Dancing people shuffle in a tight circle around a fire. The air is throbbing with the beat of their feet. He feels the warmth of the fire, follows the sparks as they fly up to join the stars. The light from the flames illuminates the dry Karoo bushes. The smell of wood smoke, minty buchu, cooking meat, dust and sweat fills his nostrils. Superimposed over this are strange human-like creatures, drifting in a forest of seaweed. The creatures are dancing and drumming as well as swimming in a sky that is water. It's as if the world of the land has met the world of underwater. The swimming creatures are secretive, moving constantly. He catches only glimpses of them behind the wafting weed. They have the heads, arms, and torsos of human beings, but from the waist down they are like dolphins. *Who are these underwater people? Where is this magical place?* He is curious to learn more. But he is leaving, fading into oblivion.

The distant drumming surges as physical pain, and his hand goes to his neck, where the source of it is. A haze is forming and swirling in the water around his head; the figures are swimming away in the red. His thoughts are slow to form. He becomes aware that he isn't breathing. His legs and arms are leaden. Held down by the weed and his clothes, he looks up at the mirrored under-surface. The need for air begins to overwhelm. Instinctively, he kicks off from the bottom. Reaches up with his right hand. His bubble is up there.

His hands grip the rim of the dam wall. With great effort he pulls himself up and hangs over the wall, gasping and coughing. He hears something and opens his eyes and she is there.

'Are you all right? My God, you're bleeding badly, man! You can't even swim, you chop. What were you thinking?' She extends her slender arms up toward him.

Klaas is desperately trying to focus on those eyes he knows are grey-blue. He pulls himself over the rim and falls next to her, a wet, bleeding heap on the dusty ground. Water beetles with silver bubbles swim behind his eyes, which are scrunched up in pain. Her smell envelops him when she kneels to tend him. The effervescent beetles, the enchanting visions, and the musk of travel entwine.

Her glorious voice, calmer now, seems to float around his ears. 'Let's get you inside. Come, you're going to need stitches, my Klasie.'

He lets her lead him, dripping and bleeding, to the farmhouse, up the steps to the stoep and across the cool threshold. Past her father and mother, who are rising from their seats and coming forward with concern. But he walks past them, eyes averted, grunts an embarrassed greeting. The Oslers are gentle folk, liberal English-speaking White South Africans, and have known him since birth. They've been generous, paid for his education, provided transport to the high school for Coloureds – a forty-minute drive each way on a winding, dusty road. But it's still a working farm in the Karoo, where the owners have always been White and the labour Coloured. They might be good to Klaas, and they might condone this close friendship, even encourage it. But Gwen's father is still 'Baas' to him, and her mother still 'Medem'.

Gwen takes him to the guest bathroom, where she makes him sit in the empty bath so he doesn't bleed on to the floor. She strips the bloodied khaki shirt off him, dries his face and stems the flow of blood from his neck with an old towel. Wraps it tight like a midwinter scarf. Catching her breath, she stands with her hands on her hips and beams at him.

'What the hell were you doing at the top of the windmill?'

'I wanted to see you arrive.'

They stare at each other. Grinning. Searching. Finally, he can see into those eyes. And it's as if he's drowning again. He swallows hard.

She breaks into her wild laugh as she turns away. 'I'll be back in a jiffy. Going to grab my mom's sewing kit and some brandy, okay?' She stops by the door and says over her shoulder, 'By the way, you're looking hot. You been lifting sheep, or what?'

When he's sure she's gone, he uses the hand not holding the towel around his neck to shift the raging erection trapped awkwardly in his wet pants. 'Eish, I'm sure she saw,' he mutters.

When she returns, Gwen fusses and dabs and sews up his skin. Klaas drinks neat brandy from the bottle for the pain – such is the way on a remote sheep farm in the Karoo.

She wipes the last bit of blood from his neck. 'You're going to have a lekker scar here. It's going to look like a gill slit.' Her laughter rings around the tiled room. Klaas can feel her breath near his ear when she whispers, 'All done, sweetheart.'

He turns to thank her. Delirious with pain and her smell, and the delicious sound of those words spoken for the first time, he finds her face right there and they are kissing. He closes his eyes, and the aroma of brandy and the faint taste of figs enter his life forever. His head fills yet again with water beetles floating upwards, ever upwards, and he's acutely aware of her breath – her nostrils breathing air into his, and his into hers.

It takes several days for the singing in his ears to clear, to hear the creaking of the windmill or the crunch of his veldskoene on the dry grass of the veld. And a few more before the neck wound becomes itchy. The sun rises above the far hills without a cloud in the sky and the days are long. Work on the farm is slowing before Christmas, with just the odd fence or leaking water pipe needing repair, as they wait for the sheep grazing on the scrubby bushes to grow their coats to be sheared. He often dreams of the strange swimming people who appeared in his watery vision. And during the day he looks toward the dam, thinks of the real creatures that live there. Water now contains magic for him. The sea becomes a dream.

He gets up well before dawn so he can complete his tasks as quickly as possible and be with her. Each day, when he sees her for the first time, he has what he calls 'warm chest flushes', and she has what she calls 'the blushes'. They take to exploring the farm on horseback while his wound heals. Gwen saddles her chocolate mare Tallulah, while Klaas borrows his father's work stallion Duiwel. On one occasion, he tumbles off Duiwel in full flight because his eyes were so fixed on her waist swerving and rising on the saddle, her blonde hair floating in the wind. Blood drips from his knees and forearms where they've struck rock. He spits out bush bits and dust as she dances around him, out of breath, flicking her blonde hair and weeping with laughter.

The day she pulls out the crude stitches, they seek out water. Gwen teaches him to swim properly in the same dam he fell into. The sensation of immersion, the way the water envelops his skin, is strangely comforting.

One morning, her father presents them with an old dive mask from a holiday in Buffalo Bay. That evening, Klaas studies the map of South Africa in his atlas to see where this place is. He imagines the colour of the waves coming in from the ocean.

With the mask, he can study the water beetles. He delights in watching frogs stretch and kick. His favourite creatures are the predatory dragonfly larvae which cling to the weed. Camouflaged, their bulbous eyes see all. When he finds one, he holds his breath and watches. Waits for an unsuspecting water beetle or a red, wriggling midge larva to swim by. Then, wham! When his eyes adjust after the explosive burst of movement, the prey is held by sharp pincers mounted at the end of the creature's hinged arm, drawing back. Eager mouthparts wait below the alien eyes.

Between turns underwater, Klaas and Gwen breathlessly share what they have seen. They stay in the cool water for hours until they get dead-man's skin and their teeth chatter. Then they jump out and lie in the heat on the warm, dusty earth. She likes to hold her forearm next to his to see if all the tanning is bringing their skin colours closer. They roll and chat and laugh and touch. And the ancient earth hums as it radiates the sun's heat. When it becomes too hot, they go back into the water again, and Klaas throws her up in the air, and they slide and touch and throw their slippery green wigs at each other.

One afternoon, Klaas is holding on to the rim of the dam, counting the seconds Gwen has been underwater, when she bursts out next to him. Spluttering.

'That was only twenty seconds, Gwen. Nowhere near your record.'

'No. I came up to tell you something. Guess what?'

'What?'

'I've worked out how to make the pain go away! In my ears.'

'Really.'

'Ja, you have to hold your nose and blow out. It makes the eardrums stop hurting. It pops them. Makes sense. I get it now. The water pressure forces the eardrum in. Pushing air from the other side flattens it again. So it stops hurting. It's amazing. Try it!'

Gwen's mother has been watching all this water-larking, and one day she presents them with a video cassette of *The Silent World*, which has arrived on inter-library loan. The farm workers are not normally allowed into their living room, but somehow this falls away. With popcorn, and furtive touches when they know her parents aren't watching, they soak up every sequence. They watch the film over and over, so they can talk about the creatures, and the way to move water with authority, and how it must feel to go deeper than the farm dam.

When Klaas lies in bed at night, in his single-room home which smells of burned paraffin and stale bed sheets, he listens to his father coughing and muttering in his sleep on the other side of the room. But when he closes his eyes, he feels the ship's bow cut through the water, moving him into an endless blue sea of adventure. He smells the Gauloises. Hears Captain Jacques Cousteau call out, 'Dolphin!' He drifts through schools of fish. Fends off sharks. Catches an octopus by surprise. In these last waking moments of each day, he knows without a shadow of a doubt that he will be a deep-sea diver.

One morning, before the cock flusters onto the donkey cart to crow, he lies awake, staring up at the low ceiling, remembering a vivid dream. In it, Klaas had turned into his forebear. In this dream, Afrikaner wasn't heroically evading the Dutch on horseback, but was swimming away from a menacing island. Guards had appeared on the shoreline and started firing at him – Klaas could almost feel the zinging bullets rip into the water right by him. He'd taken a deep breath and dived down. While he was frog-kicking through the water, he'd been joined by seals and all manner of colourful fish, including sharks. He swam on underwater with a fierce determination. Then Gwen had appeared as a grinning mermaid. Bubbles came out of her mouth as she laughed, pointing at his penis, 'Look, you're not a Baster. You're a Bushman after all. Everyone knows they have permanently semi-erect peckers.' Embarrassed, he'd swum away furiously. It was the desperate sensation of running out of air, the same as he'd felt in the dam, which had woken him.

Klaas looks down at the neat tent, his morning glory. He gets them most days now. *Does this mean I'm becoming more Bushman?* He shrugs off this silly notion, goes back to the dream. The underwater images were a mashed-up version of the Cousteau movie. And he guesses the island was Robben Island, where Afrikaner was banished after being captured in 1761.

The story of his namesake, the defiant Baster leader, is a fireside favourite with the labourers. After a few dops of brandy, his father tells with relish how Klaas Afrikaner rallied the mixed-race settlers in the north-west Cape to the point where they were talking up independence, to the alarm of the colonists. Klaas has been told he is like his forebear so many times, he's come to believe he carries a part of Afrikaner inside him. Perhaps he isn't as defiant as Afrikaner is described to have been, but he certainly identifies with the man, whom he's been told was fiercely independent. His father often reminds him that he is 'hardkoppig', always thinking he knows what's best. Every time he says this, Klaas responds in the same way, sometimes muttering it under his breath: 'Yes, I am, and I do.'

The cock crows and Klaas lies there, contemplative but content, as it heralds another cloudless Karoo day. But it isn't delicious thoughts of Gwen that fill his mind this morning, as his erection eases. It's a question. He has determination, yes; but determination to do or be what? In the dream, he'd been swimming towards something as much as away from the shooting men. And Klaas knows, in a moment of clarity, that he wants more than fireside tales. He wants to fulfil his own expression of the Afrikaner who resides within him. He knows he wants to swim. He's just not yet sure where to.

As Christmas approaches, Klaas notices the changes happening within him. He is reflecting more than ever. Dreaming. When the adult labourers get drunk on Saturday nights, with cheap wine and brandy bought with their week's wages and brought back on the donkey cart from town, he disappears. He finds himself walking alone in the veld. Weaving absentmindedly between the fragrant bushes, resting in the night air, thinking, taking it all in.

One Sunday, Gwen invites him to walk with her to the ruined Boer War encampment up on a ridge not far from the farmstead. Reaching the crest, they clamber over the low enclosure of stacked rocks so they're within the laager, and sit in the bit of shade thrown by the wall to catch their breaths. Klaas glances to his side and scratches at something sticking out of the hard earth. He spits on his thumb and rubs the dirt off to reveal the dull copper of a bullet shell. He cranes his neck and peers over the wall, down to the railway line which cuts through the farm. Imagines a train coming. Having to shoot at it, like the Boers did.

Gwen looks down at the shell in his hand, leans into him. 'Your Bushman grandfather, on your mother's side, probably worked as a tracker for the Boers.'

'Really?'

'Yes. There's a picture in the Boer War book in my dad's library. I'll show you. You should be proud. Everyone hated the British.'

'Aren't you English?'

'Not really. Not any more. We are South African now. My dad's father only bought this farm after the Boer War. The British were cruel in that war, hey, Klaas. They invented concentration camps, you know. For the Boer wives and children who they captured on the farms. That's how they won the war. By cheating. And there's a new war now, Klaas. No one talks about it. But some of the teachers at my school told us what's really going on. Apartheid has to end. My dad says so too. People are fighting for this. I am going to join this fight, Klaas. So that you and I can be South African together.'

When Gwen finds his hand resting in the dust, he can't breathe. Each time he replays her words, he forgets the 'South African' part.

Gwen is a playful soul at heart. It's natural for her to communicate her growing affection, and so, too, protect her heart, with playful banter and teasing. He is warm putty in her hands, clumsy and loyal. But she grows quiet when she senses his strength.

For Klaas, it has always been her. He knows no other. He had previously thought her out of bounds, but now he is emboldened as his defiant inner Baster man rises.

Besides, she has given him permission.

They feel these things and more. They believe that, as long as their twin souls remain true to each other, anything is possible. That forever is within reach. And when they lie on the rough wool blanket on their backs in the veld, as they do most nights now, staring up at the celestial presence of the Milky Way, they are indeed as close to seeing eternity as one can be on this earth. For the sky is so unpolluted by light here that, in decades to come, eleven governments will collaborate to construct a colossal array of radio telescopes a little way north, to see as far into time and space as is technologically possible. An outward journey that will also help the human race look inward.

Right now, they feel for the first time the mystical presence of an infinite universe, as it weaves into the meshing fabric of their love. There the comforting Southern Cross, there Orion's Belt, there a shooting star, there another musky waft of her scent, there the jackal's sharp retort in the expanding stillness.

In these moments, it feels to Klaas as though his Bushman heritage, his love for this woman, all of this and his future, which he knows will be on and under the ocean, all flow into one. In later years, when he finds himself staring up at this self-same sky while out at sea, missing her painfully as time stretches on and on, he'll experience this same longing.

'Did you see that one?' Her fingers squeeze his.

He squeezes back in reply. *Yes … forever yes.*

They discover the rock paintings on one of their long horse rides. They're following the ephemeral river that bisects the farm, venturing further up than they've ever been. All along this dry riverbed there are foetid pools choked with reeds. Here frogs and snakes survive, and dragonflies lay eggs that turn into the scary, water-breathing larvae Klaas studies in the dam.

Every few years, when big rains come, the river floods in a frothing brown fury. The stacked, bleached wood and grass wrapped around trees and bushes on the bank attest to the height of the floodwater. When the waters subside and evaporate again, Klaas and Gwen scour the newly eroded banks for treasures: garnets, rubies and rose-quartz crystals from the oldest earth. On the dried pans, the flat areas where

Bushmen used to camp, they find rounded ostrich-shell beads, animal-skin scrapers, and arrowheads made from obsidian brought from afar.

After the rain comes life. The swelling and dividing and union of cells. Seeds send forth shoots. Leaves glisten in the dawn light. Delicate blossoms appear, dots of colour on the drab sand. Bushes of kapok-bos, the wild rosemary, burst into white, as if it has snowed overnight. Even the inanimate seems to come alive as lichens spread on the rocks. Grasshoppers hatch, sometimes in multitudes, to gorge on the green. For a brief time, a week or two, there is urgent copulation, flowering, rampant growth. Devouring and assimilation. For before long the incessant sun, the singing cicadas, and the dust devils will return. The flowers wilt, the seeds harden, the ants carry the last grasshopper wings underground, and the whisperings from another time drift restlessly across the fossilising land once more.

The cliffs of a long rock ridge, set alongside the river, rise above them when they rein the horses to a halt, all hooves and dust, and dismount.

'I bet you there's a cave there, over to the left of the hamerkop nest.' Gwen is pointing to the untidy pile of sticks belonging to the brown bird with the hammer head who stabs frogs and snakes and insects along the river course.

They tether their horses to a thorn tree and clamber up the ridge toward the nest. The singing stillness of the hot rocks and dry air surrounds them – until a baboon barks. A loud, sudden resounding 'Boah-hom!' that echoes off the cliffs.

'Big male.' Klaas cups his hands around his mouth and imitates the primordial African call, with practised accuracy: 'Boah-hom!'

Gwen laughs, and points, 'There they are. Check.'

They look up to see where the troop is retreating along the cliff face with agile ease. The alpha male is leading. Some twelve baboons of various ages are following, one female with a baby clinging to the long brown fur of her belly. They put their heads down and continue up the ridge. The baboon calls again, further away this time. Plump, surefooted dassies scatter, then stop in their tracks to turn and stare deadpan before clambering away again. His father still has his mother's satin-soft kaross made of dassie fur. He'd told Klaas she used to throw it over her legs when she sat by the fire in winter.

Gwen is right. When they scramble up the last bit, squeeze past the flaking stem of a butterbush tree, they find themselves in a shallow cave. The floor is dusty and littered with drying piles of dassie dung. She grabs his arm. They look at each other in disbelief as they gather their breaths. They are not the first humans to be here.

They edge closer to examine the exquisite Bushman rock art adorning the back of the cave. Men with spears and bows and arrows are intricately captured in dark ochre. And there, in shades of faded yellow, orange and red, is a herd of springbok. Higher up, mostly orange in colour, is a long-necked creature that must be a giraffe. Some of the paintings are faded and appear ancient. Others are much fresher. Many generations of artists.

Klaas touches the rock wall below a figure. He is careful not to bring his fingers too close to the pigment. 'Wow, when last did a giraffe walk around here?'

'These are incredible, Klasie.'

He can feel her breath on the back of his neck as she leans into him. This has to be the most magical moment of his life. They move along the wall to study a depiction, in faded red and orange ochre, of the most sacred animal to Bushmen. Eland. Its rump is exaggerated. And the artist has used distinct tones to give a crude indication of depth, so it looks well rounded.

'I read about this,' Gwen whispers. 'We did *The Heart of the Hunter* by Laurens van der Post as an English setwork.'

She is running her fingers over his forearm, so Klaas has to concentrate to hear what she is saying.

'He describes how they go into a trance state before they paint. To enter through the gateway into a place that exists beyond the physical realm. And how, once there, they meet the natural spirit that resides in all living things. So, these are not just sketches of what they saw out

there' – she extends her hand out across the land. 'I think they are trying to show what they saw and felt when they ventured to the unseen
world.'

Klaas listens to the sound of their hushed breathing, merging to
carry whispers from the swimming figures he'd seen in his dam dream.
He blinks and the indecipherable voices are gone.

When they turn to each other, Klaas is instantly distracted by the
light fuzz of blonde hair below her ear.

Gwen blushes, leans into him and turns her attention back to the
paintings. 'These are magical beings, Klasie. From the other side …
painted by your people. This is your heritage. Don't forget it. When I
see these paintings, I feel like I understand you better. Be proud of who
you are. And don't change, okay? Please don't ever change.'

Gwen's quiet words tickle his ears and enter his consciousness like
the wind that comes before the rain. And there they stay – these words
that affirm.

Gwen tugs at his shirt. 'No way. Klaas, look at this lot.' She draws
him a few steps to the side, and they clasp hands as they stand before
the most exquisite composition of all. Central to this painting, executed
neatly in rich red ochre, is a thin humanoid figure which extends across
the wall for close to a metre. He, or she, is in the shape of a smile, or an
upturned bow. Fifteen smaller human figures swim around this slender
wraith. They are swimming because they have forked fins as legs – like
dolphins. Some have their arms outstretched and seem to be pointing.
One holds a strange bow-shaped object in his hands. Another holds
what looks like a short stick, perhaps for digging or starting a fire. Several have longer, pointed sticks. Klaas wonders if these are for spearing
fish underwater.

The gentle air of their open-mouthed breathing is the only sound
in the cave. Which somehow seems to be growing in size. He doesn't
tell her, but it feels like he knows these people. He is sure he has seen
this scene before. In his dreams. In the dam perhaps?

Gwen steps forward and points up at two finned figures swimming alongside each other, holding out what appears to be a long spear between them. 'This is you, and this … is me.'

'Ja. Beautiful.'

They stay in the cave for a long time that day. Klaas goes to the horses tethered in the shade and fetches the water bottles and some biltong. The loose shale clatters under his veldskoene when he scrambles to rejoin her. And he decides then that these figures are indeed magical, and that he won't forget them. Not ever. They are a part of him and he a part of them. From now on, this will be their special place. They don't talk much as they sit, chewing and sipping, staring out over the flat land, much as his forebears must have done in this exact place. When he glances over his shoulder at the merpeople, they swim into his subconscious. And when he looks away over the land and closes his eyes, his mind is filled with the fantastic creatures he will discover when he goes down there – into the ocean. Becomes the man he knows he must become.

Gwen, however, is in deep contemplation about how she will fight to right the wrongs of this beautiful, cruel land – so people can choose to be with whomever they love, in the way she believes she will be with Klaas. She runs the nails of her hand over the scar on his neck. Up through his close-cropped hair. 'Your korrelkop reminds me of a Karoo koppie,' she says, as her other hand waves across the dusty expanse.

While she is staring out, he kisses her below her ear in the secret place they have discovered. When he touches her there, she squirms with ticklish pleasure until she squeals and digs her nails into his arm to never stop.

'Before I leave, Klaas, let's come and sleep here. Here, with your eland and your merpeople.'

Without a word, he leans to the side and retrieves the gemstone, the ruby, still warm from his pocket. It's a lustrous, rich red and the size of a sheep's eye. He extends his fist, opens his fingers to reveal it for her.

'Oh my God, it's exquisite, Klaas. Where did you find this? Is this for me?'

He reaches for her hand, places it on her palm, 'I found it in the riverbank after last year's flood. I've been keeping it for the right moment. Yes, it's for you. I, I love you, Gwen.'

She doesn't reply at first, holds it up, so it catches the light. Lets his words swim around a little. Folding her fingers around it, she turns to him. 'I love you too, my Klasie.'

They lean in and kiss, not with the heated passion of previous days, but with a newfound tenderness. As she closes her hand around the ruby and brings it up between their pressed chests, Gwen vows to treasure it for the rest of her life.

They sit in silence, side by side, and gaze out over the dry Karoo. To the south, where the ocean lies. To where Klaas imagines the Bushman artist must have seen these swimming wraiths.

'I'm going away, Gwen. When you leave for university in two weeks' time, I'm going to leave as well. To join the navy, to be a diver. I saw an advert in a newspaper and showed your father. He understood. He made a phone call. He told me they said they do take Coloureds these days, and he'll write me a letter to take with me when I go. He said he'll buy a train ticket for me to get to Cape Town. Said something about me reminding him of himself when he was my age. How he sees me almost as a son. Wants to break the cycle … whatever that means. My father won't be pleased with me leaving the farm. But I don't care. I'm going. I want to be like Jacques Cousteau. I want to be with the sea animals. The navy will teach me how.' Klaas lets out his breath as if to shoo out all the remaining points he hasn't made.

She rests her hand on his forearm in the ringing silence; finds his eyes, which are luminous.

Klaas feels himself sinking deeper and deeper into those fathomless grey-blue irises, a colour he will come to recognise in the Benguela Current when it wells up off the Atlantic side of the Cape Peninsula after a good southeaster.

They carry on talking openly and sincerely, of many things, and with absolute certainty.

A few days later, when Gwen's parents are away overnight at a sheep auction, they do return, and finally consummate their forbidden love on his mother's dassie kaross, which Klaas lays out on the cave floor next to the fire they build. The baleful yelps of black-backed jackals on the plains below echo their scattered laughter and gentle cries of passion. As the moon rises in a sky full of stars, and the night wind whispers, the old iron windmill creaks to bring up water from a sea of another time.

Yzerfontein, Cape West Coast, South Africa
March 1983

Ten metres below the surface and holding on to a bull-kelp stipe, Klaas is transfixed as he stares through the clear water. He wants to stay in sight of her for as long as possible. He focuses his mind on slowing his racing heart – a freediving skill he's beginning to master. From the relative safety of the kelp, he follows her graceful lines as she moves effortlessly through the water, the sun streaming down between the swaying stems of the forest that rises around him. The playful Cape fur seals, who moments ago were flying past him, are huddled in the thickest kelp, by the rocky island that rises out of the sea closer to land. They show the bloodshot whites of their dark, swollen eyes as they strain to search the surface for movement. Klaas has dropped the spiny crayfish, a nice-sized Cape rock lobster, he'd held in his gloved hand moments before. He's alone in the water; his fellow crayfish hunters are around the next point.

She turns. He is in awe. She is magnificent. All powerful. The most beautiful creature he's ever seen. He can't tell if her round, black, ex-pressionless eye is on him or not. As the light plays on her graceful lines, her body eases through the water like it's a part of it. Without hesitation, Klaas swims out, straight towards the four-metre great white. The shark completely ignores him, but instinct tells him not to venture closer – that the shark is well aware of him. He hangs in the water, frozen. She is magnificent. Massive. Sleek. She glides away from him, and he loses sight of her black eye. When he has to blink, she's gone completely. The sudden sense of loss is overwhelming.

Klaas rises to the surface. He takes a gulp of air before immedi-ately putting his face down in the water again, scanning from side to side and into the depths. Seeing nothing, tendrils of fear creeping in, he backs up into a patch of thick kelp. Head out of the water, he looks for a fin. Water drips off the visor of his mask, obscuring his vision. Nothing. He shoves his face down again, searches the depths. A sudden movement – a streaking brown blur – and then the calm of the surface explodes, and Klaas's head bursts out of the water, eyes wide.

A surge of white frothing water, a quivering mass rising out of the water, mere metres away. The seal is held by dislocated, extended jaws. Gnarly teeth imprint in Klaas's vision before the massive bulk crashes down, dorsal fin slicing back into the water. The shark's caudal fin thrashes the water into showers, and Klaas quickly wipes the spray off his mask. Her giant jaws close, leaving pink gums exposed. Water billows out through her gill slits. There is an audible pop, followed by a burst of deep crimson, before shark and seal disappear underwater. Only ripples remain. Neither shark nor seal surface again.

Klaas is breathing in rapid, shallow gasps. His nails have bitten into the kelp stipe he's gripping. He's swearing quietly, a tense whisper, using the Lord's name in vain many times, struggling to process the enormity of what has happened in front of him. Within him. The outrageous image is etched into his mind. The adrenaline surges through his body, and he starts to feel pure joy, an overpowering natural ecstasy. He lifts his face toward the sky. 'Fu-u-u-ck! Yeah!'

Klaas stays in the water until his teeth start to chatter. He can feel the shark has moved on, but he knows she's somewhere out there in the vast heaving mass he's immersed in, that he doesn't want to leave. And he knows he will forever miss her, for she is now more than an animal. Now she lives within him. And as he stumbles out of the water, clutching his fins, he knows. He knows why he loves it down there. It's because he feels totally safe.

He doesn't tell the others when they gather around the fire that night – four other navy divers on weekend leave, camped out here on this remote coastal farm. As they lick their fingers after turning the splayed crayfish smothered in garlic butter on the coals, he listens instead, laughs at the stories of crayfish lost, of productive hunting holes discovered underwater. Perhaps he doesn't want them to take this away from him with their counter-stories, as is their way. Or maybe they won't believe him. He listens, too, to the sea as she sighs, lifting and dropping the kelp in the darkness.

They pass around the bottle of cheap wine. When it lands in his hands, Klaas snorts at the picture of 'Oom Tas' on the label. The smiling Coloured farm labourer with the felt hat bears a striking resemblance to his father. He looks up and around, doesn't say anything. He takes a sip and passes the bottle along. The men tease and slug and laugh, and Klaas zones out – allows himself to go there. To miss her.

Gwen would have clapped her hands and whooped in shared delight if she'd heard what happened today. A few months ago, she wrote to say she'd moved and no longer had a telephone. She still hasn't explained why. Something to do with her political involvement, he suspects. He'll write to tell her about today; decides he'll use the word 'majestic' to describe the shark.

Gwen's university breaks don't always coincide with his few days' naval leave. It's been three long years since they both left the farm, and almost a whole year since he last held her satin waist, which smells of honeybush when he holds his face close. That long since he felt her naked, trembling limbs around him. Tasted that teasing tongue, felt the blinding ecstasy. He runs his tongue over his lips, licks off the garlic butter. Sighs. He holds his hands toward the fire. Everything would be perfect if he could just see her more. *Can't believe she's already in her final year. What does Sociology even mean?* When she does write to him, it's all about 'the struggle'. That it's 'intensifying'. In her last letter she told him she'd joined the ANC. He didn't know one could just do that. *Aren't they terrorists?* He'd checked the letter again to make sure it hadn't been opened by naval intelligence, as they sometimes are.

He looks around at the faces of the men in the firelight. Four young men in their prime, enjoying this momentary respite in the war against 'die rooi gevaar'. The Russians, supposedly massing in

Angola and Mozambique to overthrow South Africa. The faces are all tanned, White. He's only the third man of colour to be admitted into the elite South African Navy diver course, which has been running since the Second World War.

He's earned his place around this fire. More than anyone. Their instructor, known as the Dicky, a racist White with a thick Afrikaans accent and built like a rhino, had spat the words in his face: 'I am going to get you thrown off this course, Hotnot! Since when did *you* lot even swim?' But Klaas had weathered the abuse. Grown stronger with each stupid challenge, with each frothing insult. He developed an ability, self-taught, to kick into what he calls his 'Bushman trance'. When he enters it, no one can do anything to him, for he becomes Klaas Afrikaner, riding bareback through the Karoo, laughing into the wind. At these times, he's aware of what's going on around him, but he can block out all distractions, including physical pain. When the screaming, the rib-poking and face-slapping stops, and orders are barked, he simply obeys. Without hesitation, and with a quiet determination that has won him respect and come to define him in the close-knit group of men.

Most of all, he loves being underwater. *How emotionless was that shark's black eye today?* Klaas continues to stare blankly at the flickering flames, contemplating how much he comes alive when he's down there. How he's growing into it, just as he always imagined he would. Down there, in that giant womb, he feels accepted; and there's no skin colour underwater. When he comes out of the sea and into the air world, he is stronger.

He stretches forward to put another log on the fire.

'Nothing like an open fire under African stars, hey, boys?' someone comments. Klaas settles back against the sand dune, listens to them chatting, and smiles.

In a few days' time, a couple of them will begin their special-operations diver training alongside the notorious Fourth Reconnaissance Unit, the Recces, at Donkergat, the bleak peninsula that extends into

Saldanha Bay just to the north of where they're camping. He's intent on joining the handful of select Class II attack divers. The insignia of the great white shark, central to the silver-plated mess dress badge he'll earn if he gets through the course, will carry special significance for him after today. He makes a silent vow to emulate the raging intent and absolute focus that he observed in the great fish today.

Later in life, the other two elements of the badge will come to mean more to Klaas. The anchor will signify stability. And Poseidon's three-pronged trident, more important still, will remind him of his deep love of the sea and his vow to protect all her sea creatures with all of his being.

'Hey, Klaas! I heard you almost killed the bloody Dicky.' The others crack up. The man speaking across the fire is already stationed at Saldanha, but he's heard the story going around of Klaas's now legendary altercation with the infamous dive instructor.

During the final week of training, the recruits were told to kit up and get ready, four per pontoon on the black dive boats. They had their masks taken from them and were blindfolded before being whisked away out of Simonstown Naval Harbour and into False Bay, travelling at speed. On the command, they'd executed a negative-buoyancy entry and proceeded, as instructed, straight to the seafloor to find at least one buddy and wait. For what, exactly, they weren't told. They'd practised this procedure many times before, but never blindfolded. Klaas had been a bit freaked out diving blind, not knowing what he was going down to, or even how deep.

He touched sand at what he figured was about fifteen to twenty metres of depth. He heard the other divers' rasping inhalations and the explosion of air as he breathed out. They swam until they bumped into each other. Groped around until they were settled back to back, kneeling on the bottom as they'd been taught, breathing in and out of their mouthpieces and concentrating on not allowing water up into their nostrils. Waiting for whatever was going to be done to them. For they knew there'd be some kind of attack, some kind of test.

Before long, they were set upon by seasoned navy divers, intent on ripping their regulators out of their mouths, punching them in the stomach as hard as one can through water, and unbuckling the weight belts that, if released, would send them like corks to the surface. Those who didn't react fast enough, or who panicked and rushed to the surface for air, were kicked off the course immediately.

Klaas survived. Sensing, in the way that came naturally to him, a subtle change in water pressure, he knew that someone or something was approaching at speed and with no good intention. He'd surged forward, felt for the attacking diver, grabbed his buoyancy jacket firmly by the chest straps and headbutted him as quickly and as forcefully as he could, shattering the diver's mask and breaking his nose. It was the Dicky.

Klaas smiles wryly as the others recount versions of the story. When he thinks they aren't looking, he runs his fingers over the small scar on his forehead. He enjoys this moment of affirmation within the group, this bonding talk, as the unspoken hovers in the space between them. For they all know a time is coming when they'll be called upon to do things they haven't done before. Violent things. So, they stay up swapping stories which become increasingly silly with each swig of wine. It's long past midnight when Klaas looks at the fire sending sparks up into the vast sky filled with stars, and relives that first underwater experience in the dam, the rock painting, and lying with Gwen in the cave. It all seems so long ago. He searches the evening air for the sound of animals, but all he hears is the ceaseless rumble of the cold Atlantic. When he closes his eyes and dozes, the last thing he sees is the surging rage of the shark.

A loud sound startles him. He sits up straight to find the others shrieking at him. He joins in when he sees that one of them has fashioned a horn out of a length of dried bull-kelp and is blasting a version of 'The Last Post'. When the bugler is done and their laughter dies down, and they settle back to staring contentedly into the flames, Klaas takes a lungful of the kelp-laced fog coming in from the sea.

So … I'm a Navy Diver. The piping trill of an oystercatcher carries in the night as it wings away. The call fades and the quiet crackling of the fire is the only sound. And somewhere out there, he knows, his shark is cruising.

Seaward of Inhaca Island, Maputo Bay, Mozambique
31 March 1984

In nine years' time, when his beloved suffers through morning sickness, he will feel great empathy. Right now, Klaas wants to die. He staggers through the forward gun bay, intent on making the heads before the convulsions start again. Reaching them, he grips the handrails on the bulkheads of the confined space and retches into the bowl. His stomach writhes as this painful bout of heaving deposits yellow bile. Dropping to his knees, he hugs the bowl. Moans as the acidic stench fills his nostrils. His throbbing brow sweats. Everything lurches around him.

The four powerful diesel engines scream. The South African Navy strike craft, designed by the Israelis for the Mediterranean, is a metal beast gone mad, gnashing at the massive waves. She shudders, her spine pressured to breaking point, and fights her way northwards into the post-cyclone head swells of the Mozambique Channel.

Klaas begs all the gods for it to stop. But it doesn't. It just goes on and on. When he feels enough strength, he staggers out of the heads. With hands on both bulkheads, he forces his way forward in the narrow alleyway which stinks of diesel fumes. His whole weight compresses into his knees, before he is lifted off his feet. Simultaneously he's slammed from side to side. When he reaches the forward mess, he folds clumsily into his bunk, jams himself there so he won't fly out, and clenches his eyes closed in a futile attempt to leave this reeling world. Every few minutes, the sweating starts afresh. His stomach cramps and writhes, but there isn't anything left in there.

Random clips from his memory and imagination play as an endless stream – snippets of conversations, the sun coming through a kelp bed, scenes from movies. He sees the rock paintings in their special cave.

Gwen looks over her shoulder at him for a long time while galloping ahead on her horse. Fades when he can't hold the image any longer. But it's their last conversation that tortures him the most. He replays it. Over and over. *If only I had a way of warning her.*

They'd spoken by telephone two days before he boarded ship in Saldanha. *Was the tickey box at the base bugged?* he wonders for the hundredth time.

Gwen had said that the weather was getting really hot at Rhodes University. She repeated this. And when she added, 'And the wind is blowing with a special force,' he understood. The Special Forces were onto her and her fellow activists. 'I'm *definitely* going on holiday, Klaas,' she said, and he understood the meaning of this too. 'I'm going to the place in that Bob Dylan song. You know the one I mean? We listened to it together that time. To the main city there. Me and a comrade.' She wasn't sure when they'd speak again, but she'd be in touch. She needed to call her parents.

When he'd said, 'I love you, Gwen,' she'd not responded. Too freaked out, he presumed. All she said in return was to be careful, to look after himself. She'd write if she could. And that she'd just called to say goodbye.

The same questions replay in his mind as his body struggles to endure the reeling hell. *How are you going to be in touch? Why didn't you say you love me back? Where the hell are you?*

Shortly after their phone call, Klaas had sensed that a mission was imminent. Trucks started bringing extra victuals. And their daily at-sea drills intensified – the launching and retrieving of the black high-speed inflatable craft off the sides of the adapted missile-carrier. When he'd seen the ship's officers in deep discussion on the deck with the Recce commander, he knew something was brewing. And it felt big.

One evening after dinner, the captain came into the forward mess and told them they were leaving that night on a 'high-level operation – top secret'. He said they'd been tasked with 'showing Frelimo who's in charge'; something about 'harbouring ANC terrorists'. He explained they were cooperating with Renamo, the opposition rebel movement in Mozambique, but that they must never repeat this to anyone.

Klaas hadn't really been paying attention, but went cold when he heard the words 'target' and 'strike' alongside the words 'Maputo' and 'Mozambique'.

Gwen. Fuck, what if it's true? Could it be? God, when will this hell end? He agonises as the ship shudders deep into a massive slab of ocean.

They'd gone into immediate lockdown. Level One, the highest state of security. The ship's landline had been disconnected. No one could leave. He had no way of contacting her. Final provisions and several black canvas bags, containing the Recces' high-powered explosives, guns and ammunition, had arrived on board before midnight. They'd sailed for Cape Point at two in the morning, slipping around it to steam to Cape Agulhas, and then against the Agulhas Current up the east coast past the Transkei, past Durban, on to southern Mozambique. Four torturous days and nights at sea.

Klaas drifts into a delirious half-sleep, calling weakly on his Bushman trance state to ease the pain of the shuddering chaos, the endless limbo.

Oh my Gwen, where are you? Please don't tell me …

Klaas is struggling to rise in the farm dam with the water beetles and the frogs when the bosun's despicable voice penetrates his dream. He breaks the surface into fogged consciousness.

'Rise and shine, you lazy shits! Hands off cocks and onto socks!'

Klaas groans. *My mouth tastes like the bottom of a birdcage.* He has a splitting headache, can't easily open his eyes. When he finally does, he squints up at the spitting face framed in the forward mess deckhatch.

'Come on! We've got a job to do, you fucking landlubbers! Captain's briefing on the aft deck! Now! Let's go! Let's go!'

What a prick.

Klaas registers that the ship is no longer fighting the sea. *Thank you. Oh, thank you, Lord.* He eases out of his bunk. Around him others are spilling from their pits. Groaning, muttering obscenities, scratching their crotches. Pulling shaky legs through navy-blue trousers. Clothes and toiletries lie strewn around the mess. The smell of cheap underarm deodorant, diesel fumes and vomit hangs in the air.

Klaas joins Pieter, his dive buddy on this mission, up on the grey, wet aft deck. He greets him in Afrikaans. The air is humid and warm, sweet almost, and he fills his chest with it. The smell of burned diesel lingers around the drying ship. His whole abdomen still aches. They lean their backs against the two black inflatables, which have been fitted into the space where the missile launchers usually sit.

'You alive? That was rough, hey.'

'Ja, hectic. Put me underwater in a storm any day.'

'True.'

They fall silent. Feel into the tension. The ten Recces stand in a bunch nearby, and Klaas studies them surreptitiously. None of them has a military haircut. You could easily mistake them for well-built surfers. That's the whole idea, he supposes. Men of uncertain identity doing things no one sees. When he'd first met the tall blond over there, both of them trying to force down some food in the galley, he'd looked into the man's eyes. What he'd seen had scared him. Those eyes had engaged men in close combat and won. They were quick but felt nothing. Had guided hands to spill blood.

The rest of the ship's crew saunter on board in their seagoing blue. They stand in loose groups, stretching their legs, more relaxed than the Recces. They're staying aboard. Some are smoking in cupped hands.

A spreading orange glow heralds the dawn. All around them, the glassy cobalt blue creams at the hull of the ship as she rides easily to the east of Maputo Bay. The captain arrives on deck and takes up his natural position in the middle of the circle that has formed. He's a short man, almost noble looking with his closely cropped, pointed beard.

'Men, we are in Mozambique waters. Off Inhaca.' He swivels to point to where a low island is barely visible off the port beam.

'We're going to spend the day cruising around in this approximate position. Staying out of sight of all vessels. The crew will clean the ship and ready her for our mission – we've been through that. You lot' – he motions to where Klaas stands with Pieter and the Recces – 'you get your shit ready. You know what to do. Remember to do final checks on each other, make sure no one's carrying anything that identifies you as SA Defence. Carry only the emergency survival packs you've all been given. The false passports and the local currency. Good? Understood? Good. At sunset, we will sail into Maputo Bay at no more than five knots to ensure we reach the landward side of Inhaca at approximately zero one hundred hours. I believe breakfast is ready in the galley.' With this, he strides off toward the bridge. After breakfast, Klaas and most of the others go below deck and collapse in their bunks.

Four hours later he walks back on deck, takes a deep breath as he opens his chest, cracks his neck vertebrae. Runs his hand over hair still wet from his shower. The sleep had been short but restorative. He blows on the mug of soup and stares out over the sea. *She seems to be sleeping too*. He follows an albatross as it weaves, marvelling how the bird's wings seem to caress the crests of the swells and down into the troughs without ever touching the water. Above him, crewmen are stringing additional lights on the ship's superstructure to disguise her as a prawn trawler when they come into Maputo Bay. The Recces, clad only in too-tight black shorts, are testing the silent pneumatic winches of the davits. These will launch the two inflatables, one off each side of the strike craft. He lifts his head to gulp the last mouthful of soup, places the tin mug on the deck and vaults up into the inflatable. He exchanges grunts with Pieter and joins him as they go through their final dive-gear inspections. He focuses on checking the valves and the pressures of the gas cylinders of his French-made rebreather unit, which will allow him to breathe underwater without emitting telltale bubbles.

Klaas rests his hands for a moment, looks over the sea to where Inhaca Island is showing on the horizon. Beyond this lies Maputo. *If Gwen's there she has no idea of what's coming. And there's nothing I can do about it.*

Maputo, Mozambique
1 April 1984

It's 3.30 a.m., and the bay of Maputo lies calm under the moonless night sky. Klaas and Pieter sit hunched in their inflatable, an unseen shadow in the dripping mangrove swamp to the south of the city. It hardly makes a sound as it pulls away, the powerful outboards covered in noise-reducing casings. Klaas watches as the four Recces they've just dropped off wade ashore, canvas bags slung over their backs, to join the others who came on the second inflatable, anchored nearby. The Recce platoon will be met here by Renamo rebels, who will transport them to the sprawling suburb of Matola, to the west of Maputo. There they will blow up ANC safe houses and their inhabitants. They'll be brought back to the same location and picked up before dawn.

They clear the mangroves and the skipper, a silent dark figure in the stern, guides them past the commercial harbour. And then northwards, past the lights of the city blinking quietly in the darkness to the west. The only light comes from the glow of the compass the skipper's using to navigate toward their destination, a small craft harbour known as Club Naval de Maputo. Here, if Renamo intelligence is correct, are moored two thirty-foot Mozambique Frelimo Navy gunboats.

The two divers adjust the Velcro flaps holding the limpet mines, shaped like old movie film canisters, to their rebreather units. They shoulder the black units and adjust the straps to fit them snugly to their backs. They lift the rubber air-hoses over their heads, quietly test the airflow. The skipper slows as they approach the harbour, turning ninety degrees to seaward to bring the inflatable to a slow stop about 300 metres offshore. When they look landwards, the red and green harbour-entrance lights blink back at them. The skipper cuts the engine, moves forward past the two divers to quietly drop an anchor off the bow, then steps back to the stern. He cracks the light sticks zip-locked to the mines on the divers' backs, transforming them into glow-worms in the dark. They each have matt-black boards, no bigger than a clipboard. On these are mounted luminescent under-water compasses as well as gimballed revolving-blade distance meters, which will kick in when they swim. In hushed monotones, they confirm the bearing they are to swim.

Klaas has imagined how this moment would feel, but now, as he finds himself in it, he has no thoughts. There is no contemplation. All thoughts of Gwen have receded. Without a further word and with hardly a ripple, they slip over the sides of the inflatable and head straight down.

On deck, the skipper raises a fishing rod, places a straw hat on his head, and switches on a dull yellow lantern. While the divers are com-pleting their mission, he will be a local fisherman out for the night in the bay. He lights a cigarette and the ember burns red as he drags. He sits back and waits for the bite that will never come, for there is no bait on his hook, and stares blankly out over the still waters of Maputo Bay.

The two divers find themselves in shallow water, less than ten metres; when they settle on their knees on the seafloor, they're in a meadow of seagrass. It's the warmest water Klaas has ever felt creep into his wetsuit. With only the glow of their light sticks to locate each other, the divers crouch side by side and orientate themselves for their swim. Pieter checks his compass bearing and launches up and into the water, fins off over the seagrass.

Klaas follows close behind, as they have rehearsed dozens of times. After a few minutes they locate the harbour channel, where the sea-grass gives way to sloping silt bottom where it's been dredged. Finding the deepest part of this channel, they slip undetected into the harbour.

The lights penetrate the silted water enough for the divers to see the inside edge of the southern harbour wall. They follow this along the seafloor, littered with bottles and an old deckchair, to where the two gunboats are moored, visible above them as faint silhouettes.

Pieter stops under the first gunboat and Klaas removes the limpet mines from Pieter's back. The ripping sound of Velcro strapping being pulled apart doesn't carry up into the humid night air, where on the gunboat decks the young Frelimo seamen have fallen asleep on watch, tucked into their AK-47s. Klaas presents his back to Pieter. When he hears the Velcro separating and feels the weight removed from his back, he has his first thought since getting into the water. *This is it. Action at last.* He fins off toward the second gunboat, anchored immediately ahead. The two divers rise together from the seafloor to the gunboat hulls, and with hardly a sound they attach and arm the limpet mines.

Klaas pictures the seamen being woken by the sound of screaming metal and violently pressured water and air. The men will probably not be injured, but stagger around dazed on the rocking deck. The explosions will likely cripple the boats but not sink them: shatter their prop shafts, blow a sizeable hole in the steel hulls of the engine rooms and submerse the engines in seawater, right here where he's placing the second mine. They were told during their briefing sessions that Frelimo doesn't have the capability to repair these Russian-gifted boats.

When he flips the twelve-minute timer switches and drops down to the seafloor, his thoughts finally return to her. *She could be in grave danger.* She might be murdered this very night by the same men who sat alongside him only minutes ago.

He and Pieter begin their return swim, feeling their way along the inside of the harbour wall. They reach the entrance channel and head back into the bay, where the inflatable waits for them. Klaas swims on, his physical body following training and orders, but his mind is far from calm, far from ordered.

Two minutes have ticked by on the limpet-mine fuse timers.

They clear the deeper channel and are creeping along the seagrass bed of the bay, heading due east, when he becomes aware of something to his left. He can't see what it is, but senses the disturbance of the water caused by a large creature moving near him. He stops. Feels the change in pressure again. His heart races. *Bull shark?* Breaking mission protocol, he reaches for the underwater dive light strapped to his left wrist and flicks it on. The powerful but contained beam shoots out, a light sabre in the murky water.

The dugong, not much bigger than Klaas, is easing over the seafloor, ripping up seagrass by its roots. Her forked tail fluke swishes effortlessly as she mows her way through the meadow.

Pieter, unaware that Klaas is no longer following, swims on ahead to the rendezvous position.

An intense emotion, a sadness, rises up as Klaas plays his light over her grey-brown torso, sees her front flippers lifting, almost prayerfully, to help with the feeding. He looks into a black-pea eye set deep in a leathery face, and something shifts. He has to choose. Now.

As often happens underwater, time becomes elastic. The adrenaline of the mission is keeping him in a heightened state, but at the same time, with each slowing breath, his mind has started streaming images … Jacques Cousteau and his crew laughing and free. Mystical Bushman figures swimming. He and Gwen, hand in hand on an imaginary beach. The peril to her that this day's dawn may bring. And at four in the morning, as he feels the gentle presence of the dugong in a shallow bay on the south-east coast of Africa, a question rises up through all of this: *Am I on the wrong side?*

Fuck it! I've been training to do this for years. His boyish enthusiasm and hunger for adventure have taken him this far in the navy. And he has endured so much to get here. *Why can't I do what I know?* But the frustration is momentary. Their telephone conversation replays, penetrates. It's as if he's ready to hear the message she has always brought. Is suddenly faced with the reality of the warped apartheid land he has to return to. With sudden certainty, his mind already on his next course of action, he knows that he can't go back. *I can't just leave her. It's probably too late but I must try.*

Klaas checks his compass bearings, takes one last look at the dugong and then switches his light off. Fins furiously toward the harbour.

With a minute remaining, he reaches the gunboats, rises off the dimly lit seafloor and starts to unscrew the first firing pin to flood the trigger mechanism, knowing as he does so that there is no turning back.

The pin resists. *The seal, stupid.* He fumbles for his dive knife. Hammers the pin with the flat back of the knife handle to break the waterproof seal. With a few turns, the pin is free and drops from his hand through the water. Finning furiously, Klaas swims across to the second gunboat, knife in hand.

The mines will remain, like stubborn remoras, on the hulls of the boats until they are hauled out on the dry dock for their annual cleaning. Workmen will be bewildered. The devices will end up welded into a large post-civil-war artwork by a Mozambique collective, a metal tree of hope, curated by a local Catholic priest. The same priest who will play a lead in bringing the two warring sides to their first truce. The sculpture will travel to London, Paris and New York.

Klaas is naked but for the sealed plastic package strapped with duct tape to his midriff. Keeping to the shadows of the service area at the rear of the boat club, he finds a waste skip, gags as the stench of rotting food escapes, and discards his wetsuit. His rebreather unit, mask, fins, dive light, the navigation board, and dive knife are all attached to his weight belt, which he's left on the seafloor of the harbour.

He rips the duct tape from his skin and tears open the sealed package. Places the tape and the wrapping in the skip. In an adjacent courtyard, he unpegs a pair of jeans and an African-print shirt from a washing line. He has to force the slim plastic packet into the left pocket of the jeans, as they are tight around his thighs.

As the first pinkish-orange light emerges in the east over Maputo Bay, Klaas walks barefoot and with grim determination toward the lights of Maputo, in the direction of the suburb of Matola, where he believes Gwen is. He keeps rubbing his face and eyes, desperately trying to recall the location of the target houses on the map they had to memorise during one of their briefings. A car approaches along the promenade, and he thrusts his thumb out. When it ignores him, he puts his head down and walks. He doesn't stop till he reaches Matola. Until he sees the smoke.

There's a crowd gathered across the street from the smouldering house. A makeshift fire brigade is dousing the section where explosions have collapsed most of the roof. Four Frelimo soldiers talk amongst themselves, AK-47s slung lazily over scruffy uniforms. *Really weird to see these guys close up and in the flesh.* It's all a bit surreal. He scans the crowd, sees little emotion in the sullen faces. He supposes they're used to this sort of thing. He notices a bony White man standing off to the side, discreetly taking photographs. His photo identity tag flaps around his neck. Klaas is drawn to him. Following his intuition, he moves closer, and when the man pauses between shots, engages him.

'What happened?'

'No, they are not saying. A bomb, I think.'

'Ah, I see. Who do you work for?' Klaas points to the camera.

'I am a freelancer. For AFP.'

'I see.' Klaas looks away, registering how dog-tired he is. Out of the corner of his eye, he notices the man is looking him up and down. Desperately, he considers his options. *If I run away on these blistered feet, the soldiers will catch me for sure.*

'What happened to your shoes?'

'I, uh, I had a rough night … had to walk home.'

'Oui, this I can see. Do you need a ride?'

'Yes, please.' Keeps looking forward, like he's on morning parade back in Simonstown.

'You are South African, no?'

'Uh … no, I am … um … I'm from Botswana.'

'Hmm.' He lifts an eyebrow. 'Je vois,' as he slings his camera over one shoulder and extends his hand. 'I am Christophe.'

'Hi, uh … I'm Clive,' he stammers, acutely aware of the clamminess of his hand. 'Uh, do you know of a place where I can stay around here? I … I can pay for the ride.'

Klaas self-consciously reaches into his left pocket and extracts the unmarked plastic packet. He holds it so Christophe will see the two zebras on the blue passport. What Klaas's new guardian angel doesn't see is that the Botswana passport has never been used. Klaas extracts a note from the thick fold of Mozambique meticais. When he looks up, he meets the photographer's eyes.

'Put away your money, Monsieur Clive. I know someone who can help you. Let us go. I am finished here.'

Klaas stares out of the window of the beat-up Land Rover, trying to appear nonchalant. *Can I trust the Frenchman?* Christophe asks no more questions as he dodges the potholes, winding his way through the sprawling township of Matola. Tightly packed shanty dwellings, made of variegated corrugated-iron sheets, crowd right up to the busy sidewalks. Bone-thin dogs pick at rubbish piled on street corners. Chickens rush across the road. Men on rickety bicycles balance over-sized red-white-and-blue striped bags of produce or smiling women in brightly coloured dresses on the handlebars, sometimes both.

After a ten-minute ride they come to a compound made up of ad-joining sheet-metal sheds and huts that take up a whole street block. Christophe hoots and a rusty metal gate swings open. A man closes the gate behind them as they drive in. Klaas looks around. They have pulled up in a large courtyard.

A stout, bearded man comes out of one of the buildings set around the courtyard. He isn't smiling. Christophe climbs out, and the two men speak intently in Portuguese. The man glances over Christophe's shoulder at Klaas. Klaas isn't sure what to do. Is this their final desti-nation? Is he being handed in? He decides to join them. If he must flee, then being out in the open will give him more options. He comes around from the passenger side to where they're standing, and his eyes go to the man's hands, which are covered in splatters of red. He gets a whiff of the oil paint, and his body relaxes. The last time he smelt that unmistakable odour was when he'd been with Alexander Rose-Innes.

The famous South African landscape painter had come to spend time on the farm when Klaas was about thirteen. He'd been assigned to take him by horseback to the best vistas.

The man smiles, turns to him, 'So, who have we here?' His eyes are a bit bloodshot, from the paint Klaas surmises, but they are penetrating, kind.

He extends his hand. 'Hello, sir, my name is Clive,' he says, remembering one of the few things his father taught him. *You must have a firm handshake and look them in the eye when you first meet. Be proud. Remember you are directly related to Klaas Afrikaner.*

'Welcome, Clive. My name is Malangatana. Christophe tells me you need a place to stay.'

The famous South African landscape painter he wore Klaas is and there on the eastern Klaas was out of surrounding Then been ashgem in the bion by he shooting fired out of us.

Matola township, Maputo, Mozambique
1–18 April 1984

So it is that Klaas ends up staying with the great Mozambican artist Malangatana Ngwenya. Dubbed the Picasso of Africa, Malangatana lacks the ego. He is a generous man. His talent supports many families, including several war orphans. The painter can see into the hearts of people, and he takes to Klaas. He is intrigued by the colour of the young man's eyes, neither brown nor green. And they seem to have their own light. He might look a bit like an overgrown Bushman – such interesting cheekbones, prominent yet discreet – but Malangatana suspects Klaas isn't, as he claims, from Botswana. Christophe has told him he believes Klaas is ANC, on the run after the bombings. This is why he whisked him away. Malangatana can see flecks of fear in the hazel. He'd like to paint these eyes. He can also see a young man going through the pain of loss. Mozambique is full of people like this.

As news of the bombings spreads, Klaas learns from Christophe and Malangatana that twelve people were killed. Two of the houses taken out had nothing to do with the struggle. The third was an ANC safehouse. A neighbour reported seeing four bodies covered by blood-soaked sheets being loaded onto a truck.

After two days, he can't bear it any longer. Sensing he is in a safe enough place, Klaas seeks out Malangatana in his studio, and opens up. Enough to reveal he's seeking a woman he believes may have been staying in the ANC house that was bombed. He leaves out how he swam underwater into the country with limpet mines strapped to his back. Leaves out that he's gone AWOL from the South African Defence Force. He knows he would be interrogated, likely tortured or worse, if handed over to the Frelimo government. Malangatana, perched on a stool in front of his latest canvas, a mostly red expressionistic tapestry of human faces, peers at Klaas over his spectacled nose, listens to his story, but says nothing.

The next day, as the sun is setting, Malangatana rinses his brushes and cleans his hands, first with turpentine and then with an over-sized bar of green Sunlight soap. He dries his hands on the back of his trousers as he saunters over to Klaas's room. The door is ajar and he eases it open, takes in the young man sprawled on the sheets. Klaas senses his presence and sits up suddenly; their eyes meet. Malangatana can see this is no backpacker.

'Clive, put on your shirt, young man. We're going to the bar. Time for a beer.' He doesn't tell Klaas that he's made discreet phone calls around Matola.

The two men walk into the dimly lit, low-ceilinged hall – really no more than a large shack. Klaas takes in the smells of spilled beer, stale smoke and charred chicken fat. The metal strings and lilting chorus of a looping Mozambican marrabenta tune plays from the shadows. A barman is stacking crates. Malangatana orders two quarts, pays. Klaas looks around. There aren't many patrons in yet. He wipes the sweat from his bottle and turns to Malangatana, 'Do you ever paint underwater creatures, Mr Ngwenya? Like the dugongs you get here in Mozambique?'

'No, I haven't. I am sure it's most beautiful down there. Have you been underwater?'

'Uh, yes, I have.'

'Botswana isn't known for its diving. Perhaps on your travels?'

Klaas picks up the half-smirk and squirms. It isn't in his nature to lie. Before he can answer, Malangatana continues, 'Yes, I have seen dugongs. From a boat. I was on Bazaruto Island one time' – he pauses, takes a long drink from his bottle – 'and saw a herd of them grazing in the shallows. I suppose that's why they call them sea cows ...'

Klaas has stopped listening.

The first thing he notices, after the immediate relief at seeing her alive, is that her face has aged. Her hair has been cut into a neat bob, and it's darker – dyed. He's never seen her in jeans before. She is with three men: a young White man and two who look like locals. They cross the threshold and take a good look around. Klaas notices the military bearing of the two locals and tenses. As their eyes adjust, one of them cocks his head to greet Malangatana. The White man splits off to the bar as the others head over to greet the artist.

And then Gwen approaches the table. Klaas stands up straight, and they're hugging. There is a stiffness. She hasn't kissed him, but he catches her subdued smile, this at least, as they separate. *Must be the bombings,* he reassures himself. His mouth is dry, and his mind is reeling, scrambling to interpret the signals he's getting, and not getting, not wanting to acknowledge. He notices that her eyes don't immediately meet his when they all sit down. *She smells different. Has she started smoking?*

The third man joins them, quarts in hand. Introduces himself as Duncan. *South African,* Klaas picks up immediately. Duncan's straight hair hangs on his shoulders. Below his pale, serious face, eyes obscured by little John Lennon glasses, he wears a goatee. Klaas takes an immediate dislike to him. *University lefty,* he thinks, *and full of himself.* Duncan sits down next to Gwen, directly opposite Klaas, and takes a sip of his beer. He peers through those round glass holes and says, 'So, I've heard all about you, Klaas.'

Klaas grows cold. His limbs freeze. He blinks, not sure where to look. When he briefly makes eye contact with Malangatana at the head of the table, he sees him chortle, lift his beer in a subtle 'cheers'. Klaas breathes out as the adrenaline settles.

Klaas turns back to Gwen and Duncan and is, in that instant, once again, a dumb Coloured servant, back on the farm. For Duncan is leaning in to her, grinning, has taken her hand in his. She's blushing as she looks down at the table. Klaas takes a deep slug of tasteless beer, closes his eyes. He doesn't want her to see him fight back the tears.

He's struggling to breathe, and a humming has started up in his brain. A heaviness descends, here in his sternum, like someone has planted a dive weight there. He's grateful for the conversations that have sprung up around the table, for right now he can't speak. Gwen has turned and is talking to Malangatana, sharing news of the bombings in hushed tones. Every glance at her, at them, is torture. A massive hole opens up in his soul. It will take years before it closes again.

Klaas stays with Malangatana for another two weeks and sees Gwen a few more times, but each time it's more awkward. He can see that she's wary, preoccupied. She avoids eye contact, and they don't talk about their feelings for each other. She says she and Duncan have to keep moving. His own limbs feel heavy. Most nights he gets drunk alone in his room, asking over and over, sometimes aloud, *Why did you give up on us? You said I was your soulmate* – before passing out. He is ashamed of his crying, which he can't seem to control. He avoids eye contact when in company. He helps Malangatana make up fresh canvasses and package finished works to send overseas. When Christophe announces that he's going up north to Inhambane to do a story about a French-funded orphanage filled with landmine amputees, before taking a week off in Tofo, the sleepy beachside town nearby, Klaas asks to join him. They all know it will be a one-way trip.

As happens between men in the streets here, the handshake lingers. Malangatana's hand is comforting, his eyes filled with warmth. Klaas gets into the Land Rover and places the cardboard tube he's been given next to him. He has to bunch up his eyes and wipe them before he winds down the window for a last look. 'Thank you for everything, Mr Ngwenya.'

'It has been a pleasure, my son. I hope you find some peace, Klaas. Write to me, see. Tell me if you see dugongs.'

'I will, sir. Thank you.' The artist reaches in and rests his hand on Klaas's shoulder as Christophe turns the engine.

Klaas will treasure the print, with its stylised animals, including a dugong, in vibrant shades of orange, red and azure. Malangatana has explained that it isn't only people who suffer in war. The animals' wide eyes speak of barbarism, of the deep disconnect between them and humans. The piece will fill him with a deep sense of gratitude each time he looks at it on his bedroom wall.

Even his own father did not shake his hand like that.

– TOFO TAO –

Praia do Tofo, Southern Mozambique
8 September 1991

The oystercatcher strides on the wet, mirrored sky. He is neatly dressed in black and white. A fencer, his blood-red beak the foil. The empty stretch of sand teems with life between its grains: worms, ghost crabs in their tunnels, and bivalve molluscs – his meal of choice. A telltale spurt, no more than a liquid gurgle, and he advances. Lancing into the sand as deep as his nostrils, he penetrates the mollusc in two quick stabs. Out comes the dripping sliver, impaled, twin shells parted. Held aloft for a second, then jammed back into the sand to force his rapier even deeper. All the while, his red legs are dancing. The shell is fully open now, and the juicy flesh is out with a few more slashes. Down it goes in a quick snatch. The oystercatcher struts a few metres, jab-jabbing his red beak ahead of the rest of him, and then suddenly lifts into low flight, arcing over the crumbling waves, to land behind the woman who has disturbed him.

Claire inspects the splayed halves lying on the wet beach. *How efficient,* she marvels. She turns them over, still joined, to study how the bird has completely removed the muscle of the mollusc from where it was cemented on each shell. She drops the bivalve and resumes her beach walk, listening to the ceaseless crush of the shore break, breathing out the tension of the long journey from Vancouver. Ahead, the wet intertidal stretches northwards like a highway as far as her squinting eyes can see. Out to sea, the dawn rays are lancing through the low, tropical clouds, shards of silver on the dark, cerulean expanse. Claire slowly tilts her head to the side, first this way then that, feeling the relief when her neck cracks. Her hair brushes her bare shoulders in the warm air. And she breathes in the onshore breeze: this new, sun-baked, saltwater smell coming off the Indian Ocean.

It's been three weeks since she stepped off the *Storm Dodger* in Prince Rupert and walked down the dock with her dive bag over her shoulder, past the stench of fish guts at the fish-processing plant, where they were filleting and packaging the *Viking Princess's* rockfish from SGaan Kinghlas. She'd hastily packed up all Todd's things and fled the cabin they'd shared. Away from the sympathetic looks, which only drove the guilt deeper. She'd caught the first plane down to Vancouver and holed up with his parents.

She hardly remembers those days and nights. The provincial coroner had come around to question her, returning a week or so later to share his inquest report. He'd sat in Todd's parents' living room with the autumn sun coming through the window, a cup of tea in front of him and the report on his lap, and told them Todd's death was accidental. He opened the folder and read the conclusion, which said that 'all standard safe-diving procedures had been followed', that the 'likely cause of death was probable drowning while under the influence of extreme nitrogen narcosis, consistent with diving at this depth'. And finally, the words that haunt her still: 'Dr Storstrand's body was not recovered, despite a day-and-a-half surface search conducted by the dive-support vessel.'

Reliving the numb hours spent searching the endless expanse above the seamount is painful. But it is the image of him floating, splayed in the deep void, his pale face staring unseeing up to the surface, that tortures her most when it comes uninvited in the middle of the night. When she wakes and reaches across the bed for him, she has to get up immediately. Get going, find something to do. Anything. Before the dark water rises from the depths and threatens to surround her like molasses.

No one blames her. Everyone's told her that if she'd rushed down to fetch him in those crucial minutes, she probably would have died too. After the memorial service, his parents begged her to stay on. They told her she'd always be like a daughter to them. But when she walked through Stanley Park, she found a great emptiness between the towering trees, and when she breathed in the first cold air of the coming winter, she found herself thinking of colour and of sun. Her feet led her back to Dr Eishmal at the university, and she heard herself talking to him about dugongs and about Africa.

From there it all happened very quickly. It only took one phone call to Benito Mutara in Mozambique. 'Yes, come,' he said. 'We need all the help we can get.'

'You're going to love it there,' Dr Eishmal said as he put down the receiver, holding her blank gaze with compassion.

Claire barely recalls being dropped off at the airport by Sandra, a university girlfriend. 'You're going to be okay, Claire. Just give it time.'

When she pulled away from the warmth of the embrace and turned toward the boarding gate, she was completely alone. But at least she felt like she was moving.

Claire's spirit hasn't caught up with her body yet. *Perhaps it's still flying low, a wraith, somewhere over the open sea.* An Air Canada flight attendant told her it takes as many days to recover from jetlag as time zones crossed. *That gives it a few more days.* She wonders what state her spirit will be in when it arrives.

Claire follows the undulating waterline, noticing the profusion of blue things blown in by the onshore breeze. With her big toe, she presses the bloated sack of a bluebottle, a miniature bagpipe. She knows not to touch the dark-blue stinging tentacle, which trails away on the wet sand. She hesitates for a second, then presses down. When it pops, she has to remind herself that there's a whisper of life in the warm, voiceless wind coming off the waves. But just as she can't control the waves or the tides, she can't control the thought that rises … *Todd is never coming up.*

Claire turns abruptly on her heels, as if to walk away from her thoughts. 'It's time for breakfast, for a coffee,' she says, to hear her own voice. She stretches her legs. Lifts her chin and closes her eyes. Breathes. Opens her eyes to this new reality. She will walk the full stretch of the beach on another day.

Approaching Tofo, she searches the hillside for her little cabin. There it is, the one with the rampant red bougainvillea growing up the sides of the veranda: home for the next five months. She's grateful to Benito for stocking the kitchen. *Such a lovely man,* she thinks. *So welcoming.* The cabin is up the slope from the research station where she'll volunteer during her stay, itself no more than a few thatched huts. 'You don't have to come in tomorrow,' he'd told her when he dropped her off. But she wants to.

An old man is walking toward her. He has a hessian sack slung over a shoulder and a rusty metal pole in his other hand. When he draws closer, she can see it's been flattened and sharpened to silver.

'Olá, senhor.' She'd purchased the orange Portuguese phrasebook at Maputo airport while waiting for her domestic flight.

'Olá.' He grins at her. His mouth is toothless. His eyes kind.

'Um, what is in there?' She hasn't got past page two of the phrasebook, so she lifts her hands up in a universal 'Que?', then points at the wet sack. He plants the sharpened pole, leans over to plop the sack down, fishes inside it. A dripping black mussel rests in his arthritic hand.

'Frutos do mar,' he lisps. Grins. Searches her face with sun-bleached eyes, much like Náan's in her final days. 'Mexilhões.'

'Ah, seafood. Mussels. I see. Obrigada.'

He goes into the bag and brings out several more. Extends these to her. 'Você quer comprar?' he asks. She doesn't understand, until he says, 'Dollar? Dollar?'

'Oh … no thanks,' she waves, shakes her head. 'Não. Obrigada.'

He shrugs. Drops the mussels back into the bag, shoulders it. Mutters something as he frees the pole. Walks off briskly on his bony, salt-crusted legs.

Claire reaches her cabin, steps into the cool thatched interior and makes herself a coffee. When she slides open the glass door and goes onto the veranda, she's greeted by the screeching of weaverbirds building their hanging nests up in the old mango tree. The nests are neat and rounded, the smooth-edged openings masterfully woven. Pure works of art. She notices that most of the noise is coming from the males. Their bright yellow-and-black plumage fluffs, and with wings fluttering, they watch nervously as the drabber females complete their inspections. One male is shredding a nest that must have taken days to complete. 'I would have taken that,' she tells him.

She settles into the cane chair with the faded cushions and takes a sip of her coffee, which has a thick consistency, almost Turkish. She opens up *Roberts Birds of Southern Africa* and leafs through the picture pages until she finds him. 'There you are. Eurasian oystercatcher.' The west-coast Canadian ones she grew up with are pure black, while this local species has a white belly. 'Ah, you're a vagrant, I see. Here to escape the northern winter. A bit like me.'

Claire looks up and takes in the bay. She follows the lines of swell curling around the eastern point of Praia do Tofo, Tofo Bay. Off the Casa Point Hotel, a surfer stands and weaves over the face of the wave. His tangled hair flies as he airs off the lip, paddles back doggedly. The lines of swell ripple soporifically, like a seal's skin underwater. Claire sighs. The words of the Bob Dylan song 'Mozambique', which she listened to on her Walkman on the long flight over the Atlantic, replay in her head. *I wonder if he actually danced cheek to cheek here, and fell in love … The sky really is aqua blue … Todd would have loved it here …* She blocks further thought, doesn't go there.

Out in the bay, a whale breaches. 'No way!' Claire exclaims. And just when she thinks she's imagined it, it lifts out again and a white patch appears on the blue where it crashes back. *Of course. Humpbacks. It's that time of year.* She scans the bay. One, then a pair of blows, and then another further out, confirm that there are many whales. She pictures the newly born calves, languishing with their mothers, and the bulls who'll be following them to mate before they all head south again, down the Mozambique Channel, past South Africa, through the vast Southern Ocean to spend the summer months feeding on krill in the Antarctic.

They remind her of the dolphins. She'd been leaning into the guardrail of the prow, staring down at the frothing white bow wave as the *Storm Dodger* cut across Dixon Entrance, with the frosted mountains behind Prince Rupert just beginning to rise to the east. The Pacific white-sided dolphin had appeared out of nowhere. A second had joined and together they had surfed the pressure wave as only dolphins in full flight could – with wanton delight. They burst forth and veered, puffing rapid breaths, swerving back and then surging on.

Her hands had left her leaden chest and reached down to the dolphins. Many times, on previous boat rides, she'd whooped them on, feeling the joy expressed by their taut, streaking shapes. This time she'd offered deep gratitude, and a stream of salt tears. The message she'd got from them, and it comes back to her now, is to keep moving. To just keep moving.

Down on the beach, a barefooted woman, a child strapped to her back with a colourful sarong, is walking along the water's edge. Claire goes inside to fetch a pair of binoculars.

The woman's hips sway from side to side as she balances a colourful oversized bag on her head. The silver scales of small fish that fill a straw basket catch the light as she shifts it from one hand to the other without breaking her stride. Claire focuses on her face, a picture of resignation. Then she smiles as the child's head fills the frame – chocolate cherub, jiggling in slumber. Claire takes her eyes from the binoculars and searches the waterline for the old man. He's some way up the beach already, hurrying along with his determined, hobbling gait. Resting the binoculars on her lap, she counts another seven women walking to town. All have loads on their heads, baskets in their hands.

Claire places the binoculars on the table before her and adjusts her posture, consciously straightening her spine. She closes her eyes to focus into the darkness behind her eyelids. She holds a deep, controlled breath. Feels her heart beating in its cage. Thoughts begin to emerge with her slow outbreath. She allows them to surface, without letting them overwhelm her.

The sun catching the North Pacific waters off Vancouver as the plane lifted: this is the first memory to replay. The batches of floating logs lined up like matchsticks. The fishing boats, laden with salmon on their way to the processing plants. To the south, off the Tsawwassen Terminal, she'd counted six long ships laden with mined coal. When the plane banked east, toward the snow-capped coastal mountains with their clear-cut scars, and beyond them the Rockies, Claire had closed her eyes and collapsed into a deep, pill-induced sleep.

Claire opens her eyes and they adjust to the bright, dusty green of the dune bush, the tan of the beach sand with the figures moving on it, and then the blue expanse of the Indian Ocean. She breathes into her belly, holds her yoga pose, shifts her hands to her knees, breathes out, waits for the next thought or image to show. She closes her eyes again.

As the plane broke through the low clouds coming into land at Maputo, she'd looked out to the west, where slanting grey curtains of rain were drawn across the olive-grey African scrubland and layers of hills disappeared into the haze from the smoke of many fires. Closer to the city, palm plantations filled the space between the scattered villages. Dirt roads connected them to the city, with its sprawling shanty-land outskirts. Cars and trucks trailed dusty wakes. The plane dropped lower and she could see the colourful clothes of people going about. Reds, yellows, oranges. Caught glimpses of her first African faces. People roasting food on the side of the road, walking and cycling with oversized loads. Piles of rubbish. Buses arriving and leaving. A group of children streamed like a school of fish on a barren football field with slanted, net-less goalposts, stopping their play to wave at the plane as it roared overhead. When it jolted down heavily, Claire pinched her arm, whispering through the fog of jetlag, 'Holy crap. What have I done? I'm in *Africa.*'

Claire is still struggling with the humidity that has cloaked her from the moment she stepped off the plane in Inhambane. She recalls the light breeze carrying the earthy hint of rain as she strode across the patched runway to the dilapidated terminal building. Children, dressed in faded khaki, were hanging over the fence on the edge of the runway, laughing as they jostled for a view of the new arrivals. They waved so enthusiastically, flashing their startlingly white teeth, that she had to wave back. Had even managed a half-smile herself. Oh, and the relief at spotting the red maple leaf sewn onto her dive bag, buried on the trolley trundling past her with its front wheel fluttering. And finally, seeing her name scrawled on the piece of cardboard, below a broad smile that seemed so familiar. When she took Benito's hand, it felt to her like what she imagines a turtle flipper might feel: cool and a little bony. He didn't pull his hand away immediately, and when she looked at him, his eyes dark and kind, it made her cry. Without a word, he came forward and held her.

Processing events that happened too fast at the time is having the effect of willing her spirit closer. Perhaps, she muses, it's winging its way grumpily over the hot Sahara by now, heading down the long African continent to find her.

She opens her eyes. Adjusts for the natural glare, feels around her mouth with her tongue to dilute the oily, bitter taste from the quinine in the malaria tablets she's started taking. She reaches for the mug, downs the last bit of sweetened black coffee and stares out over the bay. *What lies below these warm waves? Will her voice come to me again ... when I am down there? Or has it gone now? What will it feel like to dive again ... without him?* She sees the woman on the beach has turned, has left the harder sand near the sea, and is walking up to the northern part of town where the market is. *Time to go to work.*

The warm, powdery sand of the dirt road finds its way between her feet and her Birkenstocks as she walks down to the research station. She stops to shake them out. When she looks up, a glossy brown cock is strutting toward her, leading his flock, who are scratching in the dirt alongside the path. He lifts his head to crow loudly, his impressive red comb waving to greet the rising heat. She can't believe it's going to get even hotter in the summer. She walks on, sampling the air, lazy with the smell of sea and smoke. Hears the skinny dogs bark before she sees them coming off the beach. A gang of glistening naked children are diving after a shiny thing they're throwing and retrieving in the shallows. Further along the beach, fishermen sit huddled under the swaying casuarinas, playing some kind of board game. Nearby, their traditional wooden dhows are pulled up on the shore, waiting for the tide to turn. The faded stone-white sails are rolled up on the long yard poles attached to the masts, and the hulls are brightly painted and patched. When she walks past, the fishermen look up. Acknowledge her with broad smiles, white teeth flashing. She can't resist, and a first proper smile spreads across her face.

Before she turns away from the beach toward the research station, she notices two newer-looking fishing boats pulled up further along the beach. They're much larger than the dhows, and Claire stops for a moment to study their shiny outboard engines. Gleaming white gill nets are piled on their decks.

Benito is waiting for her, beaming like a boy as he stands framed by the door of his office. 'Good morning, Claire! How was your first night? Is everything working at the house?'

'Great, thank you. It's perfect.' She can see he's poised, can't wait to unleash that full-throated laugh she fell in love with the first time she heard it at the airport.

It's beautifully cool inside and the tension in Claire's shoulders and neck eases. The wall curves, for Benito's office is a traditional rondavel, with thick whitewashed walls and a thatched roof. Her eyes adjust and the first thing she notices is the poster. It's the same as Dr Eishmal's, only this one is tacked to the wall, and moths have been at it. There they are again. The Sirenia. She points, and he chuckles.

'Yes, a present from Adam. I miss him. I called him to say that you'd arrived safely – thanked him for the bottle of maple syrup you brought along. We had a bit of a catch-up. I'm a bit starved of academic company out here, you know. I got a lot out of his stay last year. But now I have you! For five months.'

Claire walks over to the long cabinet below the window. The bottom shelf is filled with neatly arranged field equipment. Tape measures, buckets, hand nets, glass jars, clipboards. And two butchers' knives – for dissecting beached carcasses, she guesses. She's more drawn to the spread of objects on the top shelf, illuminated by the morning light coming through the window. She lifts a dried seahorse, turns it over as dust motes turn in the sunbeams. Places it back among the assorted shells, the bits of sea-sculpted driftwood and the chunk of bleached staghorn coral. Behind it, neatly arranged by size, is a row of green urchin shells, the smallest the size of her pinkie nail. She picks up a smooth brown seed and toys with it, feeling its hardness.

'That thing wants to be touched, doesn't it? It's an African dream-bean. The sea carries them far and wide, like the dreams they induce.'

'How does it work? Do you put it under your pillow?' She tosses and catches the bean.

'No,' he laughs, a little nervously. 'You have to eat it. Beneath that tough shell is soft flesh. You grind it up and eat it before bed to induce magical dreams. Helps you commune with the ancestors.'

'You've tried it?'

'Oh, no!' he laughs again. 'I am Christian. No need for any of that.'

She raises her dark eyebrows, turns her attention to a wired skeleton. Runs her hand over the bleached bones.

'A dugong calf. She was found washed up. On Bazaruto.'

'Are they here in Tofo?' Claire asks without turning to him.

'Not really.' Benito steps over to a topographical map taped on the wall. 'See, we are on a peninsula here, with Tofo on the seaward side. Barra lighthouse is up here in the north. On the western side, over here, is Inhambane. Where the airport is. The whole region is quite flat, as you may have seen when you landed. This area here' – he uses his finger to circle the shallow, sheltered area of sea to the north of the sprawling town of Inhambane – 'is where you find the seagrass beds they feed on. There used to be a great number of dugongs, but not any more. Occasionally we do still see them. But often when it's too late. When the fishermen catch them in their nets.'

Claire runs her finger north up the coast to stop at a series of islands. 'How far is it to here? To Bazaruto.'

'About three hundred kilometres. We will fly there when we go up after Christmas to complete the marine megafauna census I mentioned when we spoke by phone. You'll like it there. We could drive, but it would take a day. The road is bad. And there are still bandits about.'

'I can't wait.' The mental image of armed guerrillas stopping the car is interrupted when she notices the small carving. She reaches for it, turns it over in the palm of her hand. *So smooth. Cute face.* Not too dissimilar in style to Otter, hanging around her neck. 'Who made this, Benito?'

'Ah, my little mermaid. It's carved from a dugong tusk. A local divemaster gave it to me. He said he was inspired by ancient rock paintings he'd seen. Painted by his ancestors.'

'I've read about southern African rock art. Is he really a Bushman? If that's the right word to use …'

'Some people say San, or Khoisan. But Bushman is the word he uses for himself. I don't think he is pure Bushman though.'

'A bit like me.' Claire chuckles.

'How so?'

'Well, my mother is Haida, and my father is White. French-Canadian, Québécois.' Claire runs her fingertips along the inscribed lines of the carving.

'Ah, that explains your surname I suppose. This is interesting to me. How is it that he came to Haida Gwaii? Is that the right pronunciation? Adam enlightened me about the geography of your country, but I am still learning how you pronounce things. Quebec is far to the east of British Columbia, not so?'

'Yes, and you say it perfectly Dr ... um, Benito.'

'Ah ah aah! That is two beers, my dear. And I drink export.'

She joins in as he laughs, can't help herself. As they walked out of the airport building yesterday, he'd told her with a straight face that he'd fine her with a beer each time she called him Doctor, and that the opening tally was one.

'Please, sit. You are probably still jetlagged.' He gestures to the two cane chairs by the round coffee table. On the crisp white tablecloth is a jug of lemon water with two glasses, and a vase with a bunch of freshly picked pink bougainvillea. She is touched.

Benito leans forward and pours them each a glass of water, sits back in his chair, 'So, tell me ... how did your father come to the west coast?'

Claire takes a drink of the refreshing water. For the first time she notices the bits of grey sprinkled like dust in his closely cropped hair. 'Yeah, so my dad came to BC after the Second World War. He said he wanted to get as far away from Europe as he could. And then I guess he gravitated to the north of the province, where things were opening up. He worked as a logger first, and then as a fisherman. That's how he met my mum. She was working in a fish-processing plant in Charlotte at the time. That's where I was born, Charlotte City. It's the biggest town in Haida Gwaii. Up in the north of the archipelago.'

'I love that word,' and he repeats it syllable by syllable, 'Ar-chi-pel-a-go. Bazaruto is also part of an archipelago. As you saw on the map. But please, continue. I am fascinated by lineage.'

'Sure. My dad is pretty much retired these days. He still has a small dive concession, for urchins. It's what got me interested in the underwater world. He took me down when I was nine. He let me walk with him on the seafloor on his hookah line.' She sees he's confused. 'You know what a hookah line is, right?'

'The only hookah I know is the one that makes you high,' Benito chuckles.

'No, I mean compressed-air hookah. Breathing off a surface line.'

'Ah, I see. *That* kind of hookah, yes.' He winks at her.

'Anyway, I became fascinated by what I saw. I spent a lot of time while I was growing up helping my dad underwater. My grandmother, my Náan, she decided my animal totem was a sea otter. On account of how otters love urchins.' With this, she puts down the mermaid on the table and pulls out her bone carving, leaning forward to show him.

'It's beautiful.'

'Thanks.'

'So, urchins, hey?'

'Yeah. I never liked the killing. Even lowly urchins. My Náan used to say you could see heaven when you opened an urchin and exposed the colourful gonads, but that if you opened up too many you would see hell.'

Claire reaches for the little mermaid and sits back in her chair, rests her hands on her lap. The smoothed bone starts to warm as she rolls it, her fingers exploring the lines. What is it about Benito that makes her feel so instantly at ease, she wonders. Is it his open, smiling face – beaming genuine curiosity? Or is it the little giggle, which can erupt into laughter at any moment, that draws one in?

'Your grandmother sounds like a wise woman,' he says. 'You must miss her.'

'I do. It's like she's still around, goes with me wherever I go. Especially underwater. Does that sound crazy?'

'No, not at all. We Africans summon our ancestors all the time. What about your mother?'

'She's a social worker, in Haida Gwaii. Many people there are dealing with the pain of loss … the loss of our identity. First the pox wiped out ninety per cent of Haida Gwaii's population. Just after Europeans arrived. And then after the Second World War, our people were sent to residential schools to westernise them. It was our own apartheid, really. They were terrible places.' Claire takes a deep breath. 'My mother helps people confront their demons by rediscovering their

Haida culture. I'm proud of her, of what she's doing. We were never close, though. I'm not quite sure why actually; you'd think with my grandmother ... My, I am babbling on. Forgive me. Must be the jet-lag.' Claire laughs shyly.

'Not at all. You have any siblings?'

'I have a younger brother. He's a bit of a redneck ...'

'What is a redneck?'

'Oh, you know ... he hangs out in bars watching ice-hockey games. Lives in a baseball cap. Swears a lot. He has an outboard-motor dealership in Prince Rupert. He's kind of turned his back on our Haida culture. We all still get along, though.'

Claire reaches for her lemon water.

As she sits back again and meets Benito's placid face, she reflects how, in recent years, she's spent more time with Todd's family than her own. And that she's comfortable with this. She drains her glass, smiles back at him, and says, 'Now it's your turn. Please tell me about *your* family.'

'Yes ... my story. Well, my father and I fled to Portugal when the civil war broke out. My father was an English teacher and worked as a translator over there until he passed away.' It's as if a shadow has come over his face.

'Your mother?'

'Sadly, she was killed before we left.'

'I ... I am sorry.' Claire blushes.

'No, no, don't be. It's fine. It's good for you to get a sense of what has happened here in Mozambique.' He holds her gaze and continues. 'Anyway, our town was raided without warning one morning by Renamo rebels. I gaze was at school with my father. For some reason, they left the school for last and we managed to flee into the bush when we heard the gunshots. That is how my father and I survived. He crept back to the village that night, and when he returned, he said the others were gone. And that we had to flee immediately. I didn't understand. He only told me later that he'd found my mother and my two sisters outside our hut. They weren't of school-going age yet. Which is why they were at home that day ...'

Claire leans into the space between them as he pauses. Feels his pain. She would like to reach out to him. Her fingers slowly stroke the little bone carving she holds in both hands on her lap.

'We walked across the border to Tanzania with nothing. Stayed in a refugee camp for a few months. And then a group of us were taken to Portugal. I think my father was given preference because he was educated.'

Claire listens in silence. Benito pauses for a drink of water. His voice lifts as he continues. 'After school, I won a scholarship to the University of Lisbon. That is where ... and I can't remember why exactly ... I developed a fascination for marine mammals. When Portugal joined the EU, my university started getting funding to do work in Africa. The civil war was ending here, so I came to do the field component of my doctorate here and in Kenya. On dugong feeding ecology, as you know. I moved back here permanently two years ago, even though the war was not quite over. It still isn't. Many of us pray for a formal declaration of peace soon. So that is me. But now, my dear' – and the radiant face is back – 'let us talk about your time here in Tofo.'

'Yes!' Claire breathes out properly. Rests her fingers on the carving.

'Well, besides the census up around Bazaruto, I had in mind that you assist me with some diving-related work here, on the reefs in the bay. I have a small grant to monitor the ecological health of the reef. I understand you are an experienced research diver. Have you dived on coral before?'

'I haven't. Is this a problem?'

'Oh, no. It is pretty basic reef-health monitoring, repeat fish-counts. We use family-level classification, so you don't even need to know all the species. You'll pick it up in a few days. And then there's my pet project, my little school programme. I could do with some help with that. You much of an artist?'

'I wouldn't say so. I did a bit of art at school. Why?'

'Excellent! That is more than I can say. Oh, you'll see.' He erupts into that laugh of his, so that she has to join him. And her fingers resume their exploration of the carved face on the dugong tooth.

Of all the fascinating smaller creatures who live on the coral reef, Klaas has grown to love the mantis shrimp the most. Firstly, because of the association with his nickname. The insect mantis is 'Hotnots-god', the Hottentots' god – which he likes to pronounce in expressive Afrikaans, so the 'g' sandpapers out of his throat and into the 'od', as if he's clearing his throat. It was Mrs Osler who explained to Klaas that Mantis isn't actually considered a god, as is often told. He's more of a super being. A kind of dream Bushman, with his wedge face and alien eyes. He is the one who brought fire to the Bushman. This is what made him so special to his ancestors, she'd told him. Once, when Klaas brought her a beautiful specimen cupped in his hands, she'd screamed and chased him off the veranda. She said it would set the house on fire.

Then there are the mantis shrimp's eyes. They always make Klaas think of Sophia, the crazy New York artist with the extraordinary eyes he'd dated shortly after settling in Tofo. She'd fallen so in love with the light and colours of the place, especially underwater, that she bought a rundown cabin by the beach. She explained to Klaas that when he, and 99.9 per cent of people on the planet, sees dark green, she, as a tetrachromat, can also see hues of violet, turquoise and blue. 'But mantis shrimp eyes are even more incredible,' she explained, while flashing hers at him. 'They have multiple eyes with tuneable eight-channel colour vision, compared to your three and my four. They can even see infrared and ultraviolet.'

He can still hear her broad Bronx accent. The technical details went over his head. All he remembers is that basically, the shrimp have the keenest eyes on the planet.

It's been a long time, Klaas realises. He can't quite remember how many years she's been away. *Wonder if she'll ever come back?* He slows his steady finning and pivots in the water to make sure his clients, a honeymoon couple, are following behind. He exhales and a shower of silver bubbles leaves his regulator and streams toward the surface of the clear water.

It's a cosy arrangement though, living in Sophia's Tofinho seaside shack in exchange for looking after the place. It's a short walk down the coast from Tofo, but far enough away from the 'scene' – Tofo beach and the bustling little market centre where all the tourists and volunteers gravitate. A trust-fund kid, she'd originally come to Tofo as a USAID volunteer. Klaas had 'looked after' her for the year or so she lived here. They'd been good together – he'd even considered falling in love. She was into tantric yoga and the sex was terrific. But they both knew they were just using each other. He was relieved when she returned to New York to take up with an older lover, who was, she told Klaas, with her intense eyes focused elsewhere, her spiritual twin.

Klaas stops and motions for his two divers to join him as he balances in the water, kneeling on the sand, below the edge of the reef. This is where they'll find his queen, as he calls the mantis shrimp he knows lives here. He knows it's a 'she' because she is with eggs, which he noticed on the last dive here, a few days ago. His divers wait patiently. They lean forward to peer where he's pointing – a little cave opening, the size of a toilet-roll end, set into the base of the coral reef where it meets the sand. In the pre-dive briefing, he'd instructed them to breathe slowly when in position. He's glad to see that they are obeying. Not all guests do. What is it about being underwater, he wonders, that transforms globetrotting first-world adults into disobedient four-year-olds? Touching everything. Even testing staghorn coral to see how easily it snaps.

A minute passes. Another. The man looks at Klaas as if to check he isn't having them on. *They're probably used to swimming mindlessly around the reef.* Klaas nods reassuringly and slowly waves his right hand up and down to indicate that they need to be patient. She will show herself to her subjects when she is ready. So, they wait.

Klaas reflects on how the life he's leading out of the water is starting to feel like one long wait, for what, he's not really sure. *Is it love?* Perhaps Gwen, or the idea of her at least, which sits there like it's a part of him, is preventing him from attracting anyone.

He's settled into a mindless but disciplined daily routine. He gets up at 5.30 a.m. each day. Urinates. Throws off the Kenyan kikoi he sleeps in. Pulls on his board shorts. Over his bowl of oats, he'll study the sea. If the surf is up, he'll grab his old surfboard and jog through the dunes to one of the local breaks for a session. Afterwards, he washes off in the outside shower attached to the shack.

He arrives at Mad Manta, Aussie Alfie's dive shop, around seven. As the resident divemaster, he repeats, sometimes three times a day, the same pre-dive spiel to the stream of adventurous world travellers who're starting to come to southern Mozambique. The time he spends each day enabling the interactions between divers and sea-life is what keeps him going. He loves being underwater, and it shows. It's the reason behind Alfie's bromance with Klaas. Alfie opted out of his Sydney-side high life after an acrimonious divorce, and is now trying to find himself as a dive-shop owner in 'this fucking beautiful African backwater'. He envies Klaas's quiet, disciplined physicality. His simple, soulful connection to the ocean. The clients love Klaas too. Like this couple. After their first dive with him yesterday, they told Alfie they only want to dive with Klaas. That he's made their honeymoon.

There's a preponderance in this scene of what Alfie calls 'bucket-list bitches'. Western women in various stages of early- or mid-life crisis who are attracted to ticking things off. And not only whale sharks and manta rays. Initially, Klaas had allowed a succession of these women to tick 'getting laid by a lean divemaster with a faraway look' off their lists. Someone who perhaps reminds them of Jacques Mayol in *The Big Blue*. It's all become a bit boring, really.

Is it time to go home? Where is home?

Ah, there she is! With a tentative show of bright-red feelers, a shifting of sand grains at the entrance to her cave, the mantis shrimp ventures out. Enough to show off her eggs. The sight of the bundle, a little scoop of orange caviar, nestled in her claspers, warms his heart. She creeps out a little further. Her abdomen is the length and thickness of his thumb, a blended array of iridescent blues, greens, reds and oranges. Her purple globe-shaped eyes pivot and shape-shift, focusing those incredible cones on the divers looming above her. *You're looking so serious, my queen.*

The mantis shrimp scuttles back into her hole. The reason becomes apparent as a sand crab, almost twice her size, advances. The mantis shrimp peeps out a few seconds later, only her feelers and eyes showing. *This could be interesting.* Crabs like this are prey for mantis shrimp, despite the size difference. *He must be after her eggs.* The crab takes a few steps closer. The shrimp retreats. Peeks out again. The two crustaceans face off, a few centimetres apart from each other. Then out of nowhere a second mantis shrimp, her mate he imagines, rushes forward. And a puff of liquid sand appears in the space between them. The movement has been too fast for human eyes to follow. But Klaas knows the weapon is a pair of clubs, at the end of hinged arms which fold away under the head. It's the third reason he loves mantis shrimp so much: they punch above their weight. Literally. They are undoubtedly, size for size, the best boxers in the world. The lightning punch has cracked the crab's rostrum, right between its stalked eyes. Dead in its tracks, the crab's innards trickle from the shattered shell. The male mantis shrimp grabs hold of a lifeless pincer and drags the crab back into their lair.

Klaas looks at his divers. They both give him enthusiastic A-okay signals. He's stoked too – he's read and heard about this killer blow, but never seen it.

Klaas isn't sure what it is – perhaps a heightened sixth sense that comes with being underwater a lot – but something makes him rise from his kneeling position on the sand and swivel around. He breathes out in a burst of bubbles when he spots them: the two divers finning above the reef behind them. He recognises Benito from his faded old wetsuit, the yellow fins, and the underwater slate he carries around on his research dives. Benito waves at him and he waves back, lifts his head in an underwater hello. Klaas's eyes go to the woman with Benito, whom he doesn't recognise. *Must be a new volunteer.* She looks at him briefly, but they're too far apart to make eye contact. She too has a slate. She turns to follow Benito. Klaas watches as she fins with slow, comfortable strokes. *This one is quite at home underwater,* he thinks, before his attention is brought back to his charges, waiting for directions. Klaas lifts his hand to indicate where they'll go next. He looks up one more time as Benito and the woman disappear into the blue.

Further along the reef, Klaas positions his two divers in front of the anemone. He glances at his dive watch. He'll give them three minutes here. The largest clownfish wiggles up to glare at the divers. The rest of the family nestle restlessly within the folds of deadly tentacles they clean in exchange for residency. Klaas studies the centrally located oral cavity, the anemone's mouth. He memorises the rippling shades of blue that flow to rich red and then delicate pink around the cavity lips. And he thinks, not for the first time, how this resembles a woman's vulva. He wants to paint this. Maybe mix in turpentine, to capture the subtle shades and voluptuous textures.

The couple have their hands extended. The largest clownfish is darting from the anemone to their fingers and back. *Hopefully, she isn't getting too stressed.* Klaas breathes out another billow of silver bubbles.

He's tried his hand at sculpting, too. Well, whittling really – turning bits of driftwood and bone into things they already resemble. Like the little mermaid he fashioned from that dugong tusk. But it's the rich colours and the sense of depth that well-applied oils can have that excite him the most. Inspired by his time with Malangatana and by Sophia's colourful abstracts adorning the walls of the shack, he's painting more and more in his spare time. Which is increasing as he cuts down on working at the dive shop. He has little need for material possessions, saves easily. He hasn't even spent all the cash he came into the country with seven years ago.

To seaward but still on the same reef, Claire and Benito have gone down low on the sand sea-floor. The coral-encrusted reef around them creates a natural amphitheatre. Two leopard sharks are circling the arena. Their colouring is striking, grey with darker spots. But it's the way they move through the water that's so mesmerising. It's as if their bodies are floating forward and it's only the long scimitar-shaped caudal fin that's moving, a hypnotic stroking of the water. She can see from the claspers extending below their tails that they're males. One swings toward Claire and she drops even lower on the sand. He passes right over her head, and she tracks the school of yellow and black-striped damselfish stationed in formation immediately ahead of his snout. She studies his neat oval-shaped mouth with its benign, sandpaper-like gums. Benito had explained before the dive, in anticipation of seeing them at this time of year, that this mouth is only good for molluscs and crustaceans. A striped remora is attached to the shark's underbelly. Claire is tempted to reach up and pluck it off. She breathes out. Her bubbles hit the shark's belly, causing the remora to slide around to the side of his body. The shark's serpentine tail passes over her.

Benito signals to her and they swim up onto the reef. Claire is struggling to decide where to look next. There's so much to see. She takes in the curtains of yellow, orange and red fish above the coral heads. A trumpetfish comes into view – swimming vertically, head down, like a levitating yellow builder's level. A spotted pufferfish, all spikes, is furiously fanning his tiny transparent fins to keep facing away from her. His oversized eyes track her as she passes. A black-tip reef shark arcs into view, sees them and accelerates out of sight. She just catches sight of a leopard eel as it snakes from one hole to another. It's visual overload, a surprise a second.

Claire runs her eyes over the sculpted bits of limestone – the cauliflower heads, the bushes, the tree branches, and the huge domed brain-like growths that form the fairy-scale coral megalopolis before her. *Crazy to think we thought these were plants for so long. What was his name again? Frederick Herschel, that's it.* The eighteenth-century astronomer who first focused a microscope on coral polyps to establish that they have animal cell membranes. Claire holds a fingertip close to an encrusting coral and sees how the tiny tentacles of the polyps retract when they sense its presence. She imagines the miniscule photosynthesising algae, the zooxanthellae, which reside within each polyp, working away to provide energy to extract calcium carbonate from seawater, which they use to build the intricate structures she's gliding over. It's one of nature's most magical symbioses. *What else are we still getting wrong?* she wonders.

Claire's hand comes up and moves involuntarily in a slow, regal wave, acknowledging the subtle shades: the greens, oranges, yellows and faded browns that indicate healthy coral growth. And in between, the soft corals, the sponges and the tunicates, in an array of colours. Bunches, branches, fans. All of these permanently attached invertebrates are filtering the seawater soup for nutrients. Feeding, cycling, recycling. And with the light angling down through the blue, catching the throngs of fish, she becomes aware of a gentle warmth spreading throughout her body as she breathes easefully. She feels into the reef's vulnerability. She knows that if the sea heats up just a few degrees, the polyps will spit out the algae and go into a kind of hibernation. And if the warm water persists, even for a few days, the polyps will starve and die. And the wonderland she is floating over will turn white overnight. Dead, bleached limestone sculptures. Millions of fish without food. With her next bubbling exhalation, the question arises: *How do we get people who can't dive down here to appreciate, and to protect, this miracle of life?* And with the same certainty that her breath rises to the surface as wobbling saucers, she knows she must pursue the answer.

She continues to drift and breathe, passing a large plate coral. The meandering grooves are reminiscent of the prehistoric rock glyphs she and Todd had found that day in the Petroglyph Provincial Park near Nanaimo. *Wonder what causes these?*

Benito has stopped at an inconspicuous metal stake hammered into the reef. It's one of a series he's placed on reefs around the bay. Attached to it is a colour-coded plastic token to identify its location. Claire knows what to do by now, and she moves into position. Comes to rest with her knees on the sand, away from the reef so as not to damage the brittle coral.

As she settles for the count, her eyes catch the telltale slither. With a jolt to her chest, she's transported back to the last time she saw an octopus. Only this time, the scene is brightly illuminated, and the octopus is very much alive. She decides it's a he. Still on her knees, she leans forward in the water, brings her face close to his – to stare into his hypnotic, opalescent eyes. The pupils, black slits, are like a cat's, but turned on their side. His eyes are set in what appear to be two stubby horns above his head. These remain still while the rest of him shifts constantly. His siphon billows as he breathes the sea, never breaking eye contact as his eight arms fiddle. Claire opens her mind to the octopus, feels into his presence. She tells him she means no harm, that he is helping *her*, and she extends her hand toward him, palm up. His skin darkens, whitens, then resumes pulsing the mottled colours of the reef. He extends a tentacle, a tendril, and she her fingers, and they meet in the space between. When his suckers attach, one by one, delicately, to her bare fingers, tears form in her eyes. She has to squeeze them tight to clear her vision. With their eyes locked, eternal seconds pass. Tentacles taste fingers, and fingers feel the pulsing tenderness. A new warmth spreads like ink in her heart space. And the presence of the Other emerges from the shroud. From that place which has been in darkness.

It's the octopus who breaks her trance. His two eye horns ease back into the rest of him. His pupils narrow, and the arm retracts. She can hear, from the sound of his rising breath, that Benito is directly behind her. The octopus slides away to continue his day on the reef.

She turns to see Benito smiling. He nods his head – as if he knows. Claire scrunches her eyes again. Gives him the A-okay sign to indicate she's ready to start their count. She brings her attention to the task at hand, to the row of names written down the left side of her slate. She places a neat pencil stroke beside the word 'octopus'.

Following Benito's lead, she starts the 360-degree scan of the reef. Positioned back to back, they work swiftly: look up, identify, tick off, turn to their right and do the same. They know there's double counting as the fish swim around in an ever-moving throng. And there's a lot of life hidden on the reef. But by combining the two lists and doing it over and over, they're building a picture of the community structure of the reef – creating a baseline to track the impact over time of fishing and recreational diving.

Benito was pleased to see that Klaas, the divemaster from Mad Manta, had positioned his two guests on the sand adjacent to the reef, and not on the reef itself, to observe whatever it was he was showing them. Clumsy fins can so easily snap off coral which has taken many years to grow.

They complete their count and continue on their dive. They haven't gone far when Claire makes out a disturbance on the sand at the base of a dome-shaped brain coral. She touches Benito's arm, points, and they swim over. At first, she thinks they are stingrays. She makes the universal thumb-on-fingers repeated clasping signal to indicate feeding. But Benito shakes his head. Lifts his left hand and makes a neat circle with his thumb and index finger. Shoves his right index finger in and out of the circle. She can see his eyes smiling, and from the froth of his outbreaths she knows that he's laughing.

There isn't a dive signal for electricity. But somehow Benito manages to communicate with jagged finger wags that these are in fact electric rays. They are the size of dinner plates, drab tan in colour. And now she can see that they lack the long tail and stinger of a stingray. The ray on top, the male she presumes, looks like he's trying to force the female into the sand. *Oh Felicity, Felicity, you fill me with electricity.*

Claire chuckles, recalling the silly line from a British send-up TV show she watched in high school. And wonders if indeed sparks are flying between them, or if the male is shocking the female into submission.

The male ray lifts up. She can see that his small mouth has a firm hold on the skin covering the female's back. He flails about, pulling his mate's skin up like a dropped serviette, launches down into her again in a flurry of muscular convulsions. *Wow, that's some love bite.* She turns to Benito, who is nodding knowingly. They watch until the rays have completed their mating and floated off, up and over the reef, trailing bits of sand like flying carpets above a desert. Claire glances at her dive computer. Sadly, it's time to leave this dreamland.

Klaas and his guests are following a creature that looks like a compressed hand with its bunched fingers extended. The diminutive reef cuttlefish is staying just out of reach with controlled jets. The cuttlefish slows, angles toward the reef. Hovers. It moves closer still, imperceptibly, pulsing a hundred shades of rust red. Klaas catches a glimpse of the little adapted tentacle as it eases out between the others. *Oh yes!* Then it flashes. A white chameleon tongue retracts, holding a tiny crab he hadn't even seen was there. The squid turns, squirts off out of sight to enjoy its meal in peace. After acknowledging his divers' delight, Klaas places two forefingers on his left palm to ask, *How much air do you have?* From their responses, he gauges there's just enough time.

They reach an extensive flat area, coated with encrusting plate coral. Klaas points down to where it looks like someone has taken a red-hot poker and gouged random grooves. He can see they are a bit perplexed. He drops lower and, making eye contact with them, holds up his index and middle finger to his eyes to indicate 'look'. And then with a pointed finger traces the outline of the crude stick figure etched into the coral. Uses the same fingers to indicate walking or running – he thinks of this one as 'the running man'. But they still don't get it. So he rolls his hand, touches his ear and points to the surface to indicate, *I'll explain when we get back to the boat.* He loves these creations, which he's come to call coralglyphs, because they're reminiscent of Bushman rock engravings. The guidebook at the dive shop explains that they're made by an Alpheus shrimp, near-transparent and no bigger than a fingernail. These diminutive farmers carve out crevices in the coral, and cultivate algae for themselves in the grooves. The rims of the crevasses are lined with tiny hydroids, which gives the glyphs a dot-drawing look – reminiscent of the Australian Aboriginal art in the book he'd studied in Malangatana's studio. *I should do something with these coralglyphs as well.* He turns in the water to face the couple, gives them a bobbing two-thumbs-up to indicate that it's time to rejoin the world up there.

They're hanging in the water at five metres, their ascent safety stop, when they become aware of the whale song carrying clearly through the water. Klaas smiles and cups his hand to his ear. His divers nod enthusiastically. *Must be stragglers. Most have left for the year.* The calls grow louder and louder, so that Klaas is convinced they'll appear out of the depths. He swivels around. Searches. A thunderous gurgle, a male humpback's call, erupts, penetrates Klaas's chest. His guests bring their hands to theirs. Again, it ripples, blasts. Makes every fibre of his being feel alive. When the call thunders once more, it is so much inside his chest, it tickles. He tries to produce a rumbling bass imitation, but it just produces giggles, so that water spills into his mouth and he splutters and coughs. The calls, the whistles, the grumbles and the gurgles slowly fade as the pod of whales passes unseen.

The skipper on Claire and Benito's inflatable takes their weight belts from them as they hang off the side of the boat, lifts their dripping scuba tanks. Claire dips her face into the water, blows her nose and wipes her face vigorously. Nothing more embarrassing than an 'oyster' lurking on your face after a dive. With two strong fin strokes, she lifts her body up and onto the pontoon. Benito is already on board, busy stowing dive gear as the skipper hauls up the anchor. Claire strips off her wetsuit, takes the towel Benito is holding out for her.

'Thanks! Holy crap! How were those whale calls, hey! Humpback, right?' She takes a few deep breaths to calm herself. Pulls her hair to the side and squeezes the water out of it.

'Yes, it must have been a group of them. That deep call was a bull.'

'Wow, that was so cool! It hits you right in the chest. Right here.' Claire slaps her flat hand on her sternum. 'What a way to finish an awesome dive. Thank you!' She raises her hand, palm out.

'You're welcome.' Benito smacks her high-five.

The skipper starts the engine. Claire and Benito sit down, beaming, hold on for the ride home. They don't talk as the inflatable lifts and falls over the swells. Claire revels in these rides. Heading out, there's the anticipation of the dive. Heading back, there's the after-glow from being underwater. Closing her eyes, she relives moving through the schools of fish. Holds the animals she's met in positive regard. And today's octopus ... *What a blessing.* With her eyes still closed, and feeling the hull caressing the waves, a fluid mantra, she begins to swim in her newfound lightness. The deep bass thunder of the bull whale replays. The wind whips her hair around her face. The octopus's suckers attach, detach. In this blissful state, in the darkness behind her eyelids, there is a stronger sense of the swimming Other. The omnipotent being who lurks in the shadows, swirling, flowing. The one whom she believes will provide answers to the questions her heart has been asking. But in this travelling moment, Claire submits to the physical glow for its own sake. She feels the salt-water dry on her neck, so that when she turns her head, it tugs at her skin. And as she does so, the gentle but firm thought comes: *I love it here.*

'Flying fish!' Benito cries out. Claire's eyelids fly open and her eyes adjust to the brightness. Just in time to see the iridescent indigo-blue fish, pectoral fins snapped into wings, streak low over the face of the sea like an arrow. It disappears back into the sea. Another bursts out of the water directly ahead of the speeding boat. Glides. When its body touches the water, it thrashes to lift off once more. Claire wonders if they think the boat is a lunging predator. She and Benito whoop as more erupt and fly out. As abruptly as they arrived, they're gone, and then the drone of the outboard and the sensation of sliding over the endless azure lulls her into a state of bliss once more.

The skipper slows as they approach Tofo beach. A white pick-up truck with a trailer is reversing down the beach. It stops above the high-tide line and the driver gets out, waves to them. Several teenage boys, and the old man, the one she met that first day on the beach, have gathered to help with the retrieval. They know Benito will hand out a few coins for their trouble. Their skipper swings the boat around. He studies the swells, waiting for a gap between sets. With a quick warning for them to hold on tight, he throws the control fully forward. The boat surges, rides on the back of a swell and up onto the beach as it breaks, coming to a sudden stop as the wet sand sucks its weight. They jump off the boat and onto the sand. The boys scramble into action, lifting the sides so the driver can navigate the trailer under the hull. The old man is hopping around, screeching toothless instructions which they ignore. Claire turns away so he doesn't see her laughing.

They have to step away as the trailer slides under the boat, picking it up like an upturned hand. Once it's on, the old man hobbles over, says a few words to Benito, too quickly for Claire to understand. But he is clearly pleased. And then he hastens up front to help the skipper secure the bow of the inflatable to the trailer.

She turns to Benito as they walk up to the truck. 'What was that all about?'

'Oh, he wanted to thank us. For looking after the reef.'

Claire is about to respond when the scream of another outboard going full throttle turns their heads. It's the inflatable from the dive shop, thrusting through the surf. The skipper cuts the engine and it slides up the wet sand like a beaching bull seal. The man standing next to the skipper, wetsuit peeled down to reveal his broad chest, turns to the two recreational divers behind him. They immediately follow his instruction and slide off the boat. He stays onboard. Claire watches him bend to move gear around, his arms and hands moving quickly, efficiently. When she lifts herself into the truck's passenger seat, she glances over her shoulder to see if he's looking their way, but he isn't.

Jangamo Village, south of Tofo, Mozambique
15 November 1991

When Claire follows Benito into the coolness of the classroom, a palpable expectancy emanates from the sea of shining faces. She is forced to take a slow, deliberate breath to calm herself. She looks up at the high ceiling, where thin lasers of sunlight angle through holes in the rusted roof sheets. Glassless windows set high in the whitewashed walls allow the room to breathe, keeping it cooler than the searing playground outside, visible through the lower windows, which do have panes. She's aware of the exquisite realisation, which she's felt many times underwater, that she doesn't want to be anywhere else in this moment.

The schoolteacher comes across from the blackboard, with its neatly inscribed alphabet set out to the side, to greet them. She smiles shyly, as she holds Benito's stare.

'Claire, it is my pleasure to introduce you to my, um, my special friend, Miss Assamulo.'

Oh, I see. Claire tucks the cardboard box she's carrying under her arm, extends her hand. 'Hi. I'm Claire.'

'I am Miriam.' She rests her slender hand gently in Claire's, brings her left hand to her own right forearm and holds it there. Claire follows suit, the first time she's done this. Their grasp lingers as they study each other's faces, and there is, within a few heartbeats, an instant female bond. Benito is shuffling in delight beside them. Miriam releases Claire's hand and steps away with quiet authority. She lifts up her hands to her class and raises her voice in perfect English. 'Class, I want you to welcome Miss Lutrísque. She works with Doctor Mutara at the marine station. You will remember our field trip there. She is from Canada!'

'Good morning, Miss Lutries! Welcome to our school!' thirty-five beaming faces chime in unison, at the tops of their voices. Claire brings her hands together in delight. From nowhere, tears well, but are stopped mid-duct by another loud chorus: 'Good morning, Doctor Mutara!' Benito chuckles at her side.

Claire takes a seat to the side of the blackboard. She places her box on the polished cement floor beside her as Benito addresses the class in animated Portuguese. Their faces are transfixed. She smiles when they sneak looks at her. Innocence, pure inquisitiveness, is written there. Each time a pair of eyes meets hers, something melts, deep inside. Miriam is unrolling the poster of endangered marine species that Benito has brought along, tacking it to the back of the door. Low enough so the children – Claire estimates they are ten or eleven years old – can study the pictures later. Benito walks over to the poster, points at the picture of a leatherback turtle. As he walks back, he flaps his arms like flippers, to the great delight of the children. He steps to the board and draws a turtle mother laying eggs in her hole, talking all the while. He grows silent as he completes his crude sketch, with a drift net entangling a second turtle. He turns to them, and he isn't smiling any more.

I must learn as much Portuguese as I can while I'm here, Claire resolves. She studies their faces to see how his words are having effect.

A movement outside catches Claire's attention, and she looks through the dirty window to see four goats trotting across the dusty schoolyard. They stop under the acacia tree growing by the slanting wire fence, and one by one rise up on their hind legs and stretch into the thorny branches, pink tongues reaching to their fullest extent for the meagre bits of green. She looks back into the room, and as her eyes adjust she takes in the children anew. None are wearing shoes. The boys are dressed in khaki shorts, the girls in black skirts, and all of them have clean white shirts. Their school desks, built for one but shared by two, are battered. Many have been repaired with makeshift planks.

Benito has rubbed out the leatherback and is drawing the outline of a manta ray. Alongside it, he sketches a knife with exaggerated drops of blood dropping off the blade. When he slices off the manta's wingtips with violent strokes of the chalk, the sound penetrates Claire's teeth. She grimaces, puts her hands to her ears. The children nearest her giggle as they copy her. Benito turns to face them. His face is grave, and the class grows quiet. He pauses many seconds for effect. Scans the class from side to side, from back to front, looking into each set of eyes. A boy sniffs to break the silence.

When Benito is done with his performance, Miriam walks forward and explains to the class that Claire will take over, and that they are going to do an exercise. Claire's heart is thudding. *Ridiculous*, she thinks, *how can a group of kids make me this nervous?*

It's been ten years since she last stood up in front of school children. She'd been the first student from Graham Island to win a university scholarship. Everyone was so proud of her. She'd been paraded at the school assembly, had mumbled a few words about the importance of knowing your roots and working hard to achieve your goals, and mentioned her grandmother. Even as a qualified marine biologist, she'd remained crowd-shy. Todd naturally did all the talking at the conferences and meetings they attended. She always felt like she would be judged, mostly by older men. Now, when she surveys these expectant young faces, she knows her current nervousness has to do with caring deeply about the outcome of this interaction. In the past it was always about her, but here it's about these children. And about Ocean. *Just bring my truth*, she reassures herself as she goes to the blackboard.

Without a word, she turns her back to the class, closes her eyes for a moment and fills her nostrils with the smell of chalk. Then she reaches for the longest piece of chalk resting on the wooden runner, and begins to draw. The pregnant silence in the room, the muffled coughs and the snuffles, all fade as she goes within, brings her Haida gifts to this gathering of village children on this dusty African day. She draws the outline of a turtle, and inside it she 'carves' with chalk, first in white and then in shades of colour, her interpretation of what she feels is the essence of sacred Turtle. Using her fingers, Claire smooths and shades the motifs, her hands gathering coloured dust. She prays that the Haida-styled drawing will speak to these children, will make a difference, even if it's only to a few.

When her drawing is complete, she stands before the class and explains as simply as she can, pausing every few sentences for Miriam to translate, that if we open our hearts and our minds we can sense, can see, can feel the sacred spirit that is in all living creatures, even the animals we eat. She tells them how she's come to love the sea and how this love stems in part from meeting animals, like the turtle, and seeing them as individuals, like people. A boy thrusts his arm up.

'Ah, a question. What would you like to know?' Claire is taken by his dark irises, set in pure white innocence.

'But how can you talk to animals underwater?' the boy asks in his accented English.

She looks around the sea of eyes, discerning how much to reveal. 'You can't use your words underwater ... obviously!' And they laugh, briefly, so she can continue. 'But you learn to read body language, and to approach animals in a way that tells them you mean no harm. And thoughts, thoughts that don't feel like they're yours, come into your head. Like they are coming from the animal. So, yes, I believe you can talk to them. Through your mind and the way you move your body. What do you think?'

'I think so, Ma'am.' The boy doesn't take his eyes off her.

'It was my dream from when I was little to go underwater and be with the animals, to protect them.' Claire goes on to share what it felt like: the explosive delight when she first donned a mask and stuck her head under the surface and entered the watery world of colour and sway.

'How old were you, Ma'am?' a girl with a cropped afro near the front asks.

'About your age, actually. I was always a bit scared of the ocean before then. In my culture, there are a lot of scary stories about the sea.' Claire makes a mental note to tell them the story of Sedna, of She

Down There, the next time she comes here. For she is sure there will be a next time.

'I also want to go there, Ma'am. One day ...' the boy with the big eyes blurts out, and she looks into them once more.

'What's your name?'

'Almeida, Ma'am.'

'Well, Almeida, I hope that one day many of you will be able to join Benito and me underwater.' She has to pull away from his innocent eyes to tell the class, 'But now, we are going to do some art.'

Claire opens the box and hands out the sheets of paper and the coloured crayons she's brought along. Through Miriam, she asks them to draw their own turtles, or any animal for that matter. And within this shape, representing its earthly body, to draw what they consider to be the most important aspect of, or story about, that animal. They can use symbols if they want to – she explains what this word means.

The children set about drawing, and a productive silence descends on the room. When they look up and make eye contact, she smiles warmly. Some peep at their neighbours' pictures. Others, she can see, keep looking at the board, so she asks Miriam to tell them that their drawings should be their own, and that it doesn't matter how 'good' they are. They won't be judged, and there are no prizes. Even the naughty boys, who sit at the back, are having a go. The class has never had such beautiful coloured crayons before. After about ten minutes, when she can see most have finished, she asks them to wrap up.

Claire asks a few volunteers to come up and share their work. She's astounded by the art. As can be expected, many have tried to emulate her First-Nation style of representation. But many have been original, even bold. One boy has sketched a dog with grotesque teeth within his turtle outline, presumably to illustrate the threats to nests dogs pose, as Benito explained. Many have depictions of nets. One boy has depicted the turtle as a round sun rising over the sea. A girl has baby turtles spilling out of the back of hers. Miriam is about to end the exercise when a girl near the back of the classroom holds her hand up as high as she can. The girl comes forward sheepishly and holds up her turtle. The children burst into laughter, but stop abruptly when they see the change that comes over Claire's face when she takes the drawing and studies it.

She is unable to stop her tears. There on the girl's sheet of paper, staring back at her, is a mischievous face within the outline of the turtle. The eyes and the smiling mouth are beautifully shaded. And it bears a striking resemblance to the print that used to hang on the wall above Náan's bed. She hugs the girl and wants to hand back her drawing, but the girl firmly shakes her head and skips back to her desk. Claire wipes her eyes sheepishly, lets out a chortle, and the whole room immediately erupts into laughter once again.

Miriam thanks Benito and Claire, and the class stands to attention. Leaving the room, before crossing the threshold into the brightness of the day, Claire looks back. Staring intently at her is Almeida, the boy who wants to go down there.

Claire has to hold her arms across her chest to stop her breasts from jiggling as Benito pushes the pick-up truck over the potholes and the corrugations. They pass a shop with the words *Comercia Geral* and a slanting Coca-Cola sign hand-painted on the whitewashed wall. She catches a glimpse of a framed picture of the president outside the entrance of a roadside eatery. Men sit in a circle under the tree, lifting cartons of sorghum beer to their mouths. A bus parked outside a building with a faded red cross on its facade is loading people from a queue. *Is that a nurse in neat blue and white?* Many women with many children. Lines and lines of coconut palms. Men on bicycles. Lone cattle with long horns rest in the shade. People wander along dust tracks between homesteads constructed from woven palms and reed thatch. The road surface smooths and the truck settles; feels like a boat cruising on flat water. Claire's hands come to rest with the drawing on her lap, and her heavy lids drop.

She is suddenly wide awake as the truck catches the rough on her side. The roadside grass blurs as she gapes, wide-eyed, out the window. Two oversized four-by-fours roar past them, hooting, their number plates obscured by dust. Benito slews back onto the road, slows to a halt after they've passed. His one hand grips the steering wheel while the other wildly gesticulates.

'This is what I am talking about, Claire!' It's the first time she's seen him angry.

'What? Who was that?'

'Oh, who knows! They are all the same. Could be the French! Or the Norwegians! Or the British! Or whatever bloody do-good nation. They're all here. Probably doing an "inspection" of some sort. Think they own the place. You must see what a zoo it is down in Maputo, Claire. They stay in air-conditioned three-storey houses with servants, boats, big fancy four-by-fours parked outside. Which they use to drive from meeting to meeting at the embassies and the Polana Hotel and the yacht club. Fly to conferences and international meetings the whole time. All of them, even your own Canadian International Development Agency, are the same. Meetings and reports. That is all they ever seem to do …' Benito catches himself. Stares across the cab at her in dismay.

She studies his expression. Titters. Bursts out laughing.

His face melts, and his grin reappears. 'You are crazy, Miss Lutrísque. Crazy! I can't tell you how good it is to have you here. Today in the classroom was wonderful. It felt like you have always been around.'

She shoves him playfully on the shoulder as he puts the car into gear and takes off. They drive on in silence, the truck swaying and bouncing past the coconut palms and the clusters of grass huts. As the holiday homes on the hill above Tofo come into view, he turns to her. 'Can I show you something before I drop you off?'

'Sure. What is it?'

'You will see. Today we might have helped shape the future, in our little way. But I want to show you something of our past. For you to understand where these children have come from.'

Benito drives along the coast road south of Tofo to Tofinho. He steers the truck up a rutted dirt incline. The shoreline drops off to their left, and they come out onto an open area on an elevated bluff looking down on the jagged intertidal shelf below. He parks the truck, opens his window, and rests his wrists on the steering wheel to gaze out to sea through the windscreen. The smell of salt spray wafts into the cab as she opens her window too. It's quiet, the sound of the waves buffered by the bluff.

'This is an unhappy place for us Mozambicans, Claire. I don't normally bring visitors here, but after today I want to show you. I am not proud of this place, but it's part of our story. And if you want to understand Mozambique, this will help.'

Claire frowns, looks around. She sees only low bushes, an elevated view of the coastline stretching to the north and to the south. And the wide Indian Ocean before them.

'We call this place Buraco dos Assassinatos. Execution Rock. Let me show you.' He steps out of the car, and she follows him along a path that leads through the coastal bushes, down to the edge of the bluff.

They're standing next to a hole in the grey, exposed rock. A few metres seaward is vertical cliff, and below this the tidal shelf. The tide is out, exposing a series of rounded rock pools. She turns her attention back to the shaft at their feet, some four or five metres deep and about a metre in diameter. When she leans over and looks down it, she sees the wave-smoothed rock of the tidal shelf below.

'As you can see, this is a natural blowhole. When the tide comes in, the waves crash against the cliff and are forced up this hole. On a spring high tide, it blows like a whale. You can see the spout from afar.'

'Impressive. But I still don't get it.'

'It started with the Portuguese.'

'What do you mean?'

'They threw men down this hole.'

'Oh no. My God, Benito!' She grips his arm. She leans forward again to study the hole, sees how its sides are rough and jagged. 'Why?'

'Well, they were establishing coconut plantations, and ruled with an iron fist. Those who couldn't pay their land taxes were executed here. Often in front of the other farmers. When the independence movement took hold in the late nineteen-sixties and early seventies, the Portuguese Colonial Secret Police, the dreaded MIP, threw pro-independence Mozambicans down this hole. Tied them inside sisal bags.'

She scans Benito's impassive face. Shakes her head slowly. No man could survive this, even if they weren't tied up. Even if they were alive after landing on the rock below, the sea would force them back up the blowhole. Grate them down again. And eventually, broken, they would be taken out to sea.

'The saddest thing, Claire, is that we Mozambicans used this same place to murder each other during our civil war. This province was a stronghold for the Renamo guerrillas. They had no fixed base. Just operated as a shadow movement. Made them difficult to bring down. So, the ruling Frelimo party used this hole to execute captured cadres, to discourage support. Then Renamo would raid a village the next week, hack people to death or leave them maimed as retribution for turning them in. Week after week, month after month, year after year, this madness raged. It only stopped a few years ago, when we started coming to our collective senses, remembered who we are.' Benito's voice drops to a whisper, as he stares out to sea, 'Terra da boa gente … we are the land of the good people.'

For quite a while they stand there, not talking. Eventually, Claire takes her hand from his arm, and they turn away. Away from this place which Ocean flushes each spring high tide; breathing up the names of those souls wracked here.

The sunset comes early as the thunderstorm builds over Tofo. Faint flashes appear in the darkening sky to the east, out over the sea. Claire sits on her deck, feeling into the stillness, the air filled with expectant static. Birds have stopped calling. A rising onshore wind brings the first whiff of rain, an almost-sweet salt scent. The impressive cumulonimbus clouds, stacking above the sea like giant anvils, move in and rumble. She is startled as rain begins to pelt. Forked lightning reaches below the clouds and seems to strike the surface of the darkening bay. A few seconds later, the crack and rippling rumble of thunder startles her, and she covers her ears. The next barbed flash flays the sky, illuminating the darkened, flattened sea and the slanting rain above it in sudden brightness. She leaps up and runs for cover, shrieking, as the cracking thunder resounds once more. Sleeting rain drenches the deck as she pulls the sliding door closed. For half an hour she watches through the glass as the storm rages over Tofo. Then, as suddenly as it started, it moves inland, and the sky over the bay and out to sea begins to clear.

She steps out onto her deck once more. As she settles to watch the dying light, swarms of winged termites rise with the smell of wet earth, and soon the deck is covered in their throbbing bodies. They shiver to throw off their delicate wings, then wiggle around looking desperately for royal mates – for all are potential kings and queens of a new colony. She has heard of, but not experienced, this 'nuptial flight'. Swallows swirl like fighter jets, feasting on those termites still flying. As the light fades, the gorged birds retreat to their telephone lines to be replaced by a fresh wave of bombers. With greasy ears tuned to their predatory pinging, the insect-eating bats come streaming in from where they've been roosting all day, upside-down Draculas in the tall avocado trees planted by the Portuguese.

Claire lies on her back before sleep arrives, in submissive repose, allowing the heightened emotions, the rich images of the day, to wash over and settle. It has been a seminal day. It will take many more to properly process this new state, this sense of knowing, which is emerging. It's like the sea creature, whose presence she first felt that day she spread her grandmother's ashes, is finally ready to show herself, if not yet completely. It is definitely a *she*. And she isn't scary. *She isn't the angel of death.* Claire smiles. No, she is beautiful. *Some part of me, actually. Yes, that's it.*

The night sounds begin to do their work and she yawns, her thoughts exploring a new realisation: that like the cycle of violence being broken here in Mozambique, so too the cycle of abuse on Earth, and especially in Ocean, needs to be broken. It's going to be a world war, and places like Tofo will be on the front line.

'And I am going to be a part of it,' she whispers to the gecko on the wall. *Yes, I am going to be a part of it. If not here, then somewhere like here.*

Her last thoughts are images. Faces. Beautiful beaming faces. *I can't wait to see them all again.*

Claire walks home from the research station, now a familiar routine, deep in thought. *Did Benito really mean what he'd said? That he has less than a year's funding after the EU grant ends next month?*

Earlier that day, he told her that he'd written proposals to all the foreign donor agencies operating in Mozambique, but so far only the German International Development Agency had come forward with any money. The grant will cover his meagre salary and the station's running costs for the next ten months. He doesn't know what he's going to do after that. *What about the Marine Park Authority up in Bazaruto?* she'd asked. But, no, they too are stretched. He can piggy-back his dugong research with theirs, use their boat and research station when he goes there. But not more than that.

And the South African?

She was referring to the retired fisherman who'd donated the inflatable dive boat and the pick-up truck, in honour of his wife, who'd loved the sea very much. When she died, he no longer had the will to go out any more. His only condition was that they keep the boat's name, her name, inscribed on the navy-blue pontoons. *Annika*: an Afrikaans name meaning grace.

No, he's given enough, Benito had replied. *I can't ask him for more.*

Claire's thoughts are interrupted when, just before turning onto the path to her cabin, she notices the abnormally large crowd gathered on the beach, down where the fishing boats come in. To see what the fuss is all about, she pushes through the gaggle of women noisily negotiating prices for the smaller fish arranged in straw baskets and in piles on the wet sand.

Then she sees them. Gasps. Brings one hand to her mouth, the other to her chest, where it feels like Poseidon has thrust his trident into her heart. For there, discarded beside the baskets, are the blood-ied bodies of sea creatures she has barely got to know but are already sacred to her. Their life force has left them, and it's only the iodine-and-iron stench of their blood on the sand that remains.

She can see from the tail tucked under the carapace that the green turtle is a male. The memory of a recent dive replays. Tortures her soul. The old loggerhead had come right into her space, his ancient mariner's milky eyes resigned, like Náan's in the months before she passed. He'd turned his barnacled back into her, and she'd scratched his carapace, removing some of the irritating green algae with her nails, the way a wrasse would do at a cleaning station on the reef. With a last dopey glance that made her laugh bubbles of delight, the battered old turtle had flapped into the blue.

Now this.

The manta ray, a juvenile, has already been butchered: both wing-tips, as well as its small dorsal fin, have been hacked off. And alongside it are two reef sharks. Their fins have also been removed.

But it's the sight of the last sea creature that distresses her the most. A drop of dark red falls reluctantly onto the sand from the corner of the dolphin's frozen smile, and Claire's chest tightens. Her breath catches, and tears well.

Wiping the wet from her eyes and nose, she shoves her way into the crowd. She becomes aware, amidst the general melee, of a heated argument going on between a few men standing near the dead animals. She sees it's the old man. He is dancing around enraged, gesticulating to the bodies and then out to sea. She can't make out what he's saying as he spits his lisped, rapid-fire venom at the two fishermen leaning casually against the side of one of the beached boats. But he appears to be unhappy with their 'catch'. Some of the villagers are watching with bemused smiles. The fishermen have their arms crossed and are goading him, switching from feigned indignation to laughing in his face. Eventually, one of them decides he's had enough. He steps forward to confront the elder, and when he persists, shoves him back, gestures for him to leave. The old man spits into the sand and struts off, pushing people aside to get clear of the crowd.

Claire struggles through to get to him. She has to break into a run to catch him as he strides along the waterline. She grabs his arm, and when he turns to see who it is, she asks, 'Qual é o problema? What is the matter?'

'O espírito do mar está irritado!' He points out to sea and repeats, 'O espírito do mar está irritado!'

She gets it. The spirit of the sea is angry. All she can say is, 'Sinto muito … I am sorry.'

She can see the hurt in his eyes. They stare at each other without talking for what seems like a long time. He lifts his arm weakly, points out to sea once more. Looks out over the waves, then back to her, 'O espírito do mar está irritado!'

'Sinto muito,' she repeats. She reaches for his hand to hold it. But he leaves it hanging by his side. He shakes his head, gives her a half-smile, clucks his tongue loudly and turns to walk away.

After a few steps, he looks back at her briefly and calls out, 'Você é mulher do mar. You are sea woman. Boa mulher do mar. Good sea woman.'

Claire turns her face away from him, so he can't see her tears, and walks back to the dispersing crowd.

A short, slight, Chinese-looking man is talking intently to one of the fishermen who'd taunted the old man. She mingles with the crowd, stepping behind the women lifting baskets onto their heads, pretending to show interest in the piles of fish left on the sand. Edging to within earshot of their conversation, she hears the words 'dollar' and 'more' in broken English. A slender, pale hand comes out and meets a black one. There is a handshake. And a glimpse of crumpled notes. The fisherman joins his friend by the dead bodies, says something to him. She sees the knowing look they give each other, the suppressed smiles. As the man, she's sure he's Chinese, saunters past them toward their pulled-up fishing boat, they carefully ignore him, look the other way. He leans against the gunwale, glances around to make sure no one's watching, then leans into the boat, lifts out a white plastic packet, and turns on his heels to march away across the sand.

She decides to follow him. She keeps her eyes on his back, sees the wind play with his wispy hair as he makes his way into the village, but loses him as he enters the busy central market. Quickening her step and ignoring the beckoning of the stall traders, she winds through the smells of fish, spices and charred meat, and the scent of earth still lingering around the piles of vegetables. She spots him directly across the street, hunched at a public telephone on the sidewalk outside the little post office. She waits for a truck carrying goats to pass, and crosses. The Chinese man, receiver to his ear and already deep in conversation in his mother tongue, notices her as she passes on her way into the post office. The first thing Claire sees in his bloodshot eyes is pain. She'd expected something else, a hardness perhaps. She steps through the doorway, and her eyes adjust to the dimly lit interior.

Claire briefly acknowledges the only other person in the tiny room, a man who seems barely awake behind the main counter. Ignoring him, she lifts the ballpoint pen strapped with dirty masking tape to the counter and pretends to write as she studies the Chinese man through the dusty window. Barely two metres away, he's gesticulating, speaking loudly in what she surmises must be Mandarin, not concerned about being overheard. His furrowed brow shifts as his words fly, and his slender fingers flutter from his chin to his darting eyes to the air. He grows still, shifts the receiver to the other ear, listens for a long time. She sees how he's moved the receiver further away, and how his body is crumpling, eyes clenched. She can actually hear the other voice screaming through the earpiece. He mutters something when the screaming ends, hangs up, sniffs, rubs his nose, lifts the plastic packet by his feet and walks off.

Claire tails him all the way to the bar at the market. She walks past it a few times before she musters the courage to enter.

Her eyes adjust to the wide-open space, wooden benches set about the dirt floor, light leaking through the roof sheets. There aren't many patrons. A group of scraggly European overlanders. A pair of divers she recognises from the beach. A few local businessmen who can afford to drink here. Conversation and laughter mingle above the subdued, lilting music easing out of hidden speakers. She spots him in the far corner with his back to her, head lifted to drain the beer in his hand. Three more bottles are on the table in front of him.

Claire orders a beer at the bar and walks over to him. As she approaches, he looks up and takes her in, his face expressionless. Her heart is thumping, but she is determined. She has to find out.

'Mind if I join you?' She points to the seat with her free hand.

'Where you from?'

'I am from Canada. You?' As she sits down, she notices that two of the bottles are already empty. She can smell his sour breath across the table.

'From Hong Kong. I saw you on beach. Why you so sad when you speak with that crazy old man?'

Claire takes a deep swig of her beer, breathes out slowly. She wonders, *Is he drunk already?* Without really understanding why, she extends her hand across the table. 'My name is Claire.'

For a few seconds he studies her face. Finally he responds, 'I am Wang. Who you work for?' His hand reminds her of a kelp frond washed up on the last tide. Drying but still floppy. She's pretty sure that's not his real name.

'I am a volunteer, Mr Wang—'

'Volunteer for who? Who you work for?'

'Ah, sorry. I work at the marine station. With Dr Mutara. You know him?'

'No. You with police?'

'No, I am not.'

'Then what you want?'

'Who do you sell the fins to?'

His eyes narrow as he places his empty bottle down. He moves one hand to the last full one while his other hand goes to the plastic packet by his side, rests on it. 'Who are you?'

'I am a marine biologist.'

'Ah. You one of those people who love sea so much?'

'Yes. I want to know why you are buying manta and shark fins when everyone knows it's illegal?'

'Easy question. Because I can sell them, that why.' He pauses, takes a long drink, almost emptying the bottle. 'No one care, Miss Claire. Fishermen need money. Your love for fish bring no money.'

'I don't speak Mandarin, Mr Wang, but I could see you were upset at the Post Office earlier. Is it the fins? Perhaps you can't sell them.' She can't hide the hope in her voice.

He surveys her for a long time, doesn't take his eyes off hers as he finishes his fourth beer. Claire is breathing normally now that she senses he won't harm her, and she holds his stare with all the calm she can muster. He places the bottle down, looks past her, and starts to speak. Like a man who has no one else to talk to, who is utterly alone.

'I *can* sell them. This isn't problem. Problem is they too little. I am upset because my uncle says I am no good. I don't deliver what they want. Too little fins from this shithole village. He says there is no excuse any more because he knows they have new boats. His partners pay for them. They can fetch many sharks, he says. He told me he is giving the selling of rhino horn to my cousin, who is in Kenya. Not to me like he promise when I came here two month ago. This is big job. Reason I agree. Now I am stuck in this shithole place.' He waves his hand around the room. When his eyes come back to meet hers, it seems he is close to tears.

He looks down at the table to continue, his voice subdued. 'My uncle say I must drive fish in cold truck they buy for me and deliver fish to other Chinese man in Maputo. I gonna get less money for this shit job and spend many days driving up and down. No prospects with this shit job. Now I will never have good woman back home in

Hong Kong. I won't have good name. This is why I am upset, okay. What you care? You pretty. You can have any man.' He looks up and is startled by what he sees. 'Why you cry? I buy you drink. You want drink? We can be sad together.' He suddenly laughs out loud, a forced guffaw that reveals his yellowing teeth.

Claire wipes a tear away, and her eyes go to the plastic packet on the seat, and then to the patch of blood on the dusty floor. She rises to her feet and turns away.

'Where you go? I buy you drink! Come on, don't be sad. Sit down. You pretty girl! You look almost Chinese. We be sad together.'

She doesn't hear him through the rush of white water that fills her head.

Praia do Tofo
21 December 1991

Klaas blows on the surface, sucks in fresh air. The three minutes he's been freediving on the reef feel like half an hour, or more – the longest he's held his breath underwater. He enjoys the growing ability to release all tension in his body at depth, and be fully present for these long minutes. Everything slows when this 'oceanic feeling' kicks in, when his body succumbs to the pressured immensity of the sea. Little details, movements, and behaviours are more keenly observed.

At one point in today's dive, he took pleasure in following a pair of bright-yellow butterfly fish as they poked their pointed snouts into crevasses looking for prey, noticing how they constantly looked at each other, and then at him, during their hunt. The sleek black-tipped reef shark which swung past unperturbed had come much closer than it ever would have with noisy scuba. He'd enjoyed a good look into those beautiful, steely eyes swivelling to scan him as it passed.

He adjusts his new mask, a low-volume freediving design, fiddles with the snorkel mouthpiece between his teeth, clears the bit of seawater which has accumulated at its base with a short, sharp exhalation. He contemplates another dive, but notices that the sun is hanging low over the land to the west. *Better keep my date.* He's growing tired of entertaining dive guests, especially the women. What do they see in him anyway? And why do they all seem so lost? He fins back to the point at Praia Tofo, making out the darker areas below him which indicate coral reef in between the lighter patches of sand. As he gets into the shallower water seaward of the breakers by the point, and as the details of the sand troughs of the seafloor below him begin to show, he hears it: the unmistakable click-clicking which fills his ears and his chest with delight. He knows they're scanning him, and his silent message to them, as he pivots in the water trying to find them, is – *let's play!*

They appear out of the haze, coming fast and straight toward him in midwater: a posse of four bottlenose dolphins. He can't be sure, but he thinks, from their markings, that he's seen them before while surfing. Sometimes twenty or thirty dolphins join the humans riding the swells that round the point, showing off, streaking through the forming waves, pulling off bursting aerials with obvious delight.

The four dolphins surround him, and he makes eye contact with those glistening hyper-intelligent eyes before they veer off playfully, clicking and whistling all the while. He can't help himself. He 'talks' to them as they twirl around him, in what he believes is some version of Bushman language. Like most South Africans, he knows how to cluck and to click and he does this now, using his snorkel to project the sounds – which in his mind are saying things like *Hello beautiful! Yes!* And *Wow, you're sleek.* The five of them have drifted to where they can see, through the clear water, the curved, silver backs of the swells as they form to break on the shore. The next swell forms and the dolphins chase after it with powerful thrusts of their tails, crying out to him in his mind, *Come! Ride this wave with us!* He laughs out loud in his snorkel as they disappear into the swell.

I can't! I can't swim that fast. He bursts out laughing, has to spit his snorkel out and raise his head above water to gasp air as he coughs and laughs and is filled with the pure child-like joy of having played with kindred souls.

When he walks into the pub at the Casa Point Hotel, his 'date' hasn't arrived yet. Anton the barman, a fellow South African, flicks his dishtowel over his shoulder and fishes inside the fridge behind the bar counter. 'Who is she this time?' he asks as he hands Klaas his beer.

'No,' Klaas laughs, 'it's not like that. I'm not interested, hey. Not any more. Just having a drink with some Swedish clients to keep everyone happy.' He ignores Anton's sarcastic 'Hah!' and asks, 'So …

have you decided yet if you're going back to South Africa? How long has it been anyway? It feels like you've always been here.'

'Almost two years, hey. I came here just before Mandela was released. When we all thought the shit was going to hit the fan. Don't you remember? We all watched it here. I was new behind the bar.'

'Oh, ja. I remember now.'

The bar had been packed, although it was only four in the afternoon. Champagne was on the house. The owners, a homesick South African couple, weren't the only ones with tears that day. They'd all cheered and cried and hugged as the grainy live coverage showed the Great Grinning Man appear hand in hand with Winnie, lifting his fist in a defiant 'Amandla!' struggle salute. No one in the room, like millions of countrymen, had ever seen him before, this stately man they all knew would be their new leader. There was one hell of a party at the Casa Point Hotel that night.

'Feels like you've been here longer.' Klaas tilts his bottle, studies the familiar label. After seven years, he still loves his 2M local brew, his 'dosh-em'. 'So … going back?' he repeats.

'I think so, hey, Klaas. I want to be part of the new South Africa, man. Our rainbow nation. I reckon it's going to open up. My folks say a lot of people are heading back. My old man tells me overseas investment money is flooding in. I want to study as well. Hotel management. Be part of the tourist boom I reckon is coming. I'm going to wait until the end of the season, so I don't let the owners down. They've been good to me. Please don't tell anyone yet, all right?'

'I won't.'

'You ever think of going back, bro?'

'I don't have anything to go back to.'

'Haven't you got family there?'

'Only my father. He's a farm labourer. It's not home for me any more. I was never close to him, anyway. I should probably write to him more, but he doesn't write back. He can't actually, can barely read. You got any brothers and sisters?'

'Yup, a sister. She's part of the aquarium they're building in Cape Town. The Waterfront thing. She says it's going to be world class. That they'll have a tank with live kelp and a machine that makes waves, so it feels like you're actually underwater when you look through the glass.' Anton places a dried glass and lifts a wet one with dishtowel in hand in one swift movement. 'But I'll miss this place. Gets under your skin, doesn't it?'

'Yes, it does.'

The two exiles stare past each other. Klaas has the thought, for the first time, that perhaps he should go back. There isn't really anything here for him any more. *Wonder if Gwen has gone back yet?*

'You going to Benito's Christmas party?' Anton breaks the silence.

'Probably not. Not my scene. You know me, I hate crowds. You?'

'For sure. Come on, man. Join us, Klaas. It'll be fun. He has a new volunteer. From Canada. A chick. Can't remember her name. She seems nice. You could meet her if you come to the party.'

'Yes, I heard. I think I saw her underwater a few weeks ago and I've seen her in town a few times, but I haven't met her yet. I guess she doesn't come in here, hey? I'm a bit over the volunteers, actually. They pull in here, get all excited about everything, and then leave.'

'Suppose so. She came here once with Benito, but she hasn't been back. You know, she actually looks a bit like you, hey. She could be your sister.' They laugh at this. Klaas picks at the label on his bottle, his thoughts far away once more. Anton looks him over. 'Jees, Klaas, *you* are actually becoming a loner. You got some local girl you're not telling us about?'

Klaas looks up. 'Ha! I wish.'

'I saw you go out earlier today. Day off?'

'Yes, I did a great freedive off the point.' Klaas takes another sip. 'Swam with dolphins again. They are such cool creatures, Anton. They seem …' he searches for the words, 'emotionally intelligent.'

'You know they brought one in a few days ago? Right here' – Anton points down to the beach – 'on one of those new boats with the big engines. And the fancy nets. The Chinese boats.'

'What?' Klaas exclaims. 'A dolphin?'

'Ja, and they didn't even try to hide it. I could see it lying dead on the sand from up here.'

Klaas clenches his hand around the bottle, closes his eyes, sees the dolphin's innocent smile, those inquisitive eyes, the images still fresh, real. *They are brothers and sisters. Family. Fuck it!*

'That Chinaman was there too. I could see him from here, lurking around, talking like a skelm with the fishermen. The skinny shit who hangs around the bars, trying to get up the local girls' skirts. You know the guy?'

'Ja, I've seen him around.'

'Anyway, one of the fishermen comes up to the bar after he'd left and asked me for two bottles of vodka. When I asked why two, he said he was going to use one to pickle the penis in. I said the penis of what? He said a dugong. So I said, what dugong? The one he's going to catch, he said. And that 'a Chinese man' – I mean for God's sake, how many are there in this little town? – will pay top dollar for them as a good-luck charm back in China. Can you believe it?' Anton sniggers, but stops abruptly when he sees that Klaas has that frowning look. The one he wore before neatly punching that drunk tourist a few months ago when the bar was packed. The guy who wouldn't stop badgering Benito's pretty schoolteacher friend.

The two men fall silent. Anton busies himself cleaning glasses, changes the music. Klaas sips his beer, which tastes like shit, and glares at the bottles of spirits with their black pour spouts; sees only lined-up Molotov cocktails on the shelf. The last time he felt this angry was that time he was called a 'coffee kaffir' by the Dicky during his first week of diver training, and almost lost it.

He thinks of his rebellious ancestor. Wonders what Klaas Afrikaner actually did to be locked up on Robben Island by the Dutch. No one ever told him that part of the story, only that his ancestor had been 'belligerent'. Gwen had to explain what this word meant. *I wonder if he actually killed anyone.*

Anton's talking again, has changed the topic: 'Hey, are you going to build your underwater thingy, Klaas? Your reef made out of AK-47s.'

'I was just thinking about Robben Island. You're telepathic, man.'

A few weeks ago, Klaas had shared his brainwave – to build an artificial reef from the guns being handed in after the war. The idea came from Mr Mandela's words – 'Take your guns, your knives and your pangas and throw them into the sea' – spoken at a packed stadium of warring Zulus in Durban shortly after he was released last year.

'Yes, I want to,' Klaas continues. 'Someone told me about an Anglican priest in Maputo who got Frelimo and Renamo to surrender over half a million weapons.'

'Never! Seriously? That's a shit-load of guns. Nice! I love the way the Mozambicans are so positive, hey, Klaas. Rebuilding after everything they've been through. We can learn from them.'

'I agree. Anyway, they're going to create art out of them. Weld them into chairs and stuff. A 'swords into ploughshares' kind of thing. I might write to him. Perhaps I can get guns from him. The shallow sandy area out in the bay here, in between the rocky reefs, would be perfect. It would become a living reef in no time. Like that wreck that's off the point.' Klaas pauses, has a sudden idea. 'You should do a dive course before you leave, Anton. Alfie will do a deal for you. You'll love it.'

'I should, hey. I'll think about it. I'm a bit scared, to be honest. I have problems with my ears. Shit, you must do the reef thing, Klaas. You must.' Anton grows silent for a while, then says quietly, almost to himself, 'I fucking hated being in the army.'

Anton is the only person in town who knows Klaas isn't from Botswana, as his passport claims. But assumes, because Klaas is Coloured, that he left to get away from apartheid. Klaas will never tell Anton that he joined the navy to learn how to dive. That he chose to be part of the Nationalist government defence force.

The Swedish trio arrives, and Klaas catches Anton's cocked smirk before he turns and pretends to straighten bottles. The blonde in the party reminds Klaas of the Abba lead singer. Other hotel guests and volunteers saunter in for sundowners. They move onto the open deck overlooking the bay, where the sky is still aglow in fading shades of orange and blue. It's a beautiful, still evening. Out in the bay, three fishing dhows set out for the night. Their traditional triangular sails, each a unique canvas patchwork, fill and draw the wooden vessels out to sea. The fishermen move about on board readying gear, then settle in the stern to steer. Klaas sighs. The distant sound of the surf mingles with the relaxed banter and lazy laughs of the patrons. The opening twanging chords of Juluka's 'African Sky Blue' waft from the bar. Klaas finds Anton's twinkle and lifts his thumb. Anton lifts both. It's their song. The tinny guitars, once held by Johnny Clegg, the 'White Zulu', the other by his partner Sipho Mchunu, the township magician, start their rhythmic banter. It brings a little half laugh that spreads to Klaas's cheeks. When Johnny's beautiful lyrics flutter in, speaking of a new dawn in South Africa, they catch Klaas in the same place they always do. At the base of his throat. He swallows, studies the locals and the foreigners lifting their drinks and staring blankly out over the Indian Ocean. And he wonders if this is it. The African Renaissance he's heard people talking about.

The Swedes order seafood, and Klaas gets his usual, a plate of cassava chips with fresh onion and tomato salad. And peri peri – everything is spiced here. He catches a whiff of grilled fish and starts to salivate, despite himself. It's been a while since he's eaten seafood, but the smell still gets him. It was a dolphin who pushed him over the edge to become vegetarian. He'd been spearfishing, sizing up a good-sized tuna circling him out past the point in deep ultramarine water, when the dolphin swam into view, one of the resident bottlenose, and 'spoke' to him with those penetrating clicks and the mouth that seems frozen in a smile. Right there and then he unloaded his spear gun and dropped it, watched it wobble down till it disappeared from view. He hasn't touched fish, or any animal flesh for that matter, since then.

God, these people are boring. He's zoned out of their travel stories. They are young, transient, travel junkies. Klaas looks up as Aussie Alfie walks in. *My saviour.* He lifts his bottle and they grin at each other. He gets up, introduces Alfie to the Swedes, hands them over and takes his leave, says he needs to prepare for tomorrow's dive. They look forward to seeing him at the dive shop at eight, they chime. The blond one tosses her hair over her shoulder as he turns and walks away.

'So! G'day!' Alfie says as he sits, clapping his hands together and gawking intently into her iceberg-coloured eyes, set in the sunglasses-white of her sunburned face. He calls out to Anton without breaking eye contact, 'Round of bloody drinks here, mate!'

Klaas walks home alone under the stars, with the gentle sound of the surf washing over him in the dark, reliving the dolphin encounter. The image of nets drifts into his mind, tangling, angering. He looks out over the sea, the lines of waves barely visible, and imagines them hanging out there. Waiting. Waiting for a young dolphin's scan to miss a trick. Waiting for the turtles to lift up after resting on the reef. Waiting for the mantas to wing their way into ... *Argh!* He closes his eyes to see those delicate wing-tips adjusting to glide effortlessly underwater. He clicks his tongue. The doleful face of the dugong from the night he swam into Mozambique comes to him, and he wonders if he should just get away. Away from the killing of sea animals which is happening more and more, and which everyone seems to be okay with. *Yes, maybe it's time.*

As he steps off the road, swings open his back gate, and into the shadows of his cabin, an idea begins to form, and he looks for the moon.

Bazaruto Island, Mozambique
8 January 1992

Claire puts her hand to her mouth without taking her eyes off the blurring water, removing the hairs clinging to her lip. She wipes her eyes, which have teared up from the rushing air. The boat skims, leaving a curving wake on the flat water as Benito, hand on the outboard throttle, carves between the sandbanks.

A vast stand of flamingos appears before them, resplendent in pink and white. The birds shuffle in unison, their heads dipping in and out of the water between their legs like piano hammers – a shimmering, striding band on the turquoise water. This splash of colour is softened by the tan tones of the sandbanks and the dunes further back, with a touch of green where the dune grass clings. All of this is set below a vast sapphire sky, with a layer of scattered cotton-wool clouds receding inland.

Disturbed, the birds lift, and the jet black on their wings flashes. As their boat approaches, waves of them pass overhead. Benito slows the outboard engine and points. But Claire's gaze is skyward, where the blue above her is filled with pink, white and black flying sticks. The birds are ungainly flyers, with straightened necks as long as their dangling legs. Lifting her hands to them, she can virtually feel the air from their beating wings. Their eyes are such a deep burning red that she fears they might burst into flame. The cacophony of their honking recedes into the warm breeze.

'Net!' she hears Benito call out. She looks down to see where he is pointing. They've come up on a line of plastic bottles and faded cork floats, dipping below the surface in the middle. He cuts the engine as they drift onto it. And Claire sees the reason for the dip. It's a dugong, wrapped up in the net which hangs beneath the floats.

'She is too heavy to bring on board. Hold the net here.' Benito pulls the boat along the floats.

Claire kneels down, takes the line.

'I will tow the whole thing to the shallows,' he says, leaning back to start the motor with one pull and kicking the tiller into forward gear.

'How do you know it's a she?' Claire asks over her shoulder as they ease forward. She has to cling to the line with both hands as it tautens.

'I am guessing. Adult females are larger, like this one. We will check when we free her.'

The boat lists. Claire feels like her arms are being pulled from their sockets as they drag the net with the entangled dugong, but she adjusts her grip, holds on. When the prow slides onto the sandbank, she releases the line and they both jump into the water. The dugong, wrapped up well in the nylon mesh, is barely moving. Squatting on the sandy bottom, Benito tucks his arms under the animal and lifts her so her twin nose flaps clear the surface. They open as the dugong breathes out loudly, and suck closed when she's taken a quick breath. Claire has to wipe the mist of the dugong's exhalation from her face. The smell of grape must and lettuce lingers.

'Grab the knife, Claire! I will keep her up. It's in my bag under the seat.'

Claire leans into the boat, scrabbles to find the knife. She hacks furiously at the net, pulling it away from the grey hide. She's breathing heavily by the time she removes the last bit of nylon.

Benito has the dugong in his arms, feet planted on the seafloor. He squat-walks her to shallower water, where her spindle-shaped body can remain submerged but rest on the sand. The flaps of her nasal holes flare and shut. Her forked tail fluke flaps weakly.

Claire leans into the boat and fishes for her fins and her mask and snorkel.

'Also the cream, Claire. In the same bag. And the tape measure. Ah, yes, she *is* a she.'

When she rejoins them, the dugong is a little livelier. Benito has turned her to face seaward.

'See her two breasts, Claire. Here, feel.'

She runs her hands between the two stumpy fore-flippers.

'They are not valved, as with whales and dolphins. This means when the mother suckles, she has to come up vertically and cradle her calf out of the water. And her breasts swell, like those of a pubescent maiden.'

Benito falls silent as they measure her, inspect her wounds and smear fingers of waterproof antiseptic ointment on the worst net cuts. Claire notices the many scars etched into her hide. The dugong trembles as she strokes them. She runs her hand under the grizzled snout; the bristles feel like wet toothpicks. The dugong's nose flaps flutter and she mewls, a chorus of mouse-like squeaks. As Claire slips on her fins and spits in her mask, she recalls that the Australian Aborigines use the name 'whistlers' for them. To Claire, the sound is a siren call. 'It's going to be all right, sweetheart.' She stares intently into one of the dugong's deep-set eyes.

'We should let her go,' Claire hears Benito say.

'I'm going to swim out with you, my sweetheart.' Claire pulls her mask on, places the snorkel in her mouth and leans into the water as Benito releases the dugong.

The two females take a breath simultaneously and dive along the sloping, sandy bottom into deeper water. Claire has to come up for air. Finning on the surface, she follows the dugong to a meadow of seagrass. There the dugong slows, starts to feed. It's unusual behaviour for a creature recently traumatised. *She must be starving.* Claire fills her lungs with air and goes down to her once more, stays with her for as long as she can. She repeats this until she is exhausted. All this time, the dugong has surfaced only once. Little yellow damselfish, the same species she's seen piloting leopard sharks and whale sharks, have gathered to feed in the cloud of sediment forming behind the dugong's head as she ploughs out seagrass by its roots.

One last time, Claire dives down to the dugong. To Dugong. In these few seconds, while she hangs in the water at the animal's side, she hears a woman's voice, faintly, no more than a lingering whisper. It might be a figment of her imagination, but it's real enough to make her look up, scan to the edge of her vision. The vacant water makes her think, with sadness, of the extinct cousin of the dugong, the Steller's sea cow, and she has the thought: *How would Sedna have felt when that last one breathed out for the last time?*

Claire stays down with the gentle grazer, blessing her, until her lungs burn. Finally, she surfaces, gasps for air. She calls out across the water to Benito. 'She's going to be okay!'

The delicious matapa dish that Benito had served up, rice topped with cassava leaves cooked in peanut and coconut sauce, is sitting well – so much so that Claire and Benito have surrendered to the relative comfort of their weathered wooden chairs as they stare out into the evening. The chairs rest on the polished cement veranda of one of the simple huts that comprise the Bazaruto Marine Research Station. Crickets rasp their violin legs in the humid air, and the gentle white noise of surf wafts in through the darkness.

A gecko chirrups suddenly – the sound of loudly smacked lips. It is answered by another. Claire looks up at the wall as one gecko chases the other away from the dim wall-lamp – prime territory, for this is where the insects come.

A whisper of wind teases through the palms. The brown bottle of beer in her hand perspires. She shifts it to her other hand and spreads the wetness over her forehead. The gecko who owns the light snatches a moth in three quick wiggles.

Out the corner of her eye, she sees Benito lift his beer to his mouth. She yawns. It's been a long day in the field. If she closes her eyes, she can still feel the wallowing motion of the station's wooden skiff, the *Dugongo* – the same boat she'd seen in the photograph in Dr Eishmal's office that day in Vancouver. It seems so long ago. She stretches out her toes. Feels the tightness in her thighs and calves.

'You feeling a bit stiff?'

Claire turns to smile at him. 'Yeah. That was some experience.'

'Your first time with a whale shark?'

Claire snakes her arm. 'She was coming straight for me, but didn't collide. That fin knew when to swerve. I brushed her skin with the back of my hand as she passed. It felt like sandpaper. I could feel her raw power underneath that.'

'Yes, they are powerful animals, aren't they?'

She's only known this man for five months and yet feels totally at home with him, Claire reflects. His face, framed below his greying hair, looks quite handsome in the half light.

Claire crosses her legs, takes a swig of beer and shares the thought that has come into her mind. 'So, Benito, you mentioned today that you believe dugongs may have started the mermaid myth. But then we got sidetracked when we spotted the whale shark. Tell me more.' Claire smiles.

Mischievousness spreads across his face. 'Ah, yes. Well, they can be quite human-like you know. The way they mate, for instance. I have observed this. The female will go on her back in the shallows and they will copulate facing each other. But actually, I was referring to the Unguva.'

'The who?'

'The Unguva. If you travel further up the coast here, to northern Kenya and into Somalia, some Muslim communities there believe that dugongs are not normal animals, that they are supernatural. They use the name "Unguva" for them in Swahili. People of the Sea. When I was doing my doctoral research, I stayed on Lamu—'

'Ah, I have heard of this island. Where they have all those skinny cats, right? And there are no cars – only donkeys.'

'Yes. It's a fascinating place. Full of history. You know, it's the oldest Arabic settlement on the African east coast. Anyway, when I was there, I interviewed an old fisherman who told me that Unguva are sought after by necromancers. Witchdoctors who are followers of what he called the "Left-Hand Path", of which there are many in that area, apparently. These black-magic witchdoctors believe that having sex with a female dugong gives them forbidden powers over the djinns, or "creatures-other-than-man", as they call supernatural beings.'

'What?'

'Yes, I am not joking. So, when the locals catch female dugongs in their nets, even though they are devout Muslims, they get the local witchdoctors, the good ones – he called them Q'uadis – to inspect them, to make sure the animals haven't been molested. The Q'uadis even cut out the wombs to check for a man-child. Now of course, the flesh is good to eat. Many have likened it to pork. But if there is any sign of human intercourse, the Q'uadis condemn the flesh and decree that it can't be sold in the markets. Which is why, if a female dugong is caught, they won't leave the body alone until the local Q'uadi has done his poking and his cutting. Not even with the fisherman who caught her – in case he is tempted to benefit from her powers.'

'Seriously?'

'Sure. But the big question, which I did ask, is what if a woman necromancer has sex with a male dugong? As we all know, many of the most powerful witchdoctors across Africa are women.' Benito pauses, struggles to keep a straight face. 'What would come of it, I asked? But he couldn't answer me.' Benito chuckles but catches himself. 'Is this not where the mermaid myth began? What kind of half-human, half-dugong creature would result from this union? There would be a water birth, I am sure. And have you seen the size of a dugong penis, Claire?' Benito rocks his extended arm and fist. He can't contain himself any longer. He claps his hands, and cracks up into a shrieking laugh, which sets Claire off.

They laugh for a long time until they are laughing at each other's laughter, at their own laughter. Eventually, Claire is able to draw a breath. She puts her hand over her crotch where she has peed herself a little. Her belly hasn't ached this much since she was in junior school.

Claire caresses the concrete floor of the lab with her toes. After a while, she asks, 'How do we stop people killing dugongs, Benito?'

He sighs. 'Whew, that is a question that has occupied my mind for many years, Claire.' Benito's face has become serious. 'The best answer I have, at this point in my career, is carrot' – he holds up his forefinger – 'replacing fishing with alternative jobs, that sort of thing; and stick' – he whips the air with his arm – 'laws and fines and arrests.

We need both. The problem with the stick is that you can have all the laws in the world, but you need enforcement. This is the problem we are facing here. Did you know that Bazaruto,' Benito points into the darkness, 'has been a marine park since 1971? Yes, 1971! It's illegal to hunt dugongs in the park, anywhere in Mozambique in fact. But it still happens. Same with mantas, turtles and dolphins. You saw this for yourself last month.'

'Yes, that was shocking.'

'The fishermen know it's illegal to land those creatures. And they knew I was away that day. Where were the officials? The police? Hey?' He shakes his head. 'They are easily corrupted. A bottle of rum gets left at their door in the night, and suddenly they have pressing business elsewhere that day.'

'And the Chinese?'

'Yes. This worries me a great deal, Claire. A great deal. This is a new problem.' Benito looks away into the night, deep in thought, then turns back to address her. 'As I explained to you before, the Chinese government donated those boats, *officially*, working with our government. But there was no consultation. No one asked my opinion.' Benito pauses, studies her face, before continuing. 'The argument put forward by the officials is that bigger boats can go out further, supposedly to take pressure off the near-shore reefs. In reality, it means they target the same reefs with better nets, those gill nets – which catch everything – and they stay out longer. And there is no monitoring, no enforcement. The fisheries inspector has a huge stretch of coast to cover. He hardly leaves Inhambane. Comes to Tofo once a month at most.'

'I've certainly not seen him since I've been here.'

'Exactly! Then that Chinese wholesaler guy, the one you met, arrived in town. Do you think that was a coincidence?' Benito is wound up, is speaking more rapidly. 'As a result, there is a whole new market opening up. Fishermen are targeting species that are not even good to eat. I am told they can get as much as one hundred dollars a kilogram for shark and manta fins. With just a few sharks, a man can get that motorbike he's always wanted. Or buy food from the super-market instead of the village market. Or put a new roof on his house, and win favour from his family. Why is he going to say no?' Benito keeps his hands up, his voice floating off into the night air. He takes several seconds to lower them, his eyes still glaring.

'He wasn't such a bad person, Benito.'

He doesn't answer. She knows they don't quite agree on this point. Benito just wants the Chinese gone.

'I hear you, Benito,' she says, quietly, as she takes in his words. They sit in comfortable silence once more, nursing their warm bottles, listening to the surf and the night sounds.

After a few minutes Benito blurts out, 'To change the subject, I have noticed you use the word *spirit* a lot when talking about animals. And that you often refer to animals with singular reverence. Manta. Turtle. Dolphin. I like that. In our culture, back when we were all animists, this was the same. Each animal had a distinct spirit. A soul. We have lost much of this ... I have had some interesting chats with that divemaster Klaas about this. You haven't met him yet, have you?'

'No, not yet. Is he the guy who made that little mermaid carving for you?'

'Yes, him.' Benito pauses, but before she can say anything he picks up his train of thought again. 'The more I work in conservation, the more I am starting to believe that our main religions, Judaism, the Muslim faith – which is prevalent further north along the coast here – and my own Christianity. They are all the same. And they are to blame.'

'What do you mean? To blame for what?'

'In the way that they treat nature as separate from us. As if we are somehow elevated above the rest of creation. I know this might sound blasphemous for a Christian such as myself. Yet I have grown to believe that this is the root cause of the crisis we find ourselves in. This basic belief that we are different to the rest of creation. Above it all.'

'I have never thought of it that way, Benito. That's profound. It's like we are in a state of ultimate apartheid.'

'Yes! Exactly. That's an excellent phrase. Ultimate apartheid. I like that a lot. I will use that phrase from now on, if you don't mind.'

'All yours. We'll share it,' she laughs, touches his arm. 'You know, Benito, my own inner journey is moving toward a practice of connecting personally with sea creatures. As beings. Individuals. Sometimes it honestly feels like I'm talking to them. Hearing them.' She glances at him to gauge whether he gets her.

'You heard of Credo Mutwa?' he asks.

'No … why?'

'He's a Zulu spiritual healer. And a poet. I love his writing. He writes that in traditional African mythology, whales and dolphins are held in great reverence. He talks of them as supernatural beings. The redeemer fish … Ihlengethwa—'

Claire cuts him short to try out the word: 'Ie … shleng … getwa. Is that right?'

'Perfect! According to him, they were brought to earth by the great sea god, Mpangu.' Claire mouths the word silently as he continues. 'And they carry a message, which will only be revealed when we learn to communicate with them. So, it's interesting to hear what you are saying.'

'Yeah …' Claire replies quietly. Reflecting on what she experiences down there, when she's with animals.

'And Mutwa believes that the San Bushmen were able to talk to dolphins. That they understood the clicks and the whistles. Being so close to their language.'

'Fascinating. I don't know, though … for me it's not about words. It's more about how you start feeling when you're in the presence of certain creatures? They seem to transform your thoughts, somehow. The interaction produces, I don't know … a sense … a sense of *being*.'

'Hmm. I have seen the look you have on your face when you come up from a dive, Claire. Like you have been in deep meditation. Or in another place. I think this is a gift. You must explore it. Use it.

See where it takes you. And I think there is a communal aspect to encountering animals down there as well. Even I can vouch for that. Here, along the east coast of Africa, several tribes, including our local Bitonga, have the concept of "siriti". I think this is what is possibly happening too.'

'Jees, I am learning a bunch of new words tonight, Benito. What does siriti mean?'

'It is the life force that connects individuals in a community. I see no reason why this cannot be extended to other animals. I believe this is part of what we are feeling down there.'

Claire studies his face. 'Funny you should call it a gift. That's what my grandmother used to say. You know, Benito, this practice is growing within me to the extent that I am questioning pure science as my path. I want to understand what lies beyond. Beyond the names and the numbers. I want to feel into what flows between everything and everyone down there.'

'Ah, but we need science, Claire. We have to know what we are dealing with. We have to measure and to quantify, so that we can track changes and communicate progress.'

'Now you're sounding like Todd. The thing is, why do we need justification to protect that which we know, we feel, needs protection?'

'I am sorry, I didn't mean ...'

'No, it's fine.'

'What I suppose you are talking about, Claire, at the end of the day, is love, is it not? Like that Baba Dioum saying, how does it go?'

Claire knows it well, and she allows the words to float off her tongue and into the still of the evening. 'In the end we will conserve only what we love, we will love only what we understand, and we will understand only what we are taught.'

'Yes, that's it. So, this speaks to the importance of facts and figures, which bring about understanding. And to then teach what we know.'

'Sure. But what I would like to add is that we love what we *feel*. Science isn't the only way of knowing, Benito. My Haida forebears, for example, didn't need to reduce nature to numbers to make sense of it all. They connected through tuning in to the living forces that we will never really understand through logic and reduction.'

'This is true. Perhaps we can marry the two. Yes, perhaps we can.'

They search each other's eyes, gauging the nature of the mystery of these things they both care about so deeply. And of their burgeoning friendship.

Claire senses the conversation has plateaued, but has one more thing to add. 'I am intrigued how people here have a daily and direct connection with nature. Where I come from, this connection has, for the most part, been lost. There are more layers of separation. People really see nature as separate from their lives. Can't we work with his?'

'That may be true, but remember that people here want to live as you do in the north. So, it is not surprising that men in the villages will readily trade a few shark fins for a television.' Benito smiles warmly. 'I so wish you were staying longer. Would you like some rooibos tea before going to bed?'

'Love some. I'm going to take boxes of it back with me. I *do* feel at home here, Benito.' She takes the cue, switches her mind off as they get up to go inside.

The kitchen is sparsely furnished. The shelves are mostly empty, their supplies for the trip almost depleted. They lean into the shadows and watch the flame flickering below the blackened kettle as they wait for the water to boil.

'Did you know that the leatherback you saw today is one of the fastest reptiles on earth?' Benito asks, squeezing a tea bag. 'In the top three, in fact.'

'Really?'

'Oh, yes! He can swim faster than any lizard or crocodile can run. Faster even than a black mamba. He is so speedy that he has made it into the *Guinness Book of World Records*. Can you believe that? He can swim thirty-five kilometres an hour in a short sprint!'

'You're kidding me. Why, you're a walking encyclopaedia, Benito. But tell me,' Claire leans forward to poke his side, 'how do you know "he" from today was not a she?'

'Ah! You see. This time I have no answer. You have come to teach me these things.'

'That reminds me, Benito. We should get the schoolchildren out on the boat sometime. We could give them turns going out to the shallow reefs in the bay.'

Benito cuts her short. 'None of them can swim, Claire. None.'

'I assumed ... Because they all live near the sea ...'

'No. But you are right, we should look at this. They should be taught to swim. I am sure the Casa Point wouldn't mind us using their pool from time to time when they aren't busy. The owners are quite community oriented. They do a lot.' Benito pauses as he sips his tea. 'Can you see how much potential there is here?'

'Oh, I can, Benito. I can. There is so much we could do to build on what you have started.'

'I like the way you use the word *we*. I like this a lot,' he chuckles.

Claire looks away from the kitchen window. To the floor, as if her sadness has suddenly reappeared and is now part of the faint shadow that extends from her feet. She lifts her face to him, waits for her smile to spread before she asks, 'What's with you and Miriam?'

'Ha. So, you've noticed.' He shuffles around.

Claire stands to poke him playfully. He lifts his arms defensively, dances away from her, spills some of his tea, laughing as he does so.

'What? You are kidding me?' She prods his ribs again. 'God. You men are so slow. I could see from the first time we met at the school that day that she's crazy about you, Benito. And at the Christmas party. Everyone, and I mean everyone, could see what was going on. How obvious does it have to be? I really think it's time ...'

'Time for what?'

'To show your feelings, you dodo.'

Benito snorts, drains his tea, puts the mug down on the table and comes toward her with his arms open, 'Good night, my sister.'

She too puts her mug down and they chuckle into each other. The hug lingers.

When she walks to her hut under the wide sky, accompanied by the gentle sound of the ocean, she is close to tears.

Instead of going straight to bed Claire takes a skinny dip to cool off. She wallows on her back in the shallow water, gazing in wonder at the vast sky. The Milky Way is so bright that it arcs across the galaxy, its array of colours clearly visible. The sea is as warm as the balmy air, but the whispering onshore cools her face and limbs when she lifts them languidly out of the water.

She stays there for a long time, knowing the sea, and the wind, will eventually cool her. She lies back, held by the rocking water, allowing her body to be massaged by the warm water and the sand. She speaks his name out loud: 'Todd … Oh, Todd.'

She feels her heart beating. Faithfully. The blood coursing to feed, to fix. Here she is, right now, in the nurturing sea which needs so much help. On the edge of this island on the edge of this vast African continent. She recalls the sea creatures she has met. Holds each in reverence as she calls them up, one by one.

Later that night, Claire is woken by the long lilting churr of a fiery-necked nightjar. Benito explained, when they first heard it, that its call is meant to say, over and over, 'Good Lord, deliver us.' The bird is so close, she imagines it must be in the tree outside her open window, that its repeated call is expressing something more intimate – like the crippling, rippling gasps of a sexual climax. And for the first time since Todd's death there is an erotic awaking. Such that she drifts off back to sleep spooning her pillow, imagining the presence of a lover who isn't him.

Flight from Vilanculos to Inhambane
16 January 1992

Claire loosens her seatbelt and presses her forehead against the window to see out over the flat savanna, stretching all the way to the western horizon, where she knows there are mountains hidden by the haze. The plane's droning twin propellers invite daydreaming. She starts to count the rising lines of grey on the landscape, smoke from many fires that will later produce a stunning sunset; loses count in the twenties. Villages, some no more than clusters of huts in the bush, appear like glands along the winding coastal road. Claire contemplates all the people living there, drawn along this lymphatic line from the dry, burned land which can't feed them all, to the bigger towns like Inhambane, where she will land in forty minutes. For now, the plane is out to sea, so when she presses her nose to the glass and looks down she can fly her eyes over the glimmering blue and along the neat, frilled line of white on the tan sand. *Prime turtle-nesting beach.* Her mind deposits a question, and she breaks her stare to turn to Benito.

'Have you heard of this Internet thing, Benito?' He looks up from his in-flight magazine.

'What? Yes, I have. Adam spoke about it a lot when he was here.'

'What do you know about it?'

'Well, he said all the universities are linking up. The World Wide Web. He explained that it will become much more than this email thing, which all us researchers are starting to use. But I am not sure how it will work. Why?'

'Do you think it could help us? Help save the sea life here?'

'I can't really see how. As you've seen this week, we need support on the ground. All the things we've spoken about. How will linking up computers help with any of this?'

'I'm not sure, Benito. I just have this hunch that if the world is more connected, maybe people will care about more than just their own backyard. Ordinary people too. Beyond the universities.'

'So you think we will be sharing more than typed words. Is that what you are saying?'

'Yes. Pictures. Perhaps one day even video. Stories, basically.'

'That would be incredible.'

The tone of the propellers lifts almost imperceptibly as they pass through a patch of lower pressure, and her train of thought is broken, replaced by another. She taps his leg. 'The women in the villages. I see they do most of the hard work. They carry water, pound the cassava in those wooden mortars; they do all the cooking, all the child rearing.'

'You are making me feel guilty again.'

Claire elbows him. 'No, silly. I mean, women are such a powerful force here. Probably more than in my own country. What I am getting at is … can't we involve them in our programmes more?'

'Possibly. I had not thought about this so directly. It could work if we had a woman on our team.' He pauses, finds her eyes. 'Husbands in the villages wouldn't want *me* working with their women.' Benito lets out a little laugh, then continues. 'You used that word *we* again. Just remind me again why you have to leave?'

The lines on his beaming face, so close, lead her to the bits of grey in his close-cropped crown, and then back to his smiling eyes. A lot passes between them in these tacit seconds.

'You had better tell Miriam how you feel,' she says abruptly.

Benito cracks up. *It's impossible to be around this man and to be sad,* she thinks, joining him.

'Shew, you really are like an older sister, Claire. Except you are younger than me.'

'You'd hardly believe it.'

Their gentle laughter mixes, like cement and water, to form mortar to be slapped onto bricks. Benito goes back to his magazine, and Claire turns to resume her window-view dreaming, and the bricks settle atop the lovely wall growing around their friendship.

Have I done any good in the time I've been here? Claire asks herself as the shoreline snakes on into the south. *I've helped count animals. But really, what difference have I made? Well ... at least I saved a dugong a few days ago. I wish I had more time ...*

Out of nowhere, Náan's voice comes to her: 'Get out of your beautiful head, my Claire. You think too much. Listen for the voice of your animal totem, your Otter. Be still and it will speak to you. What is it telling you now?'

But when she lets go of these thoughts, the propellers' drone washes her mind along like a slow current and no answers emerge. With heavy-lidded eyes, she begins to plan her final three weeks in Mozambique. *I'd love to do more freediving while I'm still here. That's number one. Number two, go back to the school.* Number three doesn't come, for she drifts into a delicious half-hour in-flight siesta.

Praia do Tofo
1–2 February 1992

The envelope is where he'd left it on the corner of the table. *Klaas Afrikaner.* The familiar cursive is scrawled with a paintbrush dipped in black ink. *Care of: Mad Manta Dive Shop, Praia do Tofo.* It arrived yesterday, and he's thought of nothing else all day, even underwater. The couple from New Zealand finally got to see a whale shark, so they'd wanted to take him to dinner. But he'd said thank you, perhaps another time, he had to do some chores before the shops closed. He glances at the items he bought, which are now laid out neatly on the sofa and on the floor.

He stares at the envelope over his bowl of leftover vegetable curry and freshly steamed rice. Takes his eyes from it to wipe the last bit of curry from the bowl with his finger. *Why is curry always better the next day?* He places the bowl in the sink, grabs a beer from the fridge and bangs the cap off on the sink edge. Finally, he picks up the envelope and backs through the mosquito-mesh door, lets it slam behind him as he sinks into his hammock.

Klaas runs his fingers over the cursive lines, finds the edge of the flap and quickly rips it open. Inside it is another envelope, airmail, and a folded sheet of paper. He slips the sheet out first. On it is a note in thick pencil, charcoal perhaps, in the same scrawl.

Dear Klaas. I trust you are well, my son. I enjoyed hearing about your news through Christophe. He told me you two had a good time together when he visited a few months ago. Isn't it fantastic that Graça is expecting a child? They have asked me to be the godfather. Of course, I accepted! I recently travelled to Portugal for an exhibition. On my return, there was this letter for you. I hope it brings good tidings. Best wishes, Malangatana.

Klaas looks out over the black ocean, takes a slug of beer, listens to the distant sound of surf. It's so dark he can barely make out the white of the breakers. Tomorrow is the new moon. *It's dark enough*, he decides. He runs through the checklist in his mind, concludes that he is ready, before turning his attention back to the package.

He extracts the airmail letter, has to remember to breathe. The stamp is British, but the handwriting hasn't changed since school. He fills his cheeks and closes his eyes, then blows out and refocuses. Carefully, he tears the envelope open. The three powder-blue sheets are neatly folded. He can't help himself – he lifts them to his nose, and the suggestion of perfume, even if it's imaginary, grabs momentarily at his loins. Even now. He puts his beer down, has to rest his hands on his knees so they don't shake as he begins to read.

Claire isn't sure if it's the dream or the hoot of an owl that has woken her. She sits up in bed, lifts the luminous face of the dive watch on her bedside table. Two a.m. She lies back again, waits for the next haunting call, her mind filled with the vivid imagery of her dream.

She'd been paddling an old Haida whaling dugout over a calm sea, covered in thick mist. She desperately wanted to get to a place up ahead, a place she knew was there but couldn't yet see. In her dream she was unable to paddle on both sides, so she kept angling off to the left as she paddled with her stronger right side. Try as she might, she couldn't get her left side to paddle. This went on for a while, making her more and more frustrated. When she felt she couldn't take it any longer, a man appeared, and they were two in the canoe. She felt his male strength by her side immediately, paddling powerfully on the left. She couldn't see his face, but he felt familiar, like family or a lover. His shoulders and biceps flexed as he leaned into each stroke. She was happy. Wanting to match his power, she had to use all of her effort to keep up. The hull gurgled as they surged forward. As they approached the shore, she transferred to the stern. Now she was steering, using her paddle as a rudder, while the man paddled powerfully on both sides. She'd woken up before the identity of the place was revealed.

Was it Todd? Or some version of herself? She's read somewhere that everyone in our dreams represents some manifestation of ourselves. But this really did feel like another person. And what was their destination? Perhaps knowing that isn't so important. She tries instead to hold on to the sensation, the thrill, of paddling with someone. But can't. All that's left is an echo, an ache.

Klaas slips out the back door of his unlit cottage. He waits at the gate for a full minute, letting his eyes adjust, swivelling his head this way and that, listening for other noises, watching for any movement. The alluring smell of frangipani from the old tree in full blossom near his back gate fills the air, but he isn't distracted. Dogs are barking in the distance, somewhere in the main township. Closer to home, there's only the quiet chirruping of crickets in the hedges. He starts as a fruit bat crashes into the mango tree on the property next door, screeches, rustles the leaves, flaps away. An expectant stillness settles in the darkness once more.

Klaas adjusts the black evening dress he's wearing, the one the big-boned Dutch woman left behind. It's too large for him, so he's stuffed a cushion under it, so now he looks pregnant. The shiny black artificial locks of the wig, purchased from the shop near the market, fall over his shoulders. He's smeared all exposed skin, including his bare feet, with a mixture of crushed black pastel, oil paint and cooking oil that he made up in the kitchen. He shoulders the canvas bag lying at his feet, feels the weight cut, and makes his way out the back gate. Soon he is breathing heavily. He shifts the bag to the other shoulder, walking briskly along the gravel road that heads north toward Bara Point.

He comes onto the beach a full kilometre to the north of Tofo, through the dunes where the fancy beach houses stand empty. Klaas catches his breath for a few seconds, then follows the water's edge, heading south. He arrives back at Tofo main beach a little before three a.m.

Claire lies quietly, listening to the still night. The sensations of the dream linger, especially the feeling of male energy in the canoe … and an idea comes out of nowhere. Wide awake now, she checks her watch again and does the math. It should be around five in the afternoon over there. She flicks on the light and sits down next to the old telephone, dials the number she knows by heart. The line is crackling but it's ringing at least, and she sighs with relief as it changes to the familiar Canadian dial tone.

'Hello?'

'Hi, Mr Storstrand.'

'Claire! Good God. Lovely to hear your voice. Are you all right?'

'I'm fine, thank you, Mr Storstrand. It's hot here, and humid, but I'm adapting. How is Mrs Storstrand doing?'

'We are both still struggling, Claire. It's better now that Christmas is behind us. You know what a family affair it is for us. Thank you for asking. What's up?'

'I'll get straight to the point, Mr Storstrand. I think I have found a way to honour Todd's legacy.'

'Okay, I'm all ears, Claire. We miss him so much.'

When the phone call is finished, she steps out onto the balcony. The owl has gone. As her eyes adjust, she makes out a figure, no more than a shadow, moving quickly along the water's edge, heading for the point.

Klaas reaches his destination and lowers the bag beside the dark shapes of the two boats. Overhead the casuarinas sigh, a never-ending out-breath. He takes a moment, scans the empty beach, before quickly unpacking the contents of the bag onto the sand. Then he sets to work, efficiently following the drill he's rehearsed in his mind, preparing each boat in quick succession. First, he takes off the cowlings of the outboard engines, removes the spark plugs with a wrench, and shoves several handfuls of beach sand into the engine cavities. Using the other end of the tool, he levers off a few essential electrical parts, rips out some wires. Finally, he spills petrol from the plastic containers onto the exposed engines, making sure some of the fuel goes into the spark-plug holes, and then onto the driftnets which are piled on the decks. He tosses the empty containers into one of the boats, and bends down to fish inside the bag for a lighter. He has to jump back when the petrol whooshes.

He drops the lighter into the second boat as its petrol catches, slips the wrench back in the bag, shoulders it and walks quickly through the sand to disappear into the dune shadows.

Claire is leaning against the railings of her veranda as the boats and the nets catch. *Bloody hell … it's the Chinese boats!* She hears the pop as the lighter explodes. The thought does go through her head, briefly, to do something. Wake up a neighbour, feign concern. But she doesn't. She's intrigued by the woman's decisive actions. Why would a pregnant woman want to destroy *these* boats? Her movements are precise, premeditated.

'That's one strong African mama,' she says out loud, as the woman turns her back on the growing orange glow of burning fibreglass and strides off the beach. Claire stays watching until the last hull collapses onto the sand.

Klaas hurries through the empty streets of Tofo, keeping to the shadows. He's about to pull off the dress and wig, to discard them in the bins near the market, when he turns the corner and collides with a man. Instinctively, Klaas lifts his arms, dropping the bag, and feels the man's thin fingers clamp onto his wrists. The smell of rum is overwhelming. Klaas and the drunk dance around for a few steps, and Klaas takes note of the unusual strength of such a slight person. When the man's head flops back, he sees who it is.

Him! Klaas's anger surges and he assumes the crouching stance he'd learned in close-combat training, finds his centre of gravity, tenses his core in readiness to throw the Chinese man, or perhaps strike him in the throat, should he release the grip on his arms. Simultaneously he slows his mind, looks into the man's bloodshot eyes and registers that they're probably not seeing much. Before he can think of his next move, the man lurches forward and vomits, in one projectile gush, all over Klaas. The man's knees buckle, and his clawed fingers lose their grasp. The man slews sideways as he crumples onto the dirt road and lies motionless at Klaas's feet.

Klaas takes a step back, gasping. The sickly smell of puke rises up from the dress and he gags. He scans behind and ahead, but the street is still deserted. The Chinese man is sprawled with his head to the side, his mouth sneering, drooling. Klaas paces around, adrenaline raging through his body. The man groans, mumbles something in Mandarin, then opens his mouth in a crazy laugh which tails off. Klaas looks down at the wretch. It's so tempting. *God, it would be so easy. No one would ever know.* He can see the pressure point right there, presenting itself to him. He pulls back his right arm, clenches his fist, tenses his torso to strike. But in that moment, he can't do it.

He takes another step back, rips the dress over his head and holds it at arm's length. Then, without thinking, he goes to crouch next to the man, lifts the bony hands and wraps them around the fabric. Eyes closed and barely conscious, the Chinese man hugs the dress and giggles while Klaas fishes in his trouser pockets to find a wallet.

In his best woman's voice, Klaas hisses in his ear, 'If you stay in this town you will get hurt.' Then he rises, takes a quick look up and down the street, retrieves his bag and walks away.

Two cats spill out of the waste skip when Klaas drops the wig, the cushion and the emptied wallet in it. He strides home, aware of how silly he must look with his half-blackened body, walking along the deserted streets of Tofo in his underwear two hours before dawn.

Under his outside shower, the one he uses after surfing, he works off the paint with the help of liberal squirts of dishwashing liquid and a pot scrubber. Back inside, he wraps his faded kikoi around his waist and climbs into the mosquito-netted oasis of his bed.

He stares at the folded letter on the bedside table for a long time. Finally, he reaches for the bedside light switch. Staring up at the mosquito net, his eyes adjust to the darkness, and he contemplates how close he'd come to killing the man. A deep loneliness rises, and he hugs himself for a few seconds. *What the fuck is it all about?*

A few minutes later, he switches the light back on. Draws the mosquito net aside, throws off his kikoi, pulls on shorts and a T-shirt and slips his feet into sandals. He goes through to the living room and sits at his writing desk with a pen and a sheet of paper. Rummaging around in the drawer where he keeps the things he'd grab if he needed to leave in a hurry, he finds what he's looking for. And with the first hint of orange to the east heralding a new day, he hastily scribbles his own note.

Praia do Tofo
2 February 1992

Benito arrives at his office at the research station earlier than usual. For some reason, he'd struggled to sleep last night. He enters the dimly lit room, puts his keys down, pulls his chair back – and freezes when he sees the envelope on his desk. His name is written on it in crude, exaggerated capitals. He doesn't touch it yet. He looks instead to his keys, to the door, to the closed window and back to the door, double-checking in his mind that he did in fact unlock the door a minute ago. He walks over to the window and notices the loose latch. Puzzled, he goes back to his desk.

He settles in his chair, lifts the envelope, feels its weight, then turns it over to open it. A plastic bank packet stuffed with meticais, plus a handwritten note, spill onto his desk. He examines the packet first, extracts the notes. 'Unusual,' he mutters to himself. The notes are crisp, unused. And folded in with them are a few soiled, large-denomination Hong Kong dollars. He reaches into his drawer to extract a calculator. He almost drops it as the telephone on his desk rings. It's early to get a call. He lifts the receiver.

'Benito. Is that you?'

'Oh, hi, Claire. I was wondering who would be calling at this hour.'

'I'm glad I found you. I tried your home first but there was no aswer. I think you should come down to the beach. Someone burned the boats. The Chinese boats. Last night.'

'What?'

'Yes, they're all gone. Shall I meet you there?'

'I'm on my way.' Benito frowns as he hangs up, reaches for the note. The writing is child-like, like someone who doesn't want to reveal their handwriting.

Dr Mutara. This money is a donation to the research station. As I'm sure you know by now, two fishermen in the village don't have boats and can't feed their families. I'm hoping you can use this money to employ them as rangers. I know it will only be enough for a while, but it is a start. We have to stop the poaching. Yours sincerely.

He turns the single sheet over. Yours sincerely, who? There is no name anywhere. How did the person open the window? Who would donate such a large sum of money? It's all rather strange.

The fishermen stand by silently, watching the policeman poke the blackened engines and what's left of the hulls with a stick. Benito's speaking to him, but when he sees Claire, he excuses himself and joins her, away from the crowd.

'What do they say?' she asks, arms crossed.

'No one knows anything.'

She avoids his eye. 'I don't see our Mr Wang anywhere.'

'I asked. The policeman said he looked for him this morning, when he first heard the news. But he wasn't home. And his truck was gone. Seems he might have left town.'

Clare bites her lip. Decides not to say anything. About last night. Out the corner of her eye, she sees the man in the wetsuit standing on the rocks by the point, away from the crowd. He has long fins under his arm. It looks like the divemaster from the dive shop. *What's his name again?* He's staring intently at them, at her. But then he turns away, looks out to sea. She nudges Benito and points, 'Who is that over there?'

'Oh, that's him. The one I told you about. Klaas. He shouldn't be diving alone like that. I have told him before. But I guess he knows what he's doing.'

Before she can say anything, Benito continues: 'Are you coming in later?'

'Yes. Yes, I am. After my morning walk.'

'Good, I'll see you there. You go ahead, Claire. I need to stick around.

See what I can learn. Can't say I am sad to see these boats gone.' And he walks off back to the policeman.

Claire watches as this Klaas hesitates on the edge of the rocks, waits for a wave to break at his feet and then falls into the water, rolling onto his back, still holding his fins. The backwash sucks him out. Claire studies him closely now, how he lies on his back like an otter to slip on his fins, then flips easefully onto his belly to head out to sea. She turns away, clears her mind for her walk.

Why now? Klaas asks for the umpteenth time as he swims out, breathing through his snorkel. Why, after so many years of nothing? Just as he's finally starting to get over her. So what if Gwen is returning to South Africa to take up some high-up position with the ANC. He didn't even know until the letter arrived that she'd been living in exile in England. What does she mean by 'It would be nice to reconnect'? Does she think he's been waiting for her all this time? Why, he wonders, as the first bits of reef appear below him, does she still have this effect on him? How cruel of her to include the memory of that night under the stars with the red merpeople on the cave wall. *Our first time.* She knows how much that would mean to him. And how does she seem to know that he's contemplating going back as well? No, she can't possibly. It's merely a coincidence. And what are these 'feelings' of hers 'that won't go away'?

His mind is fuzzy after so little sleep last night. *Stop thinking*, he decides. But one question that wants an answer pops up as he fins along on the surface. *Do I still love her?* He thought he'd moved on, that time had given way to closure.

After last night, it's good to be in the sea. To wash away the feelings of guilt. For there are some. The fishermen's families will suffer if they don't find alternative work. *Can I trust Benito?* He hopes so. He'd added some of his own money to the dollars, denting his stash of saved notes considerably.

He's well out to sea and drifting southwards down the coast with the currents. As he looks down, making out the lighter patches of sand and the dark-coloured reefs covered in schooling fish, the thoughts come to him. *Who will protect all of this? How bad will it get before it gets better? What if it never does? Will anything be left?* His thoughts are interrupted when he picks up the black triangular shape: a manta ray gliding over the reef.

He adjusts his mask, breathes in and out three times through his snorkel. Begins to enter his dive state. All thoughts slow. He empties his lungs and inhales deeply. Gulps a few extra mouthfuls of air. Clasping his nose with his right hand, and keeping his right elbow tucked tight against his stomach, he duck-dives. Swims down to the manta with slow, steady fin-kicks, his left arm outstretched to streamline his passage.

He comes down alongside the manta, slightly from the front so it can see his approach. The manta's eye, a glistening grey bead with slitted black pupil, moves in its raised socket to meet his two eyes set behind the glass of his mask, acknowledging him. As he drops down further, his eyes go to its belly and narrow with deep appreciation when he notices the swelling. A smile spreads on his face. *You're pregnant!* He arches away. Swings around gracefully in the water to meet the mother's eye once more. Stretches out his arms. Invites her. With an effortless flap she veers and joins him, and they dance a slow three-dimensional ballet. When she banks, he follows. He attempts to mimic her smooth, effortless moves by arching his back, extending his toes in his long fins, spreading his arms out even wider, then bringing them to his side, to slowly pirouette. They glide belly to belly, and he runs his eyes over the three oblong patches of black on off-white which remind him of Mr Osler's prize milk cow, the Holstein Friesian.

Klaas feels into her presence as a living being. As he would a beautiful pregnant woman. He moves with her, and she with him. It's eurhythmy in liquid space. She is grace, she is poise, she is one with the sea. As is he. He communicates, through his movements, through his flow, all of his loneliness. All of his joy at her pup, which must be coming soon.

With a casual flap she leaves him, banks away, then comes around to hover above the crest of the reef. Klaas follows and goes down low, to the side of her. Little blue, black and white cleaner wrasse flood into her flared gill-slits and over her body. Pick-pick at the dead skin and the little parasites. Her body shivers in delight.

Nice, hey, Klaas smiles at her.

She hangs, hardly moving her wide wings, maintaining eye contact with him. Her eye bores into him and time ceases. *My spirit manta.* Eventually she lifts up with the swell, rolls the cephalic lobes that hang below her eyes into streamlined cones, and with curling flaps she glides off, fades into the endless blue. Reluctantly, and suddenly feeling the need to breathe, he too rises off the reef, makes for the air above the shimmering under-surface.

Klaas tracks her from above, breathing deeply through his snorkel. He wants to join her again, and for longer this time. First, he must recover, get fresh oxygen into his body. She has stopped, is stationed above the reef. He hangs above her, expanding his chest with each deliberate inhalation. His mind is still foggy from too little sleep, but the fogginess is also having the effect of relaxing him. When he's ready, he fills his chest with air and drops down. He closes his eyes, goes inward as the water pressure builds and he has to equalise. With each slow fin stroke he needs to fight his buoyancy less as all the air spaces in his body, and in the neoprene cells of his skin-tight wetsuit, shrink. When he opens his eyes at about ten metres of depth, she's immediately below him. He angles off to settle on the reef beside her. Her wings are hardly moving as she presents herself to be cleaned once more. As a dive guide, he lectures clients not to touch marine life. For good reason: if one can touch, then so can everyone else, and if everyone did, the creatures would be chased off the reefs. But out here, alone, the manta is choosing to be with him. She comes closer, a mere flex of a wing. They make eye contact, and he reaches for her.

Her vibrant energy flows through his fingers when she lets one of her wings brush against them. Reading her next move, he kicks off to angle downwards. When she flexes, flaps once, he is beside her, and they glide with effortless grace into deeper water.

He descends past fifteen metres and feels the ocean pull. His lungs compress as the water pressure piles on, and he surrenders to the growing weightlessness. It feels like the manta is slipstreaming him. A few more metres down, his natural mammalian diving reflex kicks in and he enters the 'doorway to the deep', a sense of delicious downward drift. His spleen has started releasing red blood cells to enhance oxygen transport. His blood is shifting from his extremities to his core. His lungs, a third of their normal size, are no longer urging him upward. The urge to breathe, brought on by a build-up of carbon dioxide, is being naturally suppressed.

At thirty metres of depth, Klaas's master-switch flicks on. His heartbeat has slowed to under half its normal resting rate. He is now in a deep, natural deep-water trance. They keep going down. He glances at his depth gauge, equalises. He hasn't gone beyond forty metres before, but feels totally comfortable; he trusts the manta. A school of chunky tuna, he counts eight, circle around a few times. Their sleek countershaded grey-blue bodies are magnificent in the half light. With casual flicks of their caudal fins they disappear. The reef has changed, coral replaced by a forest of filter-feeding invertebrates, proud sponges and splayed sea fans. It's quieter. Klaas's urge to breathe is well under control. *This is what it's all about,* the lazy thought comes in answer to last night's question. *This is my home.* His mind is switching off, thoughts are slow to form, as his body shunts blood from his brain to his core. He has become a sea creature. *So, this is what it feels like to be in a Bushman trance state.* This is the dream world Gwen spoke about that day in the cave. When he gets down to fifty metres, as the twilight zone beckons, he parts with his manta. Her flapping form slowly merges with the deepest midnight blue, until they are one. He blinks once, twice. He's in midwater, away from the reef, immersed in pressured silence. There are no earthly thoughts. He lets a tiny trickle of his breath escape from the side of his mouth. Blinks. Looks up toward the faint show of light above, for the gateway back to the world up there. But he can't make out the surface any more.

Claire's daily walk up toward Barra lighthouse has become a solitary songline. When her toes flick bits of beach and her arms lift in sway, the dreaming kicks in and her soul sings. Even if the song was awash with loss when the line was first laid. In the endless hush of the breakers, she might hear Náan's whisper, telling her that all is well.

At the junction where she usually steps onto the long stretch of sand sweeping north, Claire pauses, and on an impulse turns the other way. Continuing, she replays her disturbed night. Who *was* that person down on the beach?

She clears Tofo point, slides down the sand slope and onto the beach. The loose sand squeaks in protest as she kicks into it. Out on the rock shelf, local women dressed in colourful sarongs are bent over, scraping off any form of protein they can find. Mussels, limpets, baby oysters. Claire lifts her head and strides southward along the beach, remembering the smashed turtle carapace the boy had brought in last week. It was still reeking. He said he'd found it on the rocks below the 'big thatched house' at Tofinho. Benito had explained to the boy that he'd done the right thing, but that there could be no reward.

When Claire reaches the point at Tofinho, she makes her way up the dusty path that leads over the bluff. The sound of the sea dulls but then resumes when she comes down to the rock shelf of the Buraco dos Assassinatos. She glances at the sighing pit with renewed sadness as she passes. She looks away, to the south. Runs her eyes along the coastline.

Here Ocean uses her currents, washing south from the point at Tofo, to throw up her junk. The driftwood, seashells, coconuts, and sea beans. The grey volcanic pumice stones – spat up from a leaking seafloor far away. The flotsam and jetsam. The remains of sea creatures. And of course, the plastic, forever breaking into smaller pieces. Ocean pushes all these floating bits high up on the rocks and the sandy beaches of the coves, as high as her tide tongue will reach. Reluctantly, she has to take most of it back with each spring high tide. To float as fake food, waiting to be ingested by turtles and seabirds and mantas. Killing many of them. Then Ocean will throw up their corpses, along with the plastic that has killed them, to decay and bleach on the shore. The crumbling plastic will be retrieved again. To kill again. Again and again. A cycle that will continue each day with each tide as the plastic builds and builds. Never going away. Until one day there is more plastic than fish in Ocean.

Claire opens her shoulders and sucks the morning air deep into her lungs as she picks her way down the slope to the shoreline. The slope resembles the surface of a whipped, jagged sea, frozen into rock. She feels into the lightness of being, a buoyancy brought about by this place. It's the vibrant colours, the dusty earth and smoky smells. The beaming faces. But mostly it's the sea creatures on the reefs here. Yes, it's a love affair. And after years of numbed fingers in gloves and insulated dry suits, it's heavenly to feel warm water directly on her skin. She savours the balmy air flowing over her bare legs below cut-off jeans, wafting into the sleeves of her loose T-shirt.

Reaching the intertidal platform, she picks her way between the first rock pools – scoured hollows set in the hard shelf. Lines of flat rock crabs picking morsels off the wetted rock scurry away into crevices when she approaches. A wave spills its contents, gushes into the crevasses and fills the pools.

Claire kneels alongside one of the pools. The creamy, laced foam on the surface floats away as the excess water spills clear. At first she sees only her reflection, her eyes hiding in the shadow of her brow, and the bright blue sky an aura around her dark hair. She smiles at herself. Then she focuses past her reflection and into the pool. Magically, the little world below the looking-glass reveals itself. It's like peering into a miniature pantomime. 'An aquamime,' she whispers between her knees. The faint smell of iodine from the exposed seaweed mingles with the scent of her skin.

A transparent sand shrimp ushers her gaze across the stage, with props of black spiky urchins clustered in hollows. They wave their spines like pincushions that have come alive. A miniature forest of baubled seaweed fills a corner. Brightly coloured anemones compete for space with pink barnacles on one wall. The shrimp dances out of the way as Claire puts her hand through the surface to stroke the soft side of a purple anemone: the texture of a breast in water. The anemone's tentacles catch her fingers and pull back, shorten, retract into its mouth to transform it into a swollen plum. She retracts her hand, wipes it on her shorts and continues to survey the rock-pool theatre. Hermit crab, the old beggar, drags his shell along the patch of sand between the seaweed. Perhaps he is in search of a better home. A grumpy, fat-lipped goby comes out of camouflage. He darts across the pool, settles on his pectorals, glares up at her. She leans closer to focus on the barnacles, marvelling at the fact that these are crustaceans, inverted crabs really, and not snails as they appear to be. It's like someone took a crab, stuck its bum on a rock, and got it to grow plates of armour so that it ended up looking like a little volcano. Their delicate cirri flail in and out of the vent, combing the water for plankton. The next wash spills into the pool, closes the curtain on the magical miniature world. Claire stands up, stretches.

For the first time she notices the bright bits of plastic strewn in among the drying seaweed all along the high tide line. She steps closer and stoops to retrieve a few, fills her palm with confetti-sized pieces. She forms a fist around them, and looks down the coastline to where she's heading. The reefs off this part of the coast are where mantas like to gather. To be cleaned, and to feed on the rich plankton soup – *and this shit*. She clucks her tongue. This imponderable ocean plastic problem on top of the slaughter. The images of the bloodied manta body, fins hacked off, flash in her mind. Too many are being killed. Well, at least the Chinese boats are gone. *But ... even if Wang has left town, others will come.*

She sighs. There is so much work to do. *Can't believe my time is coming to an end.*

Claire consciously isolates the parts of the scene before her to ensure it all stays with her when she goes. The streaks of yellow light angling through. The shades of pastel pink and orange on the clouds. The liquid, crystal expanse of shifting cerulean. And she dwells on the unseen – the sea creatures hidden below the shimmering surface. *I don't want to leave!*

The rising sun begins to warm her skin, and she brushes her fingers over her forearms, first one then the other, feeling the silk of the hairs. *I must write up all my thoughts. For Benito. I'll start today.* Her head is bursting with ideas. Instead of weakening her life force, the immediacy of the ecological crisis unfolding here, as political peace brings ocean plunder, is energising her. She can be heard here, can make a difference. If not here, then somewhere like this, closer to home. Costa Rica? Mexico perhaps? *Where exactly is home, anyway?*

She steps off the rock shelf and onto the beach. Bends down to remove her sandals. The cool water of Ocean's spilled apron tickles between her toes. With her head still down, she splashes a few more steps. Feels how her feet sink into the slurry.

When she looks up, he is right there. Wading out of the sea. She lifts her hand to shield her eyes from the morning rays obscuring her view. Her first reaction to him is animal – an awakening of the coiled moray at the base of her spine. He hasn't seen her yet. Without thinking, she takes a few steps forward. The next wave washes higher around her ankles. With one hand at her brow and the other on a hip, she takes him in, as she would a sea creature. Waits for him to notice her.

Klaas lifts the two long fins and tucks them under an arm, removes his mask and stuffs it into the foot-pocket of one of the fins. He pulls back the hoodie of his black wetsuit and shakes his tightly curled hair, cleaning the water off his face with his free hand. His chest heaves beneath the tight, wet neoprene as he wades forward.

Klaas stops abruptly. He's taken aback to see her. He wasn't expecting anyone here. But then, as he reaches into her eyes, he feels a greeting from a soul he somehow already knows.

For Claire, it's in the crow's feet around his unusually light-coloured eyes, which seem to be lit from within. In the creases of his brow – *Is that a scar?* – above that cute, slightly flattened nose. And it's in the boyish grin set in that unshaven face. This is quickly followed by an emotion, a deeper epiphany, which has nothing to do with him, or perhaps everything. She knows this part will take a lot longer to figure out … or whatever. Her subconscious is racing to process it all in the four seconds before her mouth can move. She'll articulate it later, but the essence of it comes to her now, quite clearly. In this moment there is the recognition of other. A sense of a solid bass beat that her more complex song yearns for. And she finds his sturdy hands, water dripping from his fingers, and sees how they hold his fins like they might a loving arm.

Still coming out of his deep freediving reverie, Klaas feels the presence of a woman with skin the colour of his, who has appeared out of nowhere and is a little flustered, like she's been caught out. It's in the way she's standing in the shallow water, and not at its edge. This, he senses, is someone who would rather be returning to the place from where he's just come. He notices how her slender fingers lead her arms as she moves them. His mind goes quite blank when these fingers brush away her silky black hair to reveal the full extent of her broad, curious half-smile. A warm chest-flush spreads for the first time in years. When he dives into those dark-brown eyes set in fine-skinned lids, he sees endless Karoo, the ache of his youth, this woman naked. *No.* He steps forward to stop this train of thought, which is making him uncomfortable. He's relieved when she speaks first.

'What did you see?' Claire hopes he hasn't seen her blush at her own banal question.

'Manta,' he says quietly, not taking his eyes off hers. 'I've seen you before. Today with Benito. Last few months also. Walking in town. Underwater. It was you that day.'

'Yup. That was me. I'm Claire.'

'Klaas.' He tucks his fins under his left arm-pit, extends his right hand.

His hand is cool and firm. She flexes her fingers in the neat fit, and the handshake lingers as he continues: 'She was majestic. Makes me so mad that people are killing them.'

Claire's hand feels exposed when he withdraws his. 'Yes, I know. I saw the boats go up.' She pauses, makes out the momentary hint of a smile on his face. 'Benito has mentioned you a few times.'

Klaas studies her more closely. Her dark eyes set in that broad face are fathomless, inscrutably still. A lot is being said in between the words. He needs to pay attention.

Claire reaches forward. 'Here, let me help you with those,' she says softly, taking the fins from him.

They are both grinning uncontrollably. Trying to hide it. He doesn't notice her trembling. She can't know that his mind is a complete muddle as he searches around for what to say next.

They head back side by side, Claire doing most of the talking. She is aware that she's babbling, but doesn't care. When she bends down to slip on her sandals, she notices the calluses on his broad feet. He steps carefully, like a large cat, when they pass over the jagged rocks.

Klaas hangs on to each word that she utters, spoken in that beautiful, rounded accent which sounds to him like she's saying 'ooh' all the time.

They reach the crest of Tofinho Point and look out past the breakers. Klaas points to where white terns have gathered and are bombing down into the sea. 'Baitfish. Probably anchovies, or round herring. Could even be sardines. But they don't always come up this far north. Whatever they are, the birds are going off!'

'Oh, wow! Look at that!' Claire grabs his arm. The pod of dolphins is slicing the surface into a boil as they advance. A sturdy newborn, the size of a large loaf of bread, slaps the surface with its tail fluke, which causes him to fall behind the pod, so he has to leap, like a wet watermelon pip squeezed between giant fingers, to catch up. Claire claps her hands and whoops in delight. They laugh together for the first time, feel into how it can't be the last.

Claire closes her eyes and breathes in the warm salt air. With sudden certainty she knows.

Within his body Klaas is reliving the ride with the manta, which now seems like a lifetime ago, yet is lingering at the same time, as if Claire is now somehow part of the experience.

When she opens her eyes, she turns to him, her brow frowned, and blurts out, 'Klaas, there is work to do now the boats are gone.'

'What do you mean?'

'We've got to build … something. I don't know what, exactly. But we have to protect what's here.'

'What do you know about the boats?'

'I saw. I mean, I know. I … I'm supposed to be leaving. Next week, actually. But I'm not going to. I kind of just decided.'

'All right,' is all he can think of saying, as he tears his eyes away from hers.

They turn and walk together toward Tofo.

Praia do Tofo
3–10 February 1992

Seconds hold eternity in the long days that follow. The time between each delicious, awkward meeting, mere hours usually, stretches. Aches. When they're alone, the scared rabbits, those lurking fears, dart. But when they find each other in a new day, embrace once more, feel the other body lingering a little longer each time, then chests swell anew. And puff! The scared rabbits vanish. So much more is said than the words that gush between them. Claire and Klaas are hardly aware of the blood that flows to curl the toes. And to those places that swell, waiting, wanting. Their flirting is fanned by each other's latest advances. Confidence grows with each gentle imparting that makes separating a little harder each time.

Klaas finds himself waking up at odd hours, wondering where Claire is right then. 'In her bed, obviously, you idiot,' he mumbles into his pillow, turns over. He stares into the darkness. Turns back. Stares. He can't bear to fall asleep in case the thoughts of her are gone in the morning. One night he wakes with his face pressed against the wall, confused. He had been in the cave on the farm with the painted merpeople. With Gwen. A familiar dream. *I thought she would go away.* 'Don't get overexcited,' he mumbles to himself as he hugs his pillow.

Claire unpacks and makes arrangements. She finds herself in front of her mirror a lot. Scraping her tongue and putting on vanilla lipbalm. 'Look at you!' she titters at her reflection. *Careful, it might just be infatuation*, she thinks before pulling away from the mirror. Yet, the happiness extends into that place of uncertainty. There is no dark sea creature swimming around in the shadows like before.

Benito just laughs. More than ever. He makes the necessary calls, negotiates the bribes for Claire's visa extension with a poker face. If the officials had to sniff his eagerness, the price would double. And he wears a fake frown and nods a lot when Klaas slinks into his office after Claire has left, pretending he hasn't watched her leaving from behind the outhouse. Benito tells him all he knows about Todd, tells him to go slow. One evening, when he's assured Klaas that indeed his feelings are real, and yes, he does think Claire feels the same way, and has watched Klaas hasten off on the dust road after her, he plucks up the courage to call Miriam and ask her out.

Claire and Klaas love to meet at dawn. On the beach. It has become a silent pact. Arriving from different directions just before sunrise, both grinning and aching to touch. And sometimes they don't need to talk, to share secrets, as they walk. This is the best time. The future takes root in this fertile silence.

The first time his hand strays to her bare lower back, that silky dimple where it joins her buttocks – to catch her attention as he points out sandpipers ahead, their little legs trilling as they chase the receding spill – it stays there all day. In his mind.

After a week of this aching courtship, Klaas finds the courage to invite her to the Casa Point for dinner.

Claire slips on her faded turquoise cotton dress after she's dried off from her shower. Her little otter carving, which she's restrung with local beads, royal blue in colour, is beautifully framed by the shoulder straps. When she steps out of her front door, taking a deep breath, and sees him leaning by the gate, she bursts into nervous laughter. She's never seen him in a shirt with a collar before. He joins in, and as he approaches, she sees he has a single frangipani flower in one hand. He hands her the bloom and she smells it, keeping eye contact, before tucking it behind an ear.

They walk hand in hand to the hotel, not feeling the dust getting in under the straps of their sandals.

Anton offers up a Merlot before they order. 'On the house,' he says. He turns away from their table smartly, so Klaas won't see the smirk he can't wipe off. He retreats behind the bar. Steals glances as Klaas's hand slides across the tablecloth – the first time he's ever seen him do this with a date. He decides he'll call that girl in Cape Town when his shift ends.

Klaas's hand feels like home as it enfolds hers, settles there. She shakes the last drop out into her glass with her other hand. She tells him it's the best wine she's ever tasted.

They walk back to her cottage hand in hand. In blissful silence. When they fold into each other at the gate, Claire kisses him on both cheeks, her lips lingering at the corner of his smile. She feels him stir and she knows he'll probably take one of his long runs on the beach when he gets home.

Claire tries not to giggle as she sways down the garden path to her front door.

Klaas waits for her to turn. When she blows a kiss and her face flushes, he wants to rush to her. With one hand gripping the gate, he waits for the door to squeeze away her shadow.

The door eases open again, enough to reveal her elven grin, 'See you at the dive shop at seven.'

They both burst into uncontrollable laughter.

Klaas falls asleep laughing.

Claire yawns in the still half-light of predawn. The sound of the tide gently clawing the pebbled shores of SGaang Gwaay, a soothing *conkle-conkle*, replays from her waking dream. The image of her great-great-grandfather's mortuary pole fades into the mists of her mind. And the sea creatures that were there, some from the Pacific and some from here in Mozambique, slowly swim away. She holds up both hands to stare at her fingers. They seem to disappear and then reappear as she rakes the air like a barnacle's cirri, with Raven's wings beating. Beating against her chest.

Praia do Tofo
11 February 1992

Which endearment to use? Claire seeks the harder beach sand so she can stride and concentrate on this vital question. Her head is still a little thick, even though she took an aspirin and drank two glasses of water before setting out. So she swings her arms to get her blood flowing; considers her options. Todd had not warmed to 'sweetie'. Or 'honey', for that matter. He never gave her the same look that her father wore when her mother used them. When she glances over the breakers and out to sea, she slows. Stops in her tracks to take in the full extent of the brooding sky stretched over the surface of the water, the one reflecting the other, each taking on some of the other's hue.

Terns working the surface are flitting flecks of white on the dark. Black cormorants in snaking v formation beat low over the waves, heading south as if their lives depend on it. Far out, almost at the horizon where it's darkest, slanting rain draws a quiet grey curtain. Behind it, a lick of lightning, and then nothing.

The thin film of a spent wave tumbles a pelagic sea snail, *Janthina*, toward her. When it catches, settles, Claire picks it up. She turns it over in her palm, admires the vivid violet shell – a perfect Fibonacci spiral. There's a brush of the purest pink on the rim of the opening, from which cobalt-blue mucous bubbles. It's the same blue as the bluebottles this snail has evaded out there on the open ocean. Had it bumped into one, the predatory jellyfish with the bagpipe sac would have taken this blue for itself. *A floating web of blues.*

A dab of colour remains on Claire's palm after she's placed the creature back on the sand. Todd once told her the Greeks crushed up this sea snail to make purple dye. She considers rescuing it, taking it out to the waves, but knows this will be futile. Its fate has been decided. A gull or a crab will pick out the flesh, and its violet shell will be crushed to become the colour of sand.

Claire checks her dive watch. *Shit, look at the time! Can't keep the boys waiting.* She splashes her way through the spill, stooping briefly to pick up a cowrie shell for Klaas, and then strides purposefully toward town. An indignant ghost crab scuttles ahead of her, and she blows him a kiss, calls out, 'Off you go, my darling!' as she laughs him into his hole.

Klaas looks up. She's standing there on the dusty road, shielding her eyes from the glare as she peers at the dive boat, parked on the cement driveway next to the dive shop. One hand remains on the pillar valve of the scuba tank, the other holds the regulator he's just tested. His blood drains. She hasn't seen him yet.

Gwen's blonde hair bobs as she steps onto the driveway, and he hears her metal bangles jangle as she rounds the boat. She stops as their eyes meet. They're still a few paces apart, but within scenting distance – and the citrus musk catches in his throat. Scratchy reggae music leaks from the compressor room behind him. Cicadas sing in the dry bushes. In the emptiness it all comes back, all at once. He tries to swallow but can't.

She's grinning, that same cheeky grin he always sees etched into the shadows when he remembers their Bushman cave. He can't find the words he's rehearsed a thousand times. His guard, which he'd imagined would come up in this moment, is down, and he finds himself diving without breath into her cold Benguela-current eyes. The regulator clatters on the cement floor by his feet.

'Hello, my Klasie.'

'Gwen.'

She takes the final two steps, and he feels her breasts pressing into his chest. His arms lift slowly to meet her embrace. She's thinner. Before his next emotion can arise, she holds him at arm's length, beams into his face. He can feel her fingers clutching his shoulders.

'The guy at the Casa Point said I could find you here.' Like the last time they embraced, there's the hint of stale cigarettes on her breath.

Klaas steps back, feels the cold steel of the scuba tank on the back of his leg. He crosses his arms over his chest.

'Did you get my letter?' she asks, hands now on her hips.

He registers a scratchiness in her voice that wasn't there before, notices the London pallor, the coiffured hair, the red lips and red fingernails. And it's as if these differences rush to form a life raft, which he lunges for.

'I did,' Klaas replies quietly, like an outbreath.

'I didn't know your address. Thought if I wrote to …'

'Yes. He passed it on. So, you're moving back to South Africa.'

'Yup. I arrived last week.'

'You been to the farm yet?'

'No, I came straight here. Well, after Johannesburg. I had to see some comrades there. And I stayed over in Maputo on the way up here, so I saw him.'

'Who? That friend you were with?' The face with the little round glasses he's punched a thousand times in his mind reappears. The skinny comrade.

'No.' Gwen laughs. 'No, Malangatana. He told me how to find you.' Still smiling, she shifts her hands on her hips.

'Ah … of course.'

Her eyes narrow imperceptibly.

'Why are you here?' Klaas asks, one hand on the life raft.

'I thought I explained. In my letter.' Gwen steps closer, searches his face. Her hand, which comes to rest on his arm, is cool to the touch.

Klaas studies the muscle barely twitching at the corner of her smile.

'You've always been there for me, Klaas. The others meant nothing.' Gwen tucks a tuft of hair behind her ear and adjusts the chain around her neck, and Klaas notices the red ruby hanging in her cleavage. He can't take his eyes off it. Even cut and polished, it's still the size of a lamb's eye. Gwen's mouth is moving, but he's no longer following what she's saying. It's as if he's suddenly put his head into the water. He turns his head to the side. Closes his eyes. He lets go of the life raft, of the light from the ruby. He drifts down into the stillness. And the questions that he will never ask fade away into the depths.

'Hey.' Claire's voice carries in the stillness, enters Klaas's mind like a sudden humpback call. His eyes snap open and he swivels. Knocks the scuba tank over, loses his balance and falls. The steel cylinder hits the cement and rings out like a bell. His hand lands on the regulator and the snake-hiss of purged air is deafening in his ear. As he gets back to his feet, Gwen holds his shoulders – to steady herself, because she's laughing. Laughing uncontrollably. Just like on the farm, when he fell off his horse. When she catches her breath, she eases into him, slides her hands up to hold the back of his head.

Klaas, his head filled with perfume, looks over Gwen's shoulder, doesn't feel her pressing into him. Claire is standing there. Quite still. And the look on her face becomes the centre point of a kaleidoscope, around which everything else tumbles. His eyes go to Benito standing beside her, for once not smiling, then to the dive bags at their feet, and up to find those dark-brown eyes again. He blinks, as if in slow motion. He'll never forget the pained expression that spreads across Claire's face before her straight dark hair sweeps the image away, like a curtain, when she turns. His hand comes up by Gwen's side, as if to reach out to Claire as he watches her back disappear down the dusty street.

Claire paces the length of her deck, folding and unfolding her arms. The soft crepuscular glow spreading in the western sky distracts her for a moment, but then she goes back to her pacing, thoughts darting. All afternoon, she'd expected him to come around to the research station, but he hadn't. And he wasn't waiting for her at her home, either.

When Benito returned from the dive she was meant to be on, he told her that Gwen left the dive shop shortly after she did. And that despite the fact that Klaas wouldn't talk about it on the boat, he's sure it's nothing. When they left the office together at the end of the day, Benito tried to reassure her once more. 'Really, Claire. It's just an un-expected visit from a childhood friend, that's all.'

Should she just leave him be? Them? *It's been a long time. They would have a lot to talk about.* Claire stops and stares over the darkening sea. *Why didn't he tell me she was coming?* And, *Why isn't he bringing her around to introduce me? Aren't we …?* 'Fuck it.' Claire swears under her breath. Grips the wood of the balustrade, closes her eyes. She remembers the feeling of minor jealousy when Todd flirted with attractive women at conferences. But this feeling is unsettling, disempowering. *I really thought we …*

She desperately wants to make sense of what she saw. She needs him to explain. Surely, what they've shared in recent weeks means something to him, too. So, as the sun finally sets, she steps inside, showers and slips on a dress, one of the ones he's admired, and dabs a little perfume on her wrists, not too much, rubs them together and spreads some on her neck, just below her ears.

Claire's scrubbed skin breathes in the evening air and her heart lifts at the thought of being with him. The evening air is still, so she hears the bat when it wings over her. A stray dog appears out of nowhere and lopes toward her, presses his wet nose into her leg as she stops in the road to reach down and pet him. 'Hello, fella, who do you belong to?' The single white patch on his black fur, off-centre on his neck, reminds her of an orca. 'Yes, my boy, you look like SGaana. Yes, you do.' When she continues, the dog saunters beside her, looking up at her with doe eyes every few paces. *I'm sure I'm overreacting*, she reassures herself, as she rounds the corner, to be welcomed by the familiar lights of his little cabin at the end of the road.

Before she sees them, she hears Klaas's voice and then a woman's gentle laughter. Framed in the yellow glow of his living room, Gwen, seated at his table, is facing away. Her blonde hair bounces as she holds forth. Her head stops moving and her slender white hand goes up. Claire sees the red wine in the glass. The woman's movements are graceful. Sophisticated.

Claire sees Klaas draw closer and raise his glass. He's smiling. Claire sees the same luminous eyes, the same crow's feet that have greeted her these past days. Claire hears the clink of the glasses and her hand finds the little otter carving hanging between her breasts. Klaas is talking, but she can't make out what he's saying.

'In the navy, it was all about moving efficiently through the water. Perfect buoyancy. Breath control. Finning technique. Equipment and explosives.' Klaas pauses to make sure she's following. 'Then when I got up here, in the early days especially, it was all about, well, if I'm honest, it was about sun, sea and …'

'Yes. Sex. I know. Go on, sweetie.' She touches his arm.

'Now it's about connection. I don't know, Gwen, there's a life force down there. Some of the animals …' He watches the red wine lift to her red lips, her eyes blank and cold blue. 'And to meet someone who …'

Gwen places her glass on the table, holds his face gently in her hands: 'You've got a little bit of a crush, haven't you?'

Claire can't bear it any longer. It's as if her heart has slowed, and she's back there – hanging on the line, watching for Todd, unable to come up. Quite alone. Her head feels light. She has to grip one of the posts of his garden fence to steady herself. The dog whines beside her.

Klaas hears a dog bark. He gets up, goes to the window and peers out into the darkness. There's nothing. *I should go and see her tomorrow*, he thinks. When he sits down and studies her face, Gwen is smiling at him again over her wine.

Praia do Tofo
12 February 1992

Claire stares at the lines of text she's typed. She takes her eyes off the computer screen and looks across the office at Benito's desk, vacated with a warm smile a few minutes ago. Searches around the room for remnants of his laughter. This room they've shared for five months now, in between the time out there. It feels like home. She wipes a tear. Sighs. Wills herself to keep it together. She should leave for the day, but she wants to finish the report she's working on, and her cabin will feel even emptier. So, she forces her mind to engage with what she's writing. She resumes pecking at the keyboard. Animal names appear in sentences. Words that will never capture the emotions, the memories, now cut adrift.

'Benito said I would find you here.'

The gentle words end all thought. She looks up and there he is – silhouetted in the doorway. 'How long have you been standing there?' She's aware that her voice has an edge.

'Sorry, I didn't mean to startle you.'

'It's okay. I was deep in thought.'

'I can see. I'm sorry. May I come in?'

'You may,' Claire replies, with the same hint of bemused sarcasm she always gives his schooled politeness. She gestures to the easy chairs where she and Benito sat and chatted the day she arrived. They don't touch when they cross paths to take their seats.

They stare at each other across the empty coffee table until Claire breaks the awkward silence. 'I've decided to go away, Klaas.' She can see the effect her words have, though he tries to hide it. And her own heart beats a little faster at hearing them.

'All right.'

Is that all you have to say? she thinks bitterly, but says nothing. *And it's not all right. It's all wrong.* She bites her lower lip, determined not to show her vulnerability. Determined not to go there, not to ask the questions that kept her up all night. But instead to be true to some kind of higher love for him, as was her resolve when the first light brought relief from the demons. So, in these cold seconds, she retreats even further into the shadows that have grown around her these last twenty-four hours. But the question tumbles involuntarily out of her mouth: 'Did you know she was coming?'

'No. But she wrote to me.'

'When?'

'About two months ago.'

'Why didn't you tell me?'

'I ... I don't know. I thought—'

'You know what, it doesn't matter.'

'Claire ...'

'No, really. I think you need to spend time with her. I know how much history you guys share. It's okay. We probably got overexcited. A bit of time and space will give us perspective. We can stay in touch. We can be ...' But Claire doesn't say it, can't use the word *friends*. Not yet.

'You mean, you're—'

'Yes ... I think it's better this way.'

Klaas's eyes go to her hands fiddling in her lap. He catches a glimpse of white, and when her beautiful fingers turn, he recognises the mermaid carving he made for Benito. There is so much he came to say to her. To explain. But Claire's words are closing down that part of him struggling to articulate his deepest feelings. With each aching heartbeat, he begins to retreat to that all-too-familiar place. *It's happening again. Like with all the other women.* The thoughts float and fade.

'When are you leaving, then?' he stammers.

'On the weekend. I was busy writing my final report when you walked in.'

The exchange hangs in the gloomy room as they search each other's pain-shrouded eyes. A cricket's chirrup resumes outside.

'Oh, I see. All right. I'm sorry.' Klaas gets up suddenly, half knocks the chair over. 'Sorry. I'll let you get on with it then.' He scrapes the chair back into place.

'No, no, you don't need to. I didn't mean …'

But Klaas has turned so she won't see his crumpling face as he heads out the door.

Claire slowly uncurls her fingers and sees the little carving, as if for the first time. 'Fuck it,' she mutters to herself. She clenches her eyes closed and waits for the urge to run after him to subside.

Praia do Tofo
13 February 1992

'Are you quite sure, Claire?' Benito leans forward, his face a sea of concern.

She doesn't meet his gaze, just blankly continues to face the bay beyond her balcony. 'I was stupid to fall in love so quickly. So soon after ...' she says, as if to herself.

Benito sits back in his chair, sighs, opens his mouth to speak, but then closes it. Miriam made him promise to say as little as possible. He shakes his head, leans forward again, unable to contain himself. 'Listen,' he touches her knee, and her bloodshot eyes soften as they meet his, waiting for him to speak. 'All I'm saying is, don't jump to conclusions. I mean, just because you saw them spending an evening together doesn't mean ... and you said he came around yesterday. I can see he's been thrown by this woman from his past. But it doesn't mean he doesn't care about you. I know he used to have a bit of a reputation, but I've seen a changed man, Claire. Really.'

'Really? Is that so?' Her eyes search his. As if the truth is hiding there.

'I don't know. He's a closed book. All I know is you made him come alive again.'

'You *men*.' Claire spits the words as she faces the sea again. 'Sorry, I didn't mean ...' Her voice a whisper.

'I understand.'

Claire studies his dark, kind eyes, his greying, close-cropped hair.

'Just give it some time, is all I'm saying. You don't have to rush off like this. What about our work? Your plans?'

'It can't ever be the same again. I saw us together, Benito. Klaas, you and me. I can see now that I was naïve.'

'No, you were not, Claire.' His brow creases.

'I don't know. I just think we need some time apart. I … I …' But she can't continue. She lowers her face into her hands.

Benito comes to the edge of his seat and rests one hand on her knee and the other on her shoulder. He feels her take a deep, deliberate breath. Then she lifts her head, wipes her wet eyes with both hands and slowly blows out through puffed cheeks.

When she finds his face, a picture of brotherly concern, it makes her laugh and cry at once, and when this has passed, she squeezes his hand on her knee. 'I'll come back, you silly old fart. I love this place too much. I just need some space. I'll be fine. I'll get stuck into fundraising over there. I'll write. I promise.'

Claire stands and Benito rises to hug her. For precious seconds she breathes him in, the homely smell of garlic-laced food. Miriam's cooking. She pulls away, fighting off the tears. She's determined to be professional.

Benito steps towards the door, stops in his tracks and turns to her, 'Claire, at least …'

'Go now,' she cuts him short. 'I need to pack. I'll see you again before I leave. Enjoy your evening. And tell Miriam I say hi.'

When she knows he's out of earshot, Claire lets it out, feels her shoulders shake, listens to the sound of her uncontrollable sobbing.

'You comfortable at the Casa Point?' Klaas asks as he ushers Gwen into his living room. Her perfume, without the undertone of stale cigarettes this morning, envelops him as she jangles in.

'Yes, it's quite quaint. Like your place here.'

'Like some coffee? I've just made.'

'Love some.' She follows his muscled back as he walks to the kitchen, dressed only in a kikoi.

Her slender white hands come together around the mug. 'It was lovely to spend an evening with you, Klaas. It feels so good to be with you again.'

'Yes.' Klaas watches as her lips kiss the rim of the mug and leave a whisper of red.

'You know what today is, don't you?'

'No.'

'It's Valentine's Day, silly.'

'Ah … of course.' He shuffles.

'You remember that bunch of white kapokbos you gave me that one year? I'll never forget it. You knocked on my window before the sun came up, and when I opened the curtains there was this big snowy surprise on the sill, with your card made from folded cardboard. So romantic.' They laugh together, and Gwen finds his eyes from above the rim of her mug. 'So sweet. You would have been, what? Seventeen?'

Gwen's laugh trails off and he smiles at her. *Of course I remember. I remember everything.*

Through the window, a movement out to sea past the point catches his attention; he searches beyond the breakers but there's nothing. Probably just a dolphin. He wonders if Claire is up yet.

'You still with us?'

'Y-yes,' Klaas stutters as he looks back at her.

'You were thinking of her, weren't you? Your Canadian friend.'

He doesn't answer, but studies her face. Takes in the fine features. When he does speak, it's almost a whisper. 'There are some things I need to tell you, Gwen.'

She tosses her bob away from her face. Runs her fingers through her hair. Her nails flash red. 'Okay, I'm all ears.'

'You said you would stay in touch. After Maputo. But you didn't. I started thinking you'd been taken out.'

'I'm really sorry. I thought I explained ... how we couldn't talk to anyone. It was hard on my folks, too.' Gwen puts her mug down on the table and finds his free hand. 'But *now* is all that matters, Klaas.'

Klaas swallows. His mind floods with memories. Sunbaking by the farm dam. The taste of her schoolgirl mouth. And suddenly his room is filled with the dry, perfumed air of the Karoo. Taking a deep breath, he meets her eyes. 'It's been a long time, Gwen. If you'd come earlier. If—' He pulls his hand away.

Her eyes rim with tears. 'I am so sorry. But we can make up for it now, sweetie.'

'Please don't call me that,' he whispers. 'And it's not just a crush. I think I've found ...' But he doesn't complete the sentence. He stands with his eyes downcast, aware that she's standing stupefied before him. He wishes she'd leave now. But she's started talking again, words gushing.

'How can she ever replace what we had? What we still *have*. Can't you feel it too? Last night ... it was like we'd never been apart.' But he remains silent, so she continues. 'The struggle is over. So exciting. It's what we spoke about as kids ... what I fought for all these years. We don't have to be in exile any more. You don't have to hide here in this ... this place. We'll be a couple ... It's possible now, in our new South Africa. Isn't this what we always dreamed of? I came here, I came here to ask you ... Come back with me, Klasie ...' Her voice trails off in the still room.

Klaas listens to the faint buzzing in his ears as he stands before her, almost at attention, with his eyes closed, head downturned. In his mind, he feels the rush that comes through the water when a school of trevally changes direction underwater, and he hears the rumbling call of a humpback bull. And he sees Claire's face glowing when they walk on the beach at dawn. He slowly lifts his head. The taste of coffee is bitter in his mouth. Gwen's grey-blue eyes are pleading. She's close to tears. He studies her face. Eventually, he answers in a hushed voice as he holds her eyes, 'It's *your* dream, Gwen. Not mine. I am sorry. And after seven years here, I don't see colour any more. I don't need to be a part of some ... some ... rainbow nation thing. This is my home now. I'm in love with the sea here. And with her ...' He remains standing before her, his hands hanging loose by his sides. 'You should probably go now.' He's looking at her face, but he's no longer present. He is underwater. In amongst the Bushmen merpeople and his animals.

'Klaas. Klaas!' Gwen's insistent voice breaks his reverie.

Someone is banging on his front door. Klaas frowns and steps away from her.

When he opens the door, Gwen close behind him, it's not who either of them expects. It's the old man from the beach, dressed only in tattered khaki shorts. His bloodshot eyes are wild, and he's spitting words in Portuguese, the tendons on his chest and neck writhing as he gesticulates.

Klaas steps out and holds the man's shoulders but he breaks free and gestures to the sea repeatedly.

'What is it?' Gwen asks.

'He says there's trouble on the beach.'

'Eles estão a morrer! Vem! Vem imediatamente. Eles estão a morrer!' the old man lisps at Klaas and points again down the path.

'What is he saying? What's going on?'

'I'm not sure, Gwen. But it's not good. They need our help,' Klaas snaps.

The old man turns and runs off toward the town, muttering loudly under his breath. 'Onde está a Mulher do Mar? Onde está a Mulher do Mar?'

'Yes, where *is* Woman of the Sea?' Klaas repeats under his breath.

'What are you talking about?'

'Nothing. Need to go down to the beach and help. Now.'

'You go, Klaas. I'll finish my coffee and follow in a sec.'

She Down There is here this day, in the bay where the dolphins are intent on dying. Their panicked clicks and whistles fill the sea as they desperately try to understand the nature of the seismic slamming that has flayed their synapses. They gather behind the breakers, perhaps seeking solace in the white crush. But they can't escape the cacophony that swells in their heads. So, first one, and then all of them, break through the waves to abandon the water.

She Down There grows silent with grief. Even the crackling of the reefs seems muted. Her voice is reduced to a whisper, carried on the waves that have travelled from afar and must release onto the shore. It drifts onto the land, asking to be heard.

She, whose name is her destiny, rises up, surfaces. Looking over the breaking waves, she sees the villagers gather around the dolphins, glistening on the shore in the dawn, and how their concerned faces turn to the two men she knows from underwater. The short one with the greying hair and the flashing teeth, and the wide-chested one. And she sees how the women dressed in colourful cloth hold back, waiting for instructions. Through the dunes, the dark-haired woman comes running, the one who calls out to her underwater. Hobbling behind her is an old man. And she sees how everyone, including the two men, turn and wait for the dark-haired woman to join them.

When the wind shifts and comes off the land, it is full of the dolphins' musty breath, and the urgent chatter of the humans intent on putting them back. She Down There can see into the hearts of the humans, and it gives her hope, for although they only hear the animals' feeble squeaks, they are also listening to the voice that resides within each one of them.

It is the call of the sea, the womb of the human soul. The call is particularly strong within the three who are rallying the villagers. She Down There knows they have felt the pull of the currents on their limbs, the brush of living plankton on their masked faces. And they have gazed into the eyes of many sea creatures and found in those moments a deep, personal peace – a reconnection with the living universe which is everything and all that there is.

She Down There, Ruler of the Sea Creatures, calls out on the wind of the sea to the dolphins with all of her voice. She speaks to their intellect, shaped over millions of years by sound and by flow, and implores them to submit to the humans, to trust them for now, and to not let go. And to see that these humans need to care, need to connect, to feel whole.

Claire kneels beside a dolphin, her hand resting on the softer skin near his blowhole. The dolphin breathes, a quick inhalation and a slower resigned outbreath that she feels through her fingers. Claire lifts her head, squeezes her eyes to clear the tears, so she can look up and over the waves. Despite the corncerned vioces around her a stillness decends, such that she hears the message carried on the wind and in the waves, and her lips tremble to speak. She calls out to Klaas, who is beside another dolphin, 'They need to go back *now*! I think they will listen to us.'

'But the tide hasn't turned yet. It's still another hour or so. Shouldn't we wait?'

'They won't make it that long. Their lungs are collapsing under their own weight. And they're overheating, for God's sake!' She points up at the sun, which has cleared the point and is already too bright to look at.

Klaas stands, straightens, and wipes his face as he thinks. He looks around, counts thirteen dolphins. He goes over to Benito and they confer. Benito touches Klaas's shoulder as he turns away, as if to affirm. Klaas strides quickly to the biggest dolphin and gestures to a few men to join him. They grab hold of its tail and its pectoral fins and they begin to slide it toward the water. Benito calls another group together, and other men and boys down the beach follow suit. The old man hobbles on his pin legs and spits encouragement and does not allow anyone to rest.

The dolphins respond when they feel the water flowing over their skins, the pressure ease from their ribs. They breathe more easily and the oxygen flows through their veins, clears their minds. They let the humans hold them in the shallows. They hear the gabbling voices above the water, and tentatively they listen also below the waves, for the sounds that drove them to despair. But the ship has moved up the coast, along with the pulsing device it drags behind it to penetrate the seafloor to reveal oil and gas.

One by one, the dolphins swim back through the waves. Only one remains on the shore. As Klaas approaches, catching his breath and wiping his wet face, he can see that Claire, kneeling beside it, is wracked with grief. He gestures to the men who are with him to stand back and he goes down onto the sand on the opposite side of the dolphin. Claire's face is downturned, her head leaning into its dorsal fin. Her hands resting on the back of a creature whose delicate ear-bones have shattered and who has stopped breathing.

Klaas places his hands over Claire's and she looks up and into him. At first her eyes are vacant, but as he searches those dark pools, she blinks and he starts, for it is as if her soul is laid bare.

Her lower lip trembles as she speaks: 'I thought this one was the strongest. It's why I left him for last. I tried to tell him to hold on, Klaas. But he faded so fast.' Her face crumples.

Klaas steps around the dolphin and he lifts her into him. 'It's all right, Claire. I'm here. We did good. We'll take this one out in the boat.

Right away.' He feels her hands on his bare back, the softening of her head into his chest, and his heart surges. They cling to each other and many unspoken words melt away in their embrace. From some other place, he hears himself whisper over the gentle sound of the surf, 'Please don't go, Claire. Please.'

'What about her?' she asks, without looking toward the dune where they both know Gwen is standing.

'She is leaving. Today, in fact.'

'But she stayed with you last night. What about that?'

"No, she didn't. And she knows I love you.'

'Do you?'

'You know I do.' And he feels her chest shudder as she lets it all go.

Klaas tucks Claire's head into his neck. Over her shoulder, he watches as Gwen slowly releases her folded arms, pauses briefly, as if wanting to wave, and then turns to walk away.

Out in the bay, the dolphins slice the surface. In unison, their blowholes open and their quick exhalations hang as mist on the water. When they suck in the new air, it is sweet. And when they dive down to the reef, this fresh air flutters their phonic lips, and their clicks and whistles carry Her harmonic overtone. She Down There flows with the dolphins through the salt water that carries the eggs and the slime and the dead bits waiting to be food. Sunlight streaks down through this blue soup to ignite new life. Below the streaking dolphins, a billion sea creatures feed and breathe and mate and die and spawn. Through the water come the returning calls of other dolphins, and of whales. And on the shore the villagers walk, slowly and without talking, away from the sea and back to their lives on the land.

Leaning against the blue pontoons of the dive inflatable, Claire and Klaas sit facing each other. Water drips from their faces as they catch their breath. Their ankles and feet, still cool from their dive, touch and stack. The wetsuits they stripped off a few minutes ago are hanging over the stainless-steel railing on the stern.

Claire shifts the top of the floral bikini she's been wearing non-stop for almost five months. She looks at his faded shorts and wonders, *How long has he been wearing those?*

The navy-blue canvas canopy shields them from the midday sun, which paints the lazy sea around them a deep azure. To landward, the dark-green vegetated dunes and golden sand beach extend up and down the coast as far as the eye can see. The boat languishes at anchor, the surf no more than a faint, constant static. The only other sounds are drips from the anchor-line up front, and the occasional call of a passing tern. Their skipper, a former fisherman recently employed by Benito, is struggling to stay awake as he lounges, feet up, by the steering console.

Benito and Helena, a shy young Swiss volunteer who arrived a few days ago – already it feels like she's always been part of the team – are underwater, carrying on from where Claire and Klaas left off. It's the first time they've tried to tag mantas here in Tofo. The animals have unique markings on their bellies, but with coloured and numbered plastic tags attached to their backs, they can be identified from above as well. The first box of tags finally arrived from Dr Eishmal last week. He sent instructions on how to attach the sharp stainless-steel ends using the applicator tool. But they're having to improvise, as divers can't always get within arm's length of a manta's back. Klaas's spear-fishing experience is helping. He's fashioned a long applicator from an old spearfishing gun so they can attach the tags without needing to come too close. Preferably while freediving, as Klaas and Claire are doing today.

Claire slides her foot under his.

'Eish, that's ticklish.' He curls his toes, lifts his foot to tap her calf. The silken firmness reminds him of dolphin skin. He runs his eyes along her tanned arm, follows every move of her slender fingers as they adjust her bikini top to lift those firm breasts up, so that he aches from wanting to cup them. As he studies her mischievous face, he wonders if this is the time to ask her the thing he's been wanting to ever since Gwen left town. He registers that she's talking again.

'That black manta was *so* cute, eh! I love how she gave a little shiver when you tagged her, swam away in fright. But then veered around to come back and check us out. Like she was saying, "Hey! Who did this to me? Who *are* you?"'

They chuckle together. 'Mantas are smart, that's for sure.'

'I love how you described dancing with that one. The day we met. I still haven't experienced this.' Claire feels the thrill of saying these words for the first time … *The day we met.*

'You will.'

Claire examines this desert waterman, this bush merman. Her eyes caress the neat crescent-shaped scars on the bridges of both his feet. From his navy days, he'd told her – being made to swim all day in fins that were too big for him. She's in deep water with him, she now accepts. But with Gwen's departure so recent, she can't stop the thought that comes: *Can I be sure it's over between them?*

Klaas looks at her. Waits. It feels like the pregnant time before the rain in the Karoo, when all the animals and the farm people know it's coming. When you can smell it in the air, can see the sky changing, but the first drops haven't fallen yet. When she shifts her silken legs against his and flicks her long dark hair out of her face, he knows he isn't prepared for the downpour. But that when it comes, he will put his face up to the sky and lick the wetness.

'Do you want to move in with me?' Klaas blows out the breath he feels he's been holding forever. He locks onto Claire's brown, almond-shaped eyes set in that broad face, and when she doesn't say anything, he finds himself standing alone on a vast dry plain, with the only water a cruel mirage shimmering on the horizon.

'What? That's a bit forward,' Claire says eventually, backhanding his knee playfully, as a warmth spreads uncontrollably in her loins. She wishes she could hide the rising flush on her neck and face.

'I ... I, uh, um ...' he stammers.

'Oh, I don't know.' She's playing with him. To buy time, to help her make sense of her emotions, which are all over the place. Why does he affect her so, with that voice of his that sounds like rocks falling, anyway? It might have something to do with that word *Karoo*, she decides, her mind flitting like a cleaner wrasse. No, that's ridiculous. She hasn't been there yet, but his description of the place conjures up raw earth-energy and wide-open space. A male place, she imagines, unlike the feminine, misted forests of her Haida Gwaii. She will ask him to take her there.

'Why, we haven't even kissed properly,' Claire blurts, but immediately thinks, *Really? Is that the best you can do?* She attempts a wink. Has an overwhelming urge to jump overboard.

'I, uh, I'm, uh, I'm sorry. Sorry for everything. For what happened. I'm sorry I never told you about the letter,' he splutters.

Her hands grab his knees and she bursts out laughing, mostly at the relief of knowing she isn't the only one with jellyfish in her stomach.

He thinks she's laughing at him, so he looks away, far away, out over the sea.

Well, there it is. He's asked. They don't talk for agonising seconds.

'I've been waiting for you to ask, my dearest Klaas,' she says quietly. 'Ever since that special evening last week. When we both thought about it but didn't say anything.'

Klaas turns to her and she leans forward and kisses him before he can speak. On the mouth. She lets her lips linger long enough to erase all thoughts, all possible fears, from both their minds.

They lean back against the pontoons. Klaas's breathing has deepened; Claire bites her lower lip. Their eyes dart and search and flirt and say 'yes'. Klaas is tempted to pull her into his arms and kiss her deeply. But he resists the urge. The skipper snorts and looks away to hide his smirk. He mutters something under his breath.

They sit there in the heat, grinning, sipping water, staring out at the blue, blue sea, not saying much. From time to time, they find each other's eyes to make sure. A petite white tern pipes a call as it flies past.

'See the birds over there.' Claire points to where a growing number of terns are fluttering, then folding and arrowing into the sea.

'Must be baitfish.'

They go back to their languishing. Klaas has started thinking of how he will make love to her for the first time. What he will do to set the mood. But when he sees the veil come across her face, that serious, faraway look she gets whenever she goes within, his vision of scented candles and dimly lit mosquito-netted bed vaporises.

Claire is looking past him when she says, 'I'd like to form a foundation, Klaas.'

'All right.' Klaas's brow furrows. 'What does that mean?'

'Todd's parents have already agreed. There are a lot of people like them in Vancouver. All over North America, in fact. Europe even. I know the type. Rich, retired folk who care about nature, about conservation. I want to use their money to make a difference here.'

'Ah …' He lifts his eyebrows, pouts his lower lip and nods.

'I want to work alongside Benito. All the things we've spoken about: stopping the poaching. Getting the locals on board. Growing volunteer tourism. And the kids, Klaas, they really get to me. There's so much we can achieve with them. You saw their faces when you came to the school.' Claire pauses and lifts her hands, which have been tucked between her legs, to find his. 'And it would mean a great deal to me if we could … if you could, you know … help. If we could do this together. I have seen it. In my mind.'

Klaas cups her slender hands. 'That was quite a speech, Claire. Well, I'm going nowhere – *nowhere*. So, ja, for sure, I'll help you. I don't know how, though. I'm just a dumb diver.'

Her hands stir when he winks at her. 'But you haven't answered my question yet. Will you move in with me?'

Claire pulls her hands free and punches him playfully on the shoulder. She bursts out laughing, and he joins in. They laugh and laugh, like a whole flock of gulls, and even though his tongue is dry, Klaas at last tastes the rain.

The skipper shakes his head and chuckles, 'Aye yai yai.' He remembers the time when he held his beloved's slender wrist, as she balanced the bucket of water on her head at the village well. So very long ago.

Benito and Helena's exhalations break the surface in a froth near the boat, and then their heads come out of the water. Klaas and Claire lean over the side to take the tagging pole, the weight belts and scuba tanks.

Benito, still hanging in the water, wipes his face. 'We tagged one. There are two more. They're coming to the shallow cleaning stations. But they were a bit wary of us on scuba. You guys might want to get back in. And it's starting to go off down there – a lot of movement. Kingfish, trevally and barracuda coming in. We could hear dolphins as well. There's something going on.'

They look at each other. 'Dive like this?' Claire asks rhetorically. Dismisses the wetsuits with a wave. Reaches for her fins, mask and snorkel.

He doesn't reply. He's already slipped on his long fins. He quickly clips open the plastic container with the tags, takes out a couple. Retrieving the tagging pole, he spits in his mask and attaches it to his face. 'Let's go!'

Claire giggles uncontrollably as she rubs the spit around the visor of her mask. Like carefree teenagers they fall over into the water, not even waiting for Benito and Helena to get back on board, and swim off on the surface, shoulder to shoulder.

They track the two mantas gliding easefully below them, matching their every move. When the creatures swerve and veer back to hover over the reef to be cleaned, Claire and Klaas slow too on the surface.

She tunes into the sound of his breathing through his snorkel, so she knows when they will dive. In the distance, she can also hear the click-clicking of dolphins. Can hear the excitement, the urgency, in their voices. There's a rising tension – something approaching through the water. Her deep in-breath is a second behind his.

Grasping their noses, they duck-dive in unison, through the shafts of light angling down to the reef, he with his tagging pole extended ahead of him like a trident, she holding the spare tag, her untied hair wafting up her back. They drop right onto the mantas.

The first fish flinches as Klaas jabs the tag into its skin. Claire hands him the second tag and they have to fin hard to get in position above the second animal.

When that tag too is attached, Klaas turns on his back, rises. Looks at her as she hangs in midwater as if to say, *Job done, what now?*

They both hear the rush of the bait ball before they see it, and swivel to locate it. The fish remind Klaas of the biblical-sized swarm of locusts he witnessed that one year on the farm, after the really big rain. With quick flicks of their long fins, they ascend. They don't talk on the surface. Keeping their faces down, they track the ball of fish, and after deep inbreaths through their snorkels, they descend.

The fish, caught in the sunlight, go from silver to dull grey as they swirl in an ever-shrinking ball. The reason becomes apparent as dolphins streak in from behind, from below, and from around the sides of the school of anchovies.

Claire's skin tingles at the intensity of the slow tornado of fish. The cacophony of dolphin clicks and whistles, and the rush of other predators who've gathered for the coordinated feast, is intoxicating.

Four black-tip sharks come from behind her and hit the fish with intensity. A sleek copper shark, hooded eyes flashing white, appears through the bait ball. Its fins quiver as it streaks at full speed to snap up a stunned sardine. It veers to miss Claire, then turns abruptly to thrust back in.

Without another thought Claire flicks her fins, reaches out her hands and disappears into the fish.

Klaas smiles and asks himself, *Who is this crazy woman?*

Claire surrenders to the full force of the vortex. The little fish pepper and slide over her skin. She senses more than sees or hears the rushing, the jaws snapping, the juices of crushed, writhing fish driving the sharks mad, their white eye-covers opening and closing as they lunge. The dolphins' pinging clicks echo through her as they command the kill. Seabirds froth down like streaming arrows. They snap about, then awkwardly flap their way back to the surface, some with a fish, some without. Tuna, jacks, barracuda burst in. Smaller fish waggle up from the reef for the morsels. A school of silver trevally flash and tear. Though she hangs motionless in the water, with the sunlight streaming through her spreading hair, adorned with fish scales and slime, she cries out through every rapidly firing synapse, every pore. The beautiful being who has been swimming out of sight for so long is no longer out there. Instead, she feels Her presence, a white light, *within*. Spreading throughout *Claire's* own being. And there are no more questions.

Her eyes roll and her beloved sea creatures, some not even from this place or time, come to her. She surrenders completely to the trance, and they surround her, swirl around and around. Claire's siren song which goes out to them is pure love. It calls out that she will never leave them. That from this moment, she will dedicate her full life force to protecting them.

She becomes aware of the firm hand on her side, the arm slipping under her armpit. His torso moulds across her back as his other arm, with the tag pole, comes under the other armpit, and he hugs her to him, lifts her toward the surface. She opens her eyes, blinks several times, takes in the receding melee as she is drawn from it.

When she twirls, flicks her fins to come up within his encircling arms, Klaas has the sudden realisation. *This is it!* This is the image he saw all those years ago in the cave painting. Two merpeople entwining, holding forth a spear.

Claire slides up his chest and searches his eyes, sparkling behind his mask. She tries to kiss him but their masks clink. She can feel him laughing. She has to turn her head to the side so her mouth can find his, and the sweet, salt taste of him.

As they ascend to the silver under-surface, up through the lubricious sea, they both know it's only for air.

Beach south of Tofo
20 February 1992

She has been coming to this stretch of beach every year, since before
Klaas fell into a dream in the farm dam. Even before Claire took her
first suck of air from her father's dive hookah. Normally she's fast, can
swim faster than either of them can run. Right now, however, because
she's out of the water, she is lumbering. Hauling her one-tonne carapace up the beach, lit by the ripening moon.

It's gone midnight when Klaas and Claire, sauntering hand in hand
along the spilling water's edge, cross the trail of tractor-like tracks. Klaas's
hand unclasps to point. 'Here, this is what I brought you to see. It's that
time of year.'

'Oh, wow! Leatherback, right?'

'Yes. Come.' He reaches for her hand. Leads her up the beach.

Claire's body is aglow. She has just danced, truly danced, for the
first time since high school. When she closes her eyes, she's still moving around the fire, with the African bass beat, two locals on djembes,
pulsing through her. She imagines the rest of the beach-party crowd
are still at it – Benito sweating it up with Miriam, Anton from Casa
Point making love to his guitar. She'd closed her eyes and smiled
as the universal rhythms, the warm laughter of the group and the
crackling of the fire, played into her, fuelling her body to sway with
abandon. The feeling of her bare feet shuffling in the sand, the sweat
trickling down her spine and between her breasts as they rocked,
fed the relaxed ecstasy. Friends were dancing around them, but it
was really just the two of them as the sparks flew up and up into the
balmy sky. She was dancing a love dance with Klaas, but also had to
keep her eyes off him. *He might have Bushman in him*, she chuckles
to herself, *but he lacks the trance moves.* He was all elbows. When his

rock-clattering laughter rang out, he reminded her of Náan's rooster.

Circling the fire – as Náan had taught her, and as she imagines her ancestors had done, stretching back to a time when the veil between supernatural and natural was thin – the Haida chants had risen up inside her, and she'd given them full voice. When the swollen orange moon rose up over the Indian Ocean and they cheered in awe, and the music lifted in intensity, she basked in unspeakable gratitude. For the gifts of pure love and life purpose, two things she felt were finally entwining.

They follow the tracks up the beach toward the dunes, where the mother turtle is about to begin. The music is still echoing in Claire's head, accompanied by the receding rumble of surf behind her. She finds his hand, leans up to give his ear a bite.

'Ouch!' He bumps her aside with his hip as they sway up the beach onto the softer sand.

There she is, appearing out of the darkness. The great leatherback, glistening in the moonlight. When they reach her, Klaas crouches, pulls Claire down to him with a gentle tug.

'She's still making her way up. She hasn't started yet,' he whispers. 'If we disturb her now, she'll abort and head back to sea.'

'Okay,' she whispers too, nuzzling into him, filling her senses with the salt-sweat and faint aftershave perfume of his ear-neck hollow. She's taken back to the freshly cut watermelon smell of *Melibe*, the Haida Gwaii sea slug. The sound of the raven's wings, from the day she laid the ashes, echoes fleetingly.

With the sound of the waves dulled by the dune, the turtle's slow, rasping sighs hang in the night air when she rests between hauls. They follow from a distance, keeping low, as she heaves her bulk to where the dune grass starts. After an extended exhalation, she begins to dig.

With great deliberation, the turtle fashions her hole in the sand with her hind flippers – first one, and then the other. They are shorter and broader than the long front ones, which produce the bursts of speed. The flippers slow each time to carefully deposit scoops of sand to the side. Tentatively, so as not to spill too much sand into the hole, they reach into it once more.

'We can go closer – touch her, even. Now that she's digging, she'll go into a bit of an alpha state. A trance. But let's still be careful not to disturb her.' Klaas produces a flashlight, dampens the beam to a glow with his hand. When he plays it over the long ridges on her back, her white speckles and blotches show up clearly in rows on the blue-grey.

'Her markings are just like a whale shark,' Claire whispers. 'Ocean's biggest fish and her biggest turtle share the same palette. Whale Shark has no barnacles, though.' When she tentatively reaches out to feel the jagged edges of a cluster of them, she's tempted to rip them off like overdue scabs.

They move up to her head, so they can meet her. Her eyes are unseeing, bloodshot and struggling to stay moist. When her lids close, a sand-filled tear forms, drops to the sand.

The mother digs for a while. Settling in the sand near her rear, they lose track of time; their fingers sift and fiddle with the fine sand, and with each other's. It's just the turtle and them under the wide sky. When the soft sand caves in around the rim of the hole, the mother has to dig this out before gaining depth again.

Abruptly, she stops. Rests. One hind flipper remains in the hole. Klaas leans forward to shine a light on her glottis-like tail, which hangs into the space.

'She's ready,' he whispers.

Claire looks up into the night as a shooting star streaks, and the words come easily: *Me too.*

They wait.

The turtle's tail pulses, extends. The first round, white, mucus-covered egg appears and plops into the hole. Two more come in quick succession. A pause. Mucus drips. A few more drop. They've counted thirty-nine when Claire lifts her pinkie finger, enough to find his hand. A mere tender touch ... but he knows.

As the mother turtle enacts her age-old rite, Claire lifts her hand to run it, soft as gossamer, over his, and up his wrist. Barely brushing the hairs of his forearm, she traces his biceps. Continues up over his full shoulders, which stir, and onto his back. And finally, her fingers slide up his neck to entwine his curly hair. Without a word, Claire eases onto her back, pulls him to her, and their mouths find each other.

They can hear the wet plop, plop of the eggs. She glances briefly to her side, once, to see the great mother, but quickly turns back to him. She can't make out his eyes, so closes hers, arching her bare back off the cool sand as she clings to him. When he enters her, the rippled drumming and throat chanting from before surges anew. They begin to move and feel, and she gasps when she opens up to him. As his muscled back rises and falls, a self she hardly recognises emerges from the depths. Reluctantly at first, and then rising, drawn midwater, with hair spreading in the deep channel, swirling. Sedna. She *is* Sedna. Through the palls of pleasure, *She* envelops, flows, to meet him as he hastens. *She* calls out to Raven with all her voice.

Klaas's nostrils flare with the scent of Karoo air before the rain. The expectant sky is somehow the sea, and he a great white shark surging effortlessly into an enormous mid-ocean wave. The thought flashes: *It will never be the same, once it crashes.* He gathers her to him as they swirl, and her tender cries are lost in the electric sky, the unstoppable water as it masses, and masses.

Claire is swirling. Delirious. Sea creatures, from this world and the other, curl and stretch around her, in and out through the shroud. With a quiet shudder, the waves ripple and break … and spread into everywhere as a tingling effervescence, accompanied by a slow bass chant.

They cling to the moment. To the subsiding, easing other. Reluctantly, they become aware of the beach. Of each other's quick breathing. Of the sweet sweat. And eventually of the flippers moving the sand next to them. Still clinging, they turn their heads to the mother turtle. They watch as she firms the sand she's piled into the hole on top of the wet, warm eggs.

Klaas slowly lifts himself off Claire. He kisses her three times with precise tenderness, first on one breast, then the other, and then one last time, pulling himself down between her thighs, on the warm tender wetness – it makes her gasp in her throat, and release a wild gypsy cackle. He collapses on his back beside her, laughing uncontrollably from his chest.

Fingers find fingers.

Klaas takes a long, mindful breath. He opens his eyes and his heart to the vastness of the universe spread out above him.

Claire's eyes remain closed. For she is still turning in the slowing current. Reaching out to the creatures deliciously fading, fading from view. She knows they will come to her again. When she too opens her eyes, she sighs into the settled vastness, safe beside this new warmth.

'Hey! That's the Southern Cross.'

'Yes, my darling. Yes, it is.' Klaas does think, for a brief moment, back to the last time he lay in the arms of a lover under the same constellation. But the thought flees; it's a childhood memory now, no more. When Claire lays the back of her hand in his upturned palm, he has to squeeze his eyes to control the waves of gratitude. His other hand starts to fiddle with the sand. He lets it run through his fist. The gentle passing of time in one hand, the certainty of new love in the other.

They lie in silence for a long time, under the blanket of stars.

When the turtle lets out a particularly laboured sigh, Klaas speaks quietly into the night, 'Let's mark this nest with a stick and come back when the babies hatch. It's pretty amazing watching hatchlings emerge from the sand like magic and scuttle down to the sea. We can shoo the gulls and the crabs that go for them.'

'When would that be?'

'Around seventy to eighty days, think. We'll check with Benito. We can come here over a period to make sure we don't miss them.'

'I'd love that.' The thought of the delicious days ahead brings a glow. A movement catches her attention. She sits up on her elbow, touches his side. 'Look, she's turning.'

With legs that buckle with joy, they stagger to their feet, gathering their clothes. And naked and glowing, they escort the turtle mother back to the sea in the darkness.

The great turtle has to rest several times on her homeward trek. Her rasping breaths are laboured now, for she is spent. They drop their clothes and the flashlight on the beach when the spill water glints up ahead.

When the mother finally feels wetness, she rests one last time. Claire crouches down next to her. She strokes her hand along the ridged carapace, over the barnacles, and whispers the Haida blessing for a safe passage.

'Eish.' Klaas shakes his head. The warmth spreads across his chest yet again as he takes in her nipples in the moonlight, almost brushing the ridged lines of the turtle's carapace.

The turtle heaves as the next wave spills around her. They stand back in the shallows as successive waves float her. With a final flurry of fins, which briefly lights up the water with luminescence, her dark dome disappears through the white froth.

Klaas wades in after her, and Claire follows. They plunge into the warm sea. The sweat and the juices of their lovemaking slide off their slippery bodies, which feel alive and in Ocean.

The women from the village, some straddling low wooden stools, some waiting to take turns with the heavy pestles, stop their singing for a moment. Claire tunes in to the rhythmic thud-crunch thud-crunch which continues as the cassava leaves are ground to fibre in the tall wooden mortars. Palm fronds rustle overhead. A welcome breeze whispers through the warm air around the cluster of palm-clad huts, a homestead set atop the hill.

When they're done, one of the youngest women, Maria, who has a sleeping child strapped to her back with a sarong, adds the green pulp to a battered pot half-full of the same. She walks over to place it on a metal stand to steam over coals from the smouldering fire; lifts the lid of a second pot to check on the rice.

From where she's sitting, her back against the trunk of a broad cashew-nut tree, Claire has an unobstructed view over the sea, turquoise close to shore and a rich cobalt further out. In the valley below, a man walks along a well-worn path, snaking its way between the coconut palms and the scattered huts built on ancient sand dunes. The palms stretch as far as her eyes can see: a sparsely planted forest left by the Portuguese. In one hand the man holds a chicken by the base of its wings, swinging it as he walks.

A nanny goat bleats at the edge of the homestead. Claire swivels her head to find it, bringing up her hand to wipe the sweat from her neck. The goat's leg is caught in the line it's tied to, but then the leg jumps free and she bleats at her kid, who's strayed a few metres. The line jerks her head back as it pulls taut on the post. The goat's black-slit pupils, set in grey, are much like a manta's. Her kid skips back through the dry sand and headbutts up into her teats.

One of the women emerges from the little outhouse, the size of a sentry post. It's located away from the two larger main huts. One is for sleeping, and the other is a kitchen and pantry. All three have plaited coconut-palm walls with reed-thatched roofs. The woman's pure-white teeth flash as she smiles at Claire. After washing the soap off her hands with water from a plastic jug, she sways back to join the group, drying her hands on her sarong, the bright colours of the Mozambican flag.

Miriam, who's sharing the tree trunk with Claire, strikes up a conversation with Teresa, the elder in the group, who's walked over to join them in the shade. They speak in Bitonga, which to Claire still sounds like beautiful birdsong accompanied by bass guitar-string twangs. They both look at her with laughing eyes, but then gesture and point to the other women, so she assumes they're discussing the progress of the meal – the matapa.

Claire reaches for SGaana, scratches him on the muzzle where the scar from a neighbourhood scrap still itches. He collapses onto the sand next to her, like one of those wooden thumb-puppets when you press its base, uttering a lazy 'harrumph' as he puts his head on his paws. After he appeared that night on the road and followed her to Klaas's place, he kept finding her. He'd be on her doorstep in the morning, or lying on the sand under the window at the research station, scratching the fleas around his black-and-white scruff. The day she fed him, he adopted her for his own. Now all the little boys on the beach know his name.

Making matapa is women's work. And often, like now, an excuse for women's business. Normally Miriam fills her in on the village gossip on the way here, but not this morning. Instead, she'd spoken about her relationship with Benito. The fact that she wanted a proper church wedding with a white dress – not like Klaas and Claire, who'd exchanged cheap rings on the beach at sunset with half a dozen friends. 'No disrespect, Claire,' she'd checked herself, 'but my father is Catholic, you know.'

But the real problem, Miriam explained, is that Benito hasn't proposed yet. Not properly. What should she do about it? Perhaps Claire could say something to Klaas to say something to Benito, 'you know … man to man'.

A pied crow lands in a nearby palm and caws, a lazy 'craaak'. The palm fronds rustle. SGaana sighs contentedly. The women's gentle voices lilt. Claire wills her leaden eyelids open, squeezes them closed, rubs them with a finger. She shakes her head just enough so the others won't notice. It would be disrespectful to nod off.

Two women laugh in her direction, but when she looks at them, they're head down, scraping white flesh from split coconuts on the jagged metal implements attached to each of their wooden stools. When all the flesh has been removed they squeeze out the milk into a clean bowl.

Two other women approach, one with the pot of steaming cassava, the other with a bowl of crushed peanuts. The peanuts are added to the pulp and the coconut milk is poured in through a sieve to complete the matapa. Maria places the pot back on the fire to simmer as they pack away the utensils and the bowls.

When one of the women uses a dishtowel to lift the lids off the pots on the coals, the smell of steaming rice and fragrant matapa brings saliva to Claire's mouth. *I really should be helping*, she thinks, not for the first time this morning. *I'll offer to dish up.* When she stands, the sudden dizziness forces her to lean forward, and she has to hold her knees. She feels Teresa's cool hand on her arm, straightens to look into her wizened face. She's cackling, not unlike her Náan, and speaking Portuguese so Claire can understand. She tells Claire to relax. To please sit down. That they will serve her when the matapa is ready. That this is a special occasion.

The women arrange themselves in a wide circle, spoons in hand, readying their tin plates to be piled high with rice and matapa. A bowl of dried chilli flakes and salt is passed around. SGaana sits up at the smell and Claire puts her hand on his head. When they're all settled,

Teresa places her plate down and stands to address them. Claire notices that the old lady's eyes are only on her.

'Claire, we have a gift for you,' she says in Portuguese. A package, wrapped in old newspaper, appears in her hands. Claire frowns.

'What?' She looks around at the beaming faces. A few of them hide their giggles in their hands. Claire addresses Miriam under her breath, 'What's going on, Ems? It's not my birthday.'

'They know, Claire. We all know,' Miriam replies in English. There is open laughter now.

Her eyes mist as she unwraps the gift. Lifts out the bright-blue sarong. She bursts into joyful tears as she unfolds it, sees the print. The bold sea creatures.

'It's for your baby.' But Miriam's voice is drowned out by the ululating. Teresa starts the clapping, calls out the refrain. The others join, break into full song. It's an old Bitonga song, passed down through many generations. A women's song, which speaks of rain and of new life and how, if they all pull together, they can face anything, and they sing it with full voice up into the sapphire sky.

Praia do Tofo
11 November 2000

Sometime before midnight, a full moon hangs over Praia Tofo. Its golden light reaches into the water and the sea creatures feel its pull.

Claire is awake but in repose. She studies the almost imperceptibly shifting shadows of the curtains on the ceiling of their bedroom, wondering what woke her. *Was that a door being opened?* Beyond the steady breathing next to her, she isolates the night sounds. The crickets. A lonely frog. The cry of a wide-eyed night plover. The gentle calling of the waves. She comes up on her elbow to study the tranquil face in the half light. He stirs when she runs her fingers over the welt on his neck. Her bush merman. She lifts the sheet and creeps out without waking him.

All is still as she moves about. The sound of the sea is louder in the living room, and the light from the moon paints the space with subdued light. She winces when she stands on a block of Lego.

Claire slides open the glass door and steps onto the deck overlooking the bay, breathing in the smell of salt and neoprene from the wetsuits drying over the railings, and feeling the full presence of Ocean. Closing the door quietly behind her, she goes to little Alice, leaning against the balustrade. Dressed in her white night shirt, she's staring intently out over the water.

'Hi, Mummy,' Alice says without turning around.

'Thought I'd find you here.' Claire feels the warmth of the seven-year-old frame when she leans into her daughter. She takes in the bright moon painting a highway across the sea, all the way to the shoreline below them. 'Couldn't you sleep, my darling?'

'A dream woke me, Mummy. It felt so real. I was sitting in a clearing in a forest. It was night time and there was a fire, and all around the fire were animals. Sea animals. I woke up with my heart bumping. It didn't make sense.'

'Dreams are like that. But sometimes they make sense to the soul.'

'What's the soul again?'

Claire pauses, hugs Alice to her. 'I like to think of it as that special place deep within you where your most golden thoughts come from.'

'They were all staring at me, Mummy. Like they wanted me to do something. Then an old lady was there. She was smiling, and she said, "You can do it." But what, Mummy? I just know that I want to be with the sea animals. To help them. That's why I came out here.'

Claire savours the pure, precious words, spoken so seriously, sees that timeless old face, her Náan, and smiles uncontrollably. She draws the sleepy warmth, the perfume of her offspring, their offspring, even closer to her.

Down there, under the glittering waves, the coral polyps pout and take in water, extend and throb. As one, their oral cavities shyly open, and ever so gently tiny pearls, their spawn, are squeezed out to float up into the water column, transforming the reef-scape into an upside-down snowstorm, flakes falling upwards. Fish fly in to feast on these protein balls, and others on them, until the reefs become a melee of life giving life.

'Did you see that?' Alice is pointing to where a bright phosphorescent trail is fading in the dark water, as if something large had flown above the reef.

'Yes, I did. What do you think it was? A dolphin? Or perhaps it was Sedna.' Claire bumps her hip against Alice's side.

'Do you really think she's real, Mummy? I mean, have you actually ever seen her underwater?'

'Not everything that is real can be seen, my darling. Like your love for Daddy. You can't see it, but it's real, right? Often, I feel things, hear things underwater that I can't explain. And then I'm filled with that same love feeling.'

'He was so goofy today when we went out in the boat with Almeida.

He was making us laugh, trying to copy how an octopus moves under-water. Almeida has such beautiful eyes, hey. I think he is very handsome.'

· 'Oh, do you now?'

'Please don't tell him, okay? Promise. I will never ever speak to you if you do.'

'It'll be our secret. He is going to be a great waterman. He's a nat-ural.' Claire casts her mind back to that day in the classroom. To his eyes. *It's always written in the eyes.*

They hold the precious silence between them, let the words wash around, like the dark sea under the moon. And Claire feels into that which exists between the here and now and the there, and the words of her Náan float up to her, cause her to chuckle softly into the still air.

'What is it? What's so funny, Mummy?'

Claire repeats what she's just heard in her head: 'You want to live down there and serve all those sea creatures, don't you just?'

'Yes, I do, Mummy. I really do.'

'And so you will, my darling. So you will. Daddy and I will help you. You know, you remind me of her.'

'Of who?' Alice looks up at Claire.

'Of Sedna, silly. Except you can keep your fingers.' Claire grabs a hand and squeezes it.

Alice giggles with delight into the night. They stare out over the bay, both imagining what could be going on below the shimmering surface.

'Why did Sedna's dad have to chop off her fingers?' Alice asks sud-denly.

'Ah, well, people had become too greedy in that village. They'd for-gotten that we can't just take whatever we want from nature. That we are a part of it. And when you're greedy like this, you become selfish too. Sedna's father had become *so* selfish that he sacrificed his only daughter to save himself from the wrath of the raven.'

'Daddy would never ever do that.'

'No, I think Daddy would cut off his own fingers for you.'

They laugh softly together and grow silent once more. They breathe in the night air, which has just a hint of chill.

Eventually Claire gives Alice a little hug. 'Come, my sweet, let's get back to bed. We have a big day ahead. We still have to pack the car. Are you excited?'

'Yes! I can't wait. The Karoo. Rhymes with poo.'

'What?' Claire chortles.

'In the Karoo, when you're far from any houses, you can sit behind any old bush and poo. That's what Dad told me.'

Claire breaks into a full laugh.

'He said we're going to climb a windmill. Like the one that gave him his scar. And dive in water that comes from deep under the ground.'

'Yeah, that's going to be cool. I'm excited too.'

'And he said that on the way back, we're picking up some guns. From the church man in Maputo. The ones from the war. I think they're going to love Daddy's funny gun reef.'

'Who?'

'The sea creatures – and Sedna, silly!'

When Alice looks up to find Claire's face and they gaze into each other's eyes, glinting in the moonlight, they both know, see everything that they need to see. And as they turn away, another streak of phosphorescence appears down there, above the dark, thronging reef.

– ACKNOWLEDGEMENTS –

Although this story is a fiction, I have been at pains to get details about real people, places, cultures and marine life as factually correct as I could. Klaas Afrikaner was a Baster rebel leader in the 18th-century Dutch colony which is now part of South Africa, and he did end his life as a prisoner on Robben Island. Malangatana Ngwenya and Alexander Rose-Innes were indeed luminary artists, both of whom I had the privilege of meeting before they passed. I visited Mr Ngwenya at his home in Maputo in 1991, and my description of his character and his home are taken from this time, augmented with desktop research. And the South African Navy did engage in illegal cross-border covert operations to bomb ANC safe houses in Maputo in the 1980s. I know this because I was there.

Claire's nature-centric spirituality is heavily influenced by her Haida lineage. Likewise, Klaas's character is shaped by his Bushman blood. I am not from either of these cultures, and relied on my time in these geographies, and published versions and interpretations of the myths and sacred stories so central to these indigenous cultures, to craft this story. I hope I have honoured both of these First Nations in the telling of it. *Haida Monumental Art – Villages of the Queen Charlotte Islands* by George F. MacDonald (UBC Press, 2002) and *Stories that Float from Afar – Ancestral Folklore of the San of Southern Africa*, edited by J.D. Lewis-Williams (David Philip, 2002) were two works I found particularly useful as reference works. I want to thank Mary Morris for completing an initial critique of the Haida Gwaii sections. And I am indebted to SGaana Gaahlandaay *Alix Goetzinger* of the Haida Nation for completing a more thorough check of Haida names and cultural references.

There are many versions of the Inuit and Aleut origin myth of Sedna, Ruler of the Sea Creatures, which is central to *She Down There*. My research leaned heavily on two texts: *The Inuit Imagination* by Harold Seidelman and James Turner, published by Douglas & McIntyre in 1993 (Chapter 3 – 'Sedna and the

Shaman's Journey'); and 'The Acculturative Role of Sea Woman' by Birgitte Sonne, published in the journal *Meddelelser Om Grønland, Man and Society* 13 in 1990. I trust my version, as recounted by Náan and woven throughout the story, respects the underlying sacred mythology, as is intended.

I would like to acknowledge Laurel Cohn, who professionally evaluated an early as well as a near-completed draft. A heartfelt 'thank you!' to my test readers spread around the world: Tim Andrew, Robert Baldwin, Alan Burger, Andrew Duvel, Brian Emmett, Clayton Frick, Sylvia Harron, Helen Heydenrych, Hugh Joseph, Andrea Lawrence, Andrea Marshall, Catherine Marshall, Howard McElderry, Lorna Parry, Meryl Smuts and Jess Williams. My writers' group, the fabulous Binklings – Susan Perrow, Ilse van Oostenbrugge, Vicky King, Jay McKenzie, Jenni Cargill-Strong and Mitchell Kelly – made a massive contribution. I am grateful to the Byron Bay Writers Festival for the mentorship which paired me with acclaimed author Marele Day, whose experienced insights shaped my final touches. Fourie Botha and the rest of the team at Penguin Random House in Cape Town were a pleasure to work with. Thank you, Catriona Ross, for bringing such professional passion to the project. Jacques Kaiser, the cover is perfect – a work of art. My editor, Henrietta Rose-Innes, is a master. It was a privilege to have you tidy my text and polish my prose – like a supernatural cleaner wrasse. And finally, I want to thank and acknowledge you, Nici Burger, for your love and patience as a trusted sounding board throughout the gestation of this book.

Around the world, in remote coastal villages on the edge of marine biodiversity hotspots like Haida Gwaii and Tofo, there are real men and women, not unlike Claire, Klaas and Benito, who have dedicated their lives (some have even given their lives) to protecting what is left of our precious oceans, of Ocean. I dedicate this book to these often-unsung heroes.

The author with a dugong off Bazaruto Island, Mozambique